NOLAN ON BRADBURY

NOLAN

ON

BRADBURY

Sixty Years of Writing about the
Master of Science Fiction

William F. Nolan

Edited by S. T. Joshi
Introduction by Jason V Brock
Commentary by Ray Bradbury

Afterword by Greg Bear

Hippocampus Press

New York

Published by Hippocampus Press
P.O. Box 641, New York, NY 10156.
http://www.hippocampuspress.com

Cover illustration "The Pedestrian" (previously unpublished) by Joseph Mugnaini © 2013 by The Joseph Mugnaini Estate. Back cover
photograph from the archives of William F. Nolan.

Cover design by Jessica Forsythe.
Hippocampus Press logo designed by Anastasia Damianakos.

First Edition
1 3 5 7 9 8 6 4 2

ISBN13: 978-1-61498-058-2

Contents

Preface

Ray Bradbury is no longer with us. He passed away quietly in June of 2012 at the age of ninety-one, leaving a rich legacy of books and stories that will continue to inspire and entertain a host of future generations.

The title of his final essay, printed in the *New Yorker* just before his death, is "Take Me Home." And, indeed, Ray has gone home. He has joined his Martian friends in their crystal cities and echoing canals. I have no doubt that his spirit will greet us when we finally arrive on the Red Planet.

I knew him for over sixty years. He was unique, and there is no one to replace him. Eccentric, hardworking, strongly opinionated, loyal, loving, highly energized, with a wild sense of humor, he was a man who savored each day as a joy and a treasure. He greatly valued his friends, and I count myself fortunate to have been among them. In one of my last visits to his bedside, he clasped my hand, leaned close, and whispered: "Thank you for being in my life." For me, it was a deeply emotional moment.

As this collection demonstrates, I have written extensively about him: articles, essays, tributes, checklists, and reviews—but only one poem. In it, I celebrate the many adventures we shared. I call it "God Bless!," after one of Ray's favorite sayings.

God Bless!

Almost thirty when I met him.
Trips to Long Beach. Great food and jolly times on the Queen.
Signings; in the Valley.
Many lectures. ("Follow your loves!")
Good letters from Ireland. The pool in Palm Springs.
A Houdini séance at the Magic Castle, and a bicycle at MGM.

Disneyland.

Late night sessions at the house in Cheviot Hills.

Dinners with Donn and Dennis and Herb and Mayor Tom.

Wild times with Freberg—and a special night at the Nuart.

Bradbury on television. ("We'll seed the stars and live forever!")

Old radio with Vic 'n' Sade.

Plays in Pasadena.

On the set with Something Wicked, and documentary evenings at the Guild.

Dandelion Wine in Fullerton. ("Green light, Doug, green light!")

A 50th wedding anniversary at the Four Seasons.

The Halloween Tree at the Academy.

Fahrenheit 451 at the Colony.

The World of Ray Bradbury at the Coronet.

And at a gallery with Joe M. (Painted metaphors!)

In Ohio, for the dedication at Bowling Green.

Manuscript readings.

Acres of books.

The incredible cellar. (A lifetime of memories.)

Tapes with Norman on a Note of Triumph.

Afternoons at the office in Beverly Hills, and a limo to San Diego.

In Culver City, watching Logan run. . .

Listening to new stories, savoring old ones.

A Wonderful Ice Cream Suit at UCLA.

Susan's wedding reception and fine champagne.

Galleys

and contracts.

Hugs

and handshakes.

And . . . *always* . . . much laughter.

God bless!

—*Witness and Celebrate* (2000)

A final note: I was sorely tempted to update and revise all the pieces that follow, but then decided to leave them alone, allowing each to reveal Ray as I knew him, year by year, into 2012.

I'll stand aside now and let this book speak for me. It has a lot to say about Ray Douglas Bradbury—all of it from the heart.

—WILLIAM F. NOLAN

Introduction

By Jason V Brock

The late Ray Bradbury was a giant, a colossus. His impact is hard to overestimate on the world stage, even in a twentieth-century literary landscape populated by such figures as Ernest Hemingway, John Steinbeck, and F. Scott Fitzgerald. He defied genre-ghettoization and was venerated by philosopher and student alike for his keen intellect, thoughtful insight, and his fine, fine prose. Truly, he was the grand man: the Pope of Speculative Fiction.

In his prodigious output—much of it in the short fiction realm—Bradbury accomplished a considerable amount by adhering to the presumptive dictum of "the art is to conceal the art," and in his best work (of which there is an abundance) one comes away transformed by the imperceptible calculus of a master craftsman who teaches as he inspires, who informs as he entertains. Even when he missed the mark, there is still much to be gleaned from studying his oeuvre, and it becomes readily apparent that this was a talent of unusual caliber, sensitivity, and genius. Few artists ever reach such a rarefied plateau, and Bradbury was certainly among their number. He will be studied with the greats, and his place is assured alongside Dante, William Faulkner, and (his personal favorite) Edgar Allan Poe.

During his lifetime, Bradbury was already considered by many to be the preeminent exponent of science fiction, but the truth lies more in the notion that he was a tremendously gifted fabulist. Using post-industrial parlance and post-atomic anxiety, he rendered his ideas into a fictional reality that was beyond simple classification, yet which often used the trappings, tropes, and elements of science fiction, fantasy, and horror in novel ways not only to illu-minate the questions of the day (and the depths of the human heart), but also to speculate on what was to come, and how best to navigate this protean modernity, replete with beauty, joy, sadness, and terror.

He was ahead of his time, his peers, his critics; at this point in the dramaturgy, enter one of his foremost apostles, disciples, and acolytes:

By his count, William F. Nolan has produced more than 2000 pieces of writing: from profiles for magazines like *Playboy* and *Rogue* to short fiction (his omnibus horror collection, *Dark Universe*, was a finalist for the World Fantasy Award), novels (*Hell-tracks*, *The Marble Orchard*), and several full-length biographies, including books on director John Huston, actor Steve McQueen, and writer Dashiell Hammett.

What many people may not realize is that Nolan has also done several bibliographies. Perhaps his most notable efforts have been on the late author (and dear friend of Nolan's *and* Bradbury's) Charles Beaumont, and, prior to that, on the esteemed Bradbury himself. Nolan compiled *Ray Bradbury Review* early in his career (it was one of the first major attempts at delineating Bradbury's works and importance, and is still useful today), and later *The Ray Bradbury Companion*, some of which is excerpted herein.

Along the way, Nolan has found the time not only to speak at conventions, lecture and teach writing in college, but also to men-tor younger writers, such as Dennis Etchison, Joe R. Lansdale, and others (including the author of this introduction). This was an im-portant aspect of his growth and development as a writer, and is a kind of "pay it forward" philosophy that he embraced as a young man hanging out with his dear friends (and fellow scribes) Richard Matheson, George Clayton Johnson, Beaumont, and of course Ray Bradbury. This is what his friends did for him, and Nolan is determined to provide the same for talented neophytes in return. It's a beautiful philosophy, and a lasting legacy—the highest calling of mentoring and apprenticeship.

Now an elder statesman of the classic science fiction and horror genres, a recognized expert on the pulp era (particularly the works of Hammett and Western writer Max Brand), and a longtime, close friend to the departed (and sorely missed) Ray Bradbury, Nolan is here with a fine volume dedicated to his early scholarship and appreciation of one of the greatest writers of our time.

Enjoy.

Editor's Introduction

By S. T. Joshi

I have been privileged in being asked to assemble this collection of William F. Nolan's penetrating writings about Ray Bradbury, spanning sixty years of the life of these two legendary writers and encompassing fiction, essays, reviews, and poetry, not to mention tributes to Bradbury by other writers. This book was conceived and largely assembled before Bradbury's death on June 5, 2012, although it is not known whether Bradbury was fully aware of the scope and nature of the book. But since he had seen and thoroughly enjoyed the great majority of Bill Nolan's contributions to the book, it is safe to say that Bradbury approved of its contents.

It is understandable that articles on a single figure, even one so versatile as Bradbury, written over a sixty-year period would contain a certain amount of repetition. I have pruned some obvious instances of repetition in some of the articles, but have retained others in order to preserve the integrity of the given item. Nolan is anything but an academic writer, and his articles are meant to be accessible to all readers, whether they have read every word of Bradbury's work or none at all.

The several works of fiction included in this book are either affectionate parodies of Bradbury's style and manner or tales that were significantly influenced by Bradbury's vision. Nolan himself is in some senses even more versatile than his mentor, for he has done significant work in criticism and bibliography; but even these phases of his work were meant for a general audience.

I am grateful to all the hands who participated in the assembly of this book—Jason and Sunni Brock, Greg Bear, John C. Tibbetts, and especially William F. Nolan, whose sixty-year devotion to the life and work of Ray Bradbury has finally achieved the recognition it deserves.

About Bill Nolan

By Ray Bradbury

[These words by Ray Bradbury were written, first, in 1963, for my original paperback collection *Impact 20*. Ray wrote more about me in 2002, when *Impact 20* was reissued in hardcover. These two pieces have been revised and combined into this piece.—WFN.]

I am prouder of Bill Nolan and his progress through the years as a writer than I am of any other writer I have ever known.

There was a special evening in 1954 when I was attending some avant-garde films at the Coronet Theater in Hollywood with Bill, when I heard someone at the edge of the crowd, at intermission, shouting, "Extra! Extra! First published story by Bill Nolan." And plowing through the crowd was Forrest J Ackerman, the super friend to us all, waving a copy of the science fiction magazine with Bill Nolan's first story. I think we all stood there and cried just a little bit, because Bill has worked for many years to become a selling author.

He has published a shelf full of books, including many collections of short fiction, and has sold over one thousand shorter items: articles, essays, stories and poems, and done more than forty TV and film scripts, the most important item perhaps his being co-author of *Logan's Run*, which has been made into a film two times;* they keep promising to do the film over until they get it right. In any event, the novel stands alone, not needing any identification with the two pictures.

---

*[The second film, from Warner Bros., is in pre-production, with an estimated release date of 2014.—WFN.]

Beyond that, I am proud of our friendship.

He showed up at my house in Venice, California, in 1950, when I still lived on the beach with my wife, and was a half-struggling writer myself. No, come to think of it, Bill didn't show up, he didn't make an appearance—he *exploded* into our lives.

Anybody who has ever met Bill Nolan will know what I mean by this. He does not walk, he *leaps* through doors. He does not just talk, he acts life out with everything he says. He does not get ideas by the week or by the day, but by the hour and the minute.

When I think of Bill I think of a tall, lean-to, thrown together rucksack of bones. He was originally bonier and more wildly constructed, but while better years and good eats have rounded him off, the main impression is still of a windmill that runs swiftly even when becalmed. I would like to think that from time to time through my life I could look up to the horizon and see that brave, fast, furious, and engaging windmill flourishing there.

In sum, God invented a pep pill and dubbed it Nolan. You cannot resist him. He is that force of nature we are always hearing about. If you tire of a conversation, put it down, Bill will snatch it up and run off with it. He is one of the great talkers of the universe.

But, above all, he is one of the great doers.

Which means, finally, he loves well and exudes his love and gives it energy and form, no matter where he drives it, no matter what he wants. He is a sublime Sammy, on the run for the right things instead of the wrong.

I knew this from the first.

He was all over the place, illustrating, writing articles and stories for fan magazines and finishing up a wondrous compliment, a magazine he edited and paid hard cash for, a *Review* which contained the first full index of my stories and the first really critical examination of my work. The pattern hasn't changed.

Bill, like most of us down the years, resembled the athlete who races to the end of the diving board, leaps up, and comes back down still on the board, and stands to ask: "How deep is it? Is the water cold?"

On occasion over those years, Bill would slip me a short story or an article to read and, figuratively, ask: "Can I swim yet? Where's the lifeguard?"

And I had to answer: "There's no lifeguard, and nobody knows if the water is hot or cold. Just hold your nose, and *jump!*"

Well, Bill did just that. He got around to jumping off the end of that board, nose held, in the year 1956. At twenty-eight, he quit a good-paying job, bought himself a ream of paper, and began to write full time.

Here is where I will take one very small, insignificant bow. After all, I only made the suggestion; Bill followed up with the work. I suggested that he write fifty-two short stories or articles a year, one a week, to put himself in training to do good work.

As with most of us who have written over a period of time, Bill discovered that by working hard, by forming good writing habits, by discharging his emotions on paper day by day, week by week, he could move closer to discovering himself, revealing his own truths, and in the process, entertaining others. To stand still, to cogitate, to muse too long, is often to kill an Idea on its way to birth. Bill has stayed in motion.

He has always worked. He will continue, like *Battle Aces*, until someone shoots him down. And even then, he will make a splendid fall, and where he hits will be a permanent dent in our memories.

He is my friend, he is a fine writer.

More power to him, say I.

ARTICLES

R. B.: A Biographical Sketch

Ray Douglas Bradbury was born on August 22, 1920 in the town of Waukegan, Illinois. His mother, of Swedish descent, was born in Stockholm. His father's family came to America around 1630. Bradbury is a member of a literary family, since both his grandfather and great-grandfather were publishers of magazines, books, and newspapers. Ray's sister, Elizabeth, and a brother, Samuel, died in infancy. A second brother, Leonard (Samuel's twin), was born in 1916.

When he was still quite young, a shy and gangling teenage girl with a taste for unusual reading moved into his grandmother's upstairs room. She lent the inquisitive boy an old copy of *Amazing Stories*. It was Ray's initial introduction to a science-fiction magazine, and he was greatly impressed with the Paul illustrations and by the story "World of Giant Ants" by A. Hyatt Verrill.

A few years later, when he was twelve, his family moved to Arizona. There Bradbury made the acquaintance of a youth named Tucker, who possessed a fair-sized collection of *Wonder* and *Amazing Stories*. Bradbury, of course, devoured them all and, ready for more, began to read the books of Edgar Rice Burroughs. He had received a toy-dial typewriter on his birthday and with this he wrote his first story. It was a lusty sequel to one of Mr. Burroughs's books which he could not afford to buy at the time.

During this period Ray managed, by a combination of luck and persistence, to land a part-time job at radio station KGAR, reading the comic-section to the kiddies. He would imitate various dialects for the characters. During the five months he was employed, he also dubbed in as sound man and general bit-player on other programs. At holiday conventions he would perform on-stage as a boy magician. Acting, along with writing, seemed in his blood.

Two years later (1934) the Bradburys moved again—to Los Angeles. Ray discovered that his next-door neighbor had a typewriter. Within a week he was dictating stories to the family's seventeen-year-old daughter who typed them for him.

In 1937 he joined the Los Angeles Science-Fantasy Society where, during his four-year membership, he enjoyed the good friendship of Russ Hodgkins, Fred Shroyer, and Forrest Ackerman, among others. The desire to write was flaring up stronger than ever, and through the help of the Society he published his own fan magazine, *Futuria Fantasia*, which ran to four issues with covers by Hannes Bok and inside material by Hank Kuttner, Bob Heinlein, Henry Hasse, and Ross Rocklynne. Bradbury was present in the double role of editor and author. (Under two or three pen names he wrote stories in his own magazine.) At this time he was an ardent admirer of writers like Hemingway, Steinbeck, Sinclair Lewis, Thomas Wolfe, and Sherwood Anderson.

1938 saw his graduation from high school. In his senior year he wrote and acted in a series of plays and sketches. In 1940, after a year and a half with Laraine Day's theatre group, the Wilshire Players, he gave up acting, since he felt he should be devoting his time to the serious pursuit of writing.

He did not attend college. Instead he worked at the corner of Olympic and Norton selling newspapers and rented, very cheaply, a small downtown office which contained nothing but a desk, typewriter, and chair. With determination and energy he began to write. Sights, descriptions, conversations—he put them together to form stories totaling over three million words (all of which he later burned in disgust). His reward was a rapidly accumulating pile of rejection slips.

Writers like Leigh Brackett, Edmond Hamilton, Jack William-son, Kuttner, Rocklynne, Heinlein, and Henry Hasse took an in-terest in his work and gave him invaluable criticism and aid. In fact, it was through the help of Bob Heinlein and his wife that Ray made his first professional appearance in *Script*, a California maga-zine, with a story called "It's Not the Heat, It's the Hu—." This ef-fort blossomed forth late in 1940. The following year, with Henry Hasse, he sold a story to *Super Science*. And he's been selling stead-ily at an ever-increasing rate since then. Of writing and plots Bradbury has this to say:

"I'm sometimes asked what a typical story of mine is like. I don't *know* what a typical Bradbury story is. I hope the one I write tomorrow is better than the one I write today, of course, because I expect the one today to teach me more about writing. I don't be-lieve in throwing unusual words at the reader, but I *do* believe in using the *right* word. The reader should be given more than the ba-sic meaning—he should be able to *see* a given situation. Thus, every writer must *be* his character. If you describe that character's reac-tions, feelings, sensations, then the reader is able, by self-identification, to become an actual part of each story.

"I usually take from three to six months to finish a story. But I'm not working on it all that time. I try to keep about twenty-eight stories in process during one year, though these are rarely finished. When I'm not as interested in a story as I should be, I simply shift to another that exerts a stronger personal appeal to me at the mo-ment. There is always some story to fit whatever mood I happen to be in when I crawl out of bed in the morning. I think it very im-portant that a writer be at work on something, *anything*—to be writ-ing. My annual total of finished stories now is between 12 and 15.

"Instead of filing story ideas I write an opening. It may be very brief but I get words down so the idea is there and the correct moods and tensions are established. Thus, the actual narrative is under way and ready to continue at any time.

"Writers must know human behavior. They should study people with the eye of an artist; people of all kinds, shapes, and colors to provide a sort of 'backlog of human nature' for their subconscious. A story, in my opinion, is not successful through logic, or beautiful thinking, or by its appeal to the intellect (though these elements *must* be present); rather it succeeds if it 'gets under your skin'—if it is hard to forget because you have *lived* it with the characters, sharing in their hopes, fears, and happiness.

"Writing is hard work. There is plenty of discouragement and heart-break waiting along the way. And no matter how well a writer sells, his future is always uncertain, since each story submitted must stand on its own individual merits *as* a story. I have often been asked for writing tricks. I don't know any shortcuts which make writing a cinch. It's simply work and study and more work. If you want to be a writer badly enough—WRITE—and keep on writing. If you don't give up and are good enough you'll sell."

Bradbury is a family man now. In September of 1947 he married Marguerite McClure, UCLA graduate, and they have two daughters—Susan, two years old, and Ramona, six months.

In the short story field, Bradbury has reaped considerable acclaim over the past few years. He has simply proven anew that nothing worthwhile is earned without great effort. If he is a success, then it is surely an earned and a deserved success. Whether or not he will continue to rise is up to him and to no one else.

—*Ray Bradbury Review* (1952)

Portrait of a Writer

There is a shining light illuminating the field of literate fantasy in our decade. It emanates from the work of a young man whose name is rapidly becoming synonymous with the rebirth of the short story as an art form in America; who has, in less than a dozen years, achieved nationwide recognition for his particular genius in both the fields of fantasy and realistic fiction. Of a uniform and consistently high quality, the short stories of Ray Bradbury have seen publication in every market from obscure and short-lived literary journals through almost every slick and pulp magazine. He is the man who cracked the ivory tower of *Mademoiselle* with a vampire story, gained a coveted admittance to *Harper's* with a psychological fantasy, and stormed the portals of *Collier's* and the *Saturday Evening Post* with science fiction.

His second published book, *The Martian Chronicles*, drew the admiring praise of such well-known critics as Christopher Isherwood, who termed Bradbury "a writer of great and unusual talent." Other reviewers have actually placed him on an equal footing with Guy de Maupassant and Edgar Allan Poe, and he has been referred to as "the greatest original writer the fantasy field has produced in modern times." Naturally there are those who do not agree with such all-inclusive statements, yet any who read Ray Bradbury, whether or not they see eye to eye with his convictions, will have to admit that here is a writer with something to say—the will and the talent to say it, and the integrity to back it up. Integrity. That word means everything to Bradbury. To maintain it in his work has cost him years of steady rejections, uncountable days of discouragement, and anguishing periods of uncertainty. But it has paid off in a rich dividend. It has paid off in the emergence of an intensely fresh and original style, in the acclaim of an ever-increasing segment of the reading public eager for something more to chew on than the vanilla pudding published in the slicks, and in Ray's own personal satisfaction that he is always, for any market, doing the best writing of which he is capable, and saying the things he wants to say in the way *he* wants to say them.

To Bradbury each new story he writes represents a fresh challenge—a new experiment in the imaginative. Strong emotion and conflict are present, while poetic descriptions shimmer from the page. Yet basic simplicity in theme and idea is the keynote of his work. He believes in the utilization of the commonplace everyday things around us, which offer an abundance of plot material which all too many writers fail to examine—the usual turned unusual. Around a strong, direct foundation he builds mood and color and action—until the original theme (many times hoary with age), revamped by his style and imagination, becomes a completely fresh reading experience.

His stories are, in most cases, briefly told with a quiet intenseness which immediately carries the reader into the very heart of chillingly believable situations faced by the characters. Dialogue and description are balanced, one upon the other, to lend a subtle contrast to the whole. The climax is reached with unexpected suddenness, and the narrative is brought to a swift termination.

Despite the smooth delivery of the final product there is no helter-skelter plunge into writing on Bradbury's part. Before that shining, neat, beribboned package is presented to the public it has been wrapped and rewrapped, shuffled and changed, polished and tightened. Whether one page or twenty-one it is the best Bradbury can deliver at the time—and the spike-tailed self-critic that dwells in his typewriter is no easy chap to please!

I personally know of one short story Ray has been at work on, at odd times now and again, for over five years. He may finish the last rewrite job on it tomorrow or ten years from now! He has nearly half a thousand partially written ideas, plots, and stories kicking around in his studio, and he is constantly inventing new ones.

His work reveals him as a mixture of the man and the child. But this is not to say that he is an adolescent—not any more so than a great number of intelligent thinking adults. We grow to maturity so fast in this quick and hurrying world that the few really important attributes of childhood are all too often lost in the shuffle. A child is not afraid to release intense emotion; he is capable of a wonderful sense of clarity about many things which are ignored by the cynical life-hardened adult. The child's imagination is not fitted and set and molded by the constricting bonds of life's reality. Ray Bradbury has managed to retain the clarity, the emotion, the unleashed imagination of his childhood, and add to it the objective outlook and philosophical balance of the mature adult.

He delights in the creation of incredibly advanced electrical houses which cook their own meals and sing nursery rhymes to themselves and show ever-changing pictures on their walls; of tiny mechanical mice with minds of their own; of fragile golden insects capable of spinning artificial webs of thinnest silver. He recreates the fairy tale of childhood and embellishes it with the perspective of mature adulthood.

But with all this he is a bitter young man with no false illusions about the world we live in. With a coldly detached and discerning eye he dissects his neighbor—strips bare the frailties, the fears, the weaknesses, of a gadget-loving everybody-going-nowhere-fast people. Like the late George Orwell he pulls no punches, but hits us where we live—in the synthetic unreality of a movie house, in the silvered reflection of our television sets. With savage, biting slashes he drives home his rage. Few modern classics of our time carry more raw impact than "Way in the Middle of the Air," or sharper satire than "The Fireman."

On Mars he carefully fashioned his own personal utopia—his literary Shangri-La, containing jeweled and delicate cities inhabited by a lithe and golden-eyed race of Martians, who lived in the constant beauty of murmuring fountains and books which sang to them—lovers of fine arts and rich music—philosophers and dreamers who dwelled in peace and contentment along the quiet canals. And as thoroughly as he had built Bradbury destroyed. The silver locusts—man in his rockets—came down from the skies and laid Mars to waste under their feet. In reading *The Martian Chronicles* we are struck with the truth and beauty man might well achieve, yet blindly scorns for thoughts of power and war. In the creation of Mars Bradbury shows us what we *could* be, and in its destruction what we actually *are*. His Martians are a well-adjusted and quietly happy people—etched in sharp relief against the neurotic and commercial earth invaders. It is not a pleasant book in many ways, but it *is* a thought-provoking and very brilliantly conceived job of writing.

I hope I have not created the impression of a grumbling defeatist who sees in writing merely the best way to give vent to his anger with mankind. For, of course, this is far from the fact. Bradbury can see the worth as well as the shallowness of living, and his sense of humor—the ability to "laugh while crying"—is acute, and put to frequent use in most of his stories. He has a great fondness for the things most of us tend to take a little too much for granted—the simple greenness of the grass, the sun on a crisp summer day, the way a beach can look at sundown. It is in this final awareness, this essential humanness, in the ability to temper the sorrow with the joy that he emerges as the fully three-dimensional creative artist that he is.

To borrow from Dorothy Baker—he is the "Young Man with a Horn." His horn is the realm of fine storytelling and his notes are pure and clear and brilliant, and descend on a multitude of ears. Let us hope he continues to play for us.

—*Ray Bradbury Review* (1952)

The Bradbury Years

That tempest in the science fiction teapot, Ray Bradbury, has sold nearly a million words of fiction during his thirteen-year professional career. His total stands at 185 originals with at least a dozen new stories bought and scheduled for the coming eighteen months. Beyond initial printings, well over 50% of the Bradbury output has been re-sold to magazines, books, radio, television, and, recently, movies. Some titles have seen as many as ten reprintings, with the classic "Mars Is Heaven!" selling twenty-five times in six languages!

In this article I intend to point out those particular stories which I personally feel represent Bradbury at his best and present a generalized picture of his growth throughout the years.

1940

Emerging from the protective womb of science fiction fandom (a period in which his stories, poems, and parodies gained wide acceptance in fanzines) Bradbury achieved definite, if somewhat shaky, professional status in November of 1940 shortly following his twentieth birthday. "It's Not the Heat, It's the Hu—," a satirical slap at clichés, appeared in *Script*, a West Coast humor magazine, unable at that point of its uncertain existence to pay for material used (a fact which in no way diminished Bradbury's immense joy at seeing his name at last in professional print!). This vigorous one-page short demonstrated his annoyance at a cliché-spouting society and is worthy of note as an example of a philosophy he was to pursue to a much greater extent in future work.

1941

Bradbury's first actual sale occurred when *Super Science Stories* purchased "Pendulum," a collaboration with Henry Hasse—an extensively rewritten and vastly improved draft of one of their earlier fanzine efforts.

1942

"The Candle," his fifth sale, appeared in the November issue of *Weird Tales*, initiating a long series for this magazine. Shallow, complete with contrived climax, "The Candle" was wholly typical of the standard weirdie, offering no hint of the unique originality which was to trademark his work in *Weird Tales*.

1943

The Bradbury talent began to assert itself in 1943, a year especially notable for "King of the Gray Spaces" (*Famous Fantastic Mysteries*), one of the first in a group of stories responsible for shifting the emphasis in science fiction from the bug-eyed-monster-scientific-gimmick tale to the emotional-human-interest type of story. Of course this is not to say that Bradbury singlehandedly engineered this shift. Writers like Bob Heinlein and Ted Sturgeon did a great deal toward changing ossified patterns. "Promotion to Satellite" (*Thrilling Wonder Stories*), another Bradbury yarn of 1943, qualifies in this progressive category but lacks the polish and depth of "Gray Spaces."

In the realm of pure fantasy, "The Wind" (*Weird Tales*) is easily outstanding for the year. Like "Gray Spaces," it represents a radical departure, in that Bradbury began to draw upon his own dreams, hopes, and fears of childhood. And the quality of his work, gaining impetus from the utilization of genuine emotion, increased immeasurably.

1944

In 1944, however, Bradbury was still a confused and unsettled young man. He was simultaneously producing very good and very bad fiction. The type of science fiction he wanted to write met stiff resistance among editors. In fact, the only editorial encouragement and help he ever received came from the detective pulps, while science fiction editors ignored his work, bluntly advising him to conform or remain unsalable. Bowing to pressure, he wrote three painfully obvious imitations of Leigh Brackett for *Planet* and, still unsure of his field, energetically plunged into the detective magazines with a total of seven crime tales appearing in 1944. These stories were trite, conventional vehicles, in which Bradbury forced wooden characters into unreal acts and situations.

His really original work was confined almost solely to the pages of *Weird Tales*. Such excellent stories as "There Was an Old Woman," "Reunion," "The Lake," and "The Jar" saw print in *Weird Tales* in 1944. By harking back to the early small-town days of boyhood in Illinois, he was able to write with a conviction and authority noticeably lacking in his science fiction and detective tales.

1945

Despite a continuance of sorry excursions into the detective field (possibly the worst of these, "Corpse Carnival," appeared under the pseudonym of D. R. Banet in *Dime Mystery*), his careful attention to mood and story structure landed him, at last, in the slicks. The poetic and moving "Big Black and White Game," based directly upon an incident in his youth, appeared in the *American Mercury* and was immediately chosen by Martha Foley for her annual anthology, *Best American Short Stories* of 1946, while his *Mademoiselle* story, "The Invisible Boy," a brilliant study in loneliness, achieved Honor Roll listing among distinctive American short stories printed in 1945. Two other quality stories from *Weird Tales*, "Skeleton" and "The Dead Man," strengthened his growing reputation in fantasy.

1946

Undoubtedly the biggest Bradbury success of the year came with publication of "Homecoming" in *Mademoiselle*. Chosen for the 1947 anthology of O. *Henry Memorial Prize Stories*, this remarkably original and beautifully written fantasy placed Bradbury at the top of his field. Other superb exercises in terror continued to appear in *Weird Tales*, among them "The Night" and "The Smiling People." *Charm* presented "The Miracles of Jamie" and *Collier's* the nostalgic "One Timeless Spring."

With "The Million Year Picnic" in *Planet Stories*, Bradbury staged a successful return to science fiction after a year's absence. "Chrysalis" (*Amazing Stories*), though overlong and lacking the concise impact of "Picnic," evidenced strong original treatment of a familiar theme. The short novel "Lorelei of the Red Mist" (*Planet*), written in collaboration with Leigh Brackett (Bradbury wrote the entire last half), was largely experimental, since it represented the only space-opera he had ever tackled.

1947

Bradbury's first published book, *Dark Carnival*, a collection of macabre gems, was released by Arkham House. At least three outstanding stories appeared for the first time in its pages—"The Next in Line," "Jack in the Box," and "Uncle Einar."

"I See You Never," Bradbury's realistic *New Yorker* short, was chosen for *Best American Short Stories* of 1948, and although two of his best fantasies appeared in smooth paper publications ("The Man Upstairs" in *Harper's* and "The Cistern" in *Mademoiselle*), slick editors remain stubbornly unconditioned to science fiction. The

Collier's-Post reject, "Zero Hour," caused a major stir within science fiction circles when it finally sold to *Planet*.

1948

This year Bradbury's original sales jumped to twenty-one! His science fictional break into the slicks occurred with "The Long Years" in *Maclean's Magazine*, the Canadian counterpart of *Collier's*.

His forceful study in faith, "Powerhouse" in *Charm*, qualified for the O. *Henry Memorial Award Prize Stories* of 1948, winning third prize in that anthology. In addition, "The Meadow," the only story he ever wrote directly for radio, won inclusion in *Best One-Act Plays* of 1947–1948.

Beginning a four-year-straight run in the annual *Best Science Fiction* anthologies, two of his yarns were chosen for the 1949 volume—"And the Moon Be Still as Bright" (*Thrilling Wonder Stories*) and "Mars Is Heaven!" (*Planet*). Other top-grade science fiction of the year included "The Earthman" (*Thrilling Wonder*), "Asleep in Armageddon" and "Pillar of Fire" (both in *Planet*). In 1948 Bradbury bowed out of *Weird Tales* with three shorts ("Fever Dream" best among them), ending a seven-year twenty-five-story association.

Detective Book Magazine carried his superb study in mental terror, "Touch and Go," which surely ranks with the finest contemporary crime fiction.

Two neglected classics, a fantasy and a bit of nostalgic realism, remain to round out a highly successful year: "The Women" (*Famous Fantastic Mysteries*) and "End of Summer" (*Script*). Neither story has seen reprinting. Unpicked fruit for some wise anthologist!

1949

In marked contrast to earlier years (prior to 1948) when Bradbury was selling little or no science fiction, fifteen of the sixteen originals printed in 1949 fall under the science fiction heading. The one exception was "The Great Fire" from *Seventeen*, the lightly whimsical tale of moonstruck adolescence later chosen for the anthology *Best Humor of 1949–1950*.

A host of feminine readers were no doubt genuinely astounded to find a science fiction novelette in the reserved and selective pages of their fashion magazine, *Charm*, but that is precisely where the original longer version of Bradbury's "The Silent Towns" appeared. He had managed, by dint of unending effort, to crack a major U.S. slick with a Martian story! *Maclean's*, in Canada, followed up its Bradbury of the previous year with another science fiction yarn, "The Exiles" (under the gaudy editorial title of "The Mad Wizards of Mars"!). The crop of notable science fiction continued with "Holiday" and "The One Who Waits" (both from the *Arkham Sampler*), "I, Mars" (*Super Science*), and "The Naming of Names," "The Man," and "Kaleidoscope" (from *Thrilling Wonder*).

1950

With Doubleday's publication of *The Martian Chronicles*, a book that earned unreserved praise from critic and reader alike, Bradbury firmly established himself among leading short story craftsmen. "Ylla," the lead story in the collection, appeared in *Maclean's* under the title "I'll Not Look for Wine."

This year also witnessed his science fictional invasion of U.S. slickdom's big two—*Satevepost* and *Collier's*. His lyric masterpiece, "There Will Come Soft Rains," preceded, by one week, the oft-reprinted "To the Future" ("Fox in the Forest") in *Collier's*, while the *Post* gave the feature spot in their September issue to his savage short "The World the Children Made" ("The Veldt").

His carnival fantasy of the tattooed giant, "The Illustrated Man," was presented in *Esquire* with loud editorial fanfare.

Equally excellent non-fantasies of the year (each of them based upon incidents in his Illinois hometown) included "Miss Bidwell" (*Charm*), "The Window," "Season of Disbelief" (both *Collier's*), "All on a Summer's Night" (the *Philadelphia Inquirer's Today*), and his suspense classic "The Whole Town's Sleeping" (*McCall's*).

Planet featured "Forever and the Earth" and the poetic "Blue Bottle" (which the editors, in extreme error, retitled "Death Wish"). His bitter attack on Southern race prejudice, "Way in the Middle of the Air," was finally accepted by *Other Worlds* after having been rejected by almost every editor in the field as too controversial.

At least seventeen of the twenty-three original stories printed in 1950 qualify as superior examples in the highly competitive field of the "serious" short story. Five of these later earned a place on the Distinctive American Short Stories list in Foley's *Best American Short Stories* of 1951.

1951

On the heels of *The Martian Chronicles* Doubleday released *The Illustrated Man*, a mixed collection of fantasy and science fiction. His fourth Canadian science fiction original, "The Rocket Man," previewed in *Maclean's*, saw first U.S. printing in this volume. It received Honor Roll listing in the same anthology that included his "The Other Foot" (*New Story*)—*Best American Short Stories* of 1952.

Bradbury's longest effort, "The Fireman," a 25,000-word short novel in *Galaxy*, drew enthusiastic response, as did "Here There Be Tygers," a stylistically beautiful account of man's "dream world," written especially for the anthology *New Tales of Space and Time*.

A number of excellent slick stories appeared in 1951—"The Pumpernickel" (*Collier's*) and "These Things Happen" (*McCall's*). The *Post* went "all out" in the presentation of his "Beast from

20,000 Fathoms" ("The Foghorn") with one of the most impressive double-page illustrations ever to grace its pages. And rounding out the year, Bradbury's science fiction vignette, "The Pedestrian," appeared as the first piece of fiction to be printed by that astute political publication, the *Reporter*.

1952

With book publication in England of *The Illustrated Man*, Bradbury altered the contents to include a powerful new fantasy, "The Playground," which must surely be counted among the best work he has done to date. (This story will make its U.S. debut in *Esquire*.)

The *Post* presented his delightful fantasy love story, "The April Witch." *Today* featured his haunting portrait of future frontiers, "The Wilderness."

In Canada *Maclean's* previewed yet another Bradbury (in this case a "realistic"), "Cora and the Great Wide World," a fine story of warmth and human understanding. Perhaps his best short of the year appeared in the *California Quarterly*, "A Flight of Ravens," providing the reader with a soberly chilling insight into a family crushed by the pressures of big city life.

1953

Bradbury's fifth book, *The Golden Apples of the Sun* (Doubleday), is specifically designed to appeal to a much wider audience than his previous short story collections. It contains a large percentage of realistic work from selected sources (many "best" anthology items are included) along with scattered fantasy and science fiction tales, thus constituting a representative mixture of Bradbury under one cover. Among new originals appearing in its pages, "The Flying Machine," "Hail and Farewell," and "The Murderer" are outstanding.

Beyond this volume he has written an excellent time fantasy for the anthology *Star Science Fiction* entitled "A Scent of Sarsaparilla," while the *Reporter* has printed a second story of top quality, "Sun and Shadow."

As mentioned in the preface to this article, at least a dozen more new stories are sold and scheduled for publication in book and magazine form in 1953 and 1954. Two new collections of Bradbury's short stories will have been published by the end of 1954. The comparative worth of all this material, as related to superior work of past years, remains to be determined.

–Inside (September 1953)

Bradbury: Prose Poet in the Age of Space

I've known Ray Bradbury for over a dozen years. When I met him, in June of 1950, a month after *The Martian Chronicles* had been published, he was living modestly in Venice, California, and his first daughter, Susan, was less than eight months old. Now Susan is a young lady of thirteen, with three sisters, and Ray is one of the most famous and popular contemporary writers in America, having gained an international reputation with the *Chronicles* (which has sold more than a million copies) and the many books which followed. He currently owns a warmly furnished, rambling upstairs-downstairs house in Cheviot Hills, large enough for his family and their two automobiles, one of which is a Thunderbird, prized by his wife Maggie, who drives it with élan. Bradbury still refuses to learn to handle a car, just as he steadfastly refuses to board a jet—and these are perhaps his last "holdouts" against the atomic age in which he lives. In 1955, when the Bradbury clan was beset with mumps, Ray allowed his girls to rent a TV set. Once the Monster was installed the battle was lost; the set was soon purchased. For years Ray even fought to keep telephones out of his house, and now periodically changes his phone number to offset a host of unwanted calls which cut into his writing time.

"His has consistently been the voice of the poet raised against the mechanization of mankind," a critic once declared, and this fear of engulfment has often been echoed in his stories. Bradbury has never mistrusted machines, yet he has always mistrusted the men who use them.

"The machines themselves are empty gloves," he has often stated. "And the hand that fills them is always the hand of man. This hand can be good or evil." Bradbury elaborates: "Today we stand on the rim of Space, and man, in his immense tidal motion, is about to flow out toward far new worlds . . . but he must conquer the seed of his own self-destruction. Man is half-idealist, half-destroyer, and the real and terrible fear is that he can still destroy himself before reaching for the stars. I see man's self-destructive half, the blind spider fiddling in the venomous dark, dreaming mushroom-cloud dreams. Death solves all, it whispers, shaking a handful of atoms like a necklace of dark beads . . . We are now in the greatest age in history, and we will soon be capable of leaving our home planet behind us, of going off into space on a tremendous voyage of survival. Nothing must be allowed to stop this voyage, our last great wilderness trek."

These are the words of a space age moralist, and Bradbury has often demonstrated his deep concern for mankind's future in the stories he has written. Aldous Huxley calls him "one of the most visionary men now writing in any field," and an English reviewer added to this image: "He sees man standing like Faustus, god-like power in his grasp, but aware of his own mortal frailty."

In person, Ray is anything but a somber moralist; he is, in fact, disarmingly cheerful, with a lively sense of humor, often wild, sometimes ribald, an ebullient fast-talking fellow whose enthusiasms tend to overwhelm the meek. At forty-two, he seems much younger, even with his heavy glasses, and his personality strikes sparks in any room. The warmth he generates is contagious and always welcome. But he is also very sensitive, is easily hurt, and is quick to anger if he feels that he has been unjustly dealt with in a situation.

A prime example of Bradbury the outraged in action was his suit against the famed TV show, *Playhouse 90*. A few seasons back, when this show was at its height, it presented a 90-minute drama, *A Sound of Different Drummers*, dealing with a time in the future when censorship ruled and the "Bookmen" were called out to burn the houses of those who defied their society by secreting

books. Bradbury exploded when he saw this show, called his law-
yer and immediately sued *Playhouse 90* and the network for plagia-
rism. This show, he declared, was simply a rewritten version of his
own *Fahrenheit 451*. After a pitched legal battle, Ray eventually
achieved victory in the higher courts and received a handsome set-
tlement. "Most of us would never *dream* of trying to sue that outfit," admitted one Hollywood writer, "but Bradbury not only sued,
he won! This is like trying to pin down Khrushchev for slander!"

In *New Maps of Hell*, Kingsley Amis calls Bradbury "the Louis
Armstrong of science fiction," and explains this by saying: "He is
the one practitioner well known by name to those who know nothing whatever about his field." This is certainly true. No other SF
writer has reached so vast an audience, and it is doubtful that any
writer, whatever his field, has been anthologized more than
Bradbury. His work has appeared in over 130 anthologies, including the following: *Best American Short Stories* (four times), *O. Henry
Memorial Award Prize Stories* (twice), *Best Science Fiction Stories* (five
times), *Best from Fantasy and Science Fiction* (twice), *Best Short-Short
Stories* (three times), *Year's Best SF* (twice), *Saturday Evening Post Stories* (seven times), *Best One-Act Plays*, *Best Detective Stories*, *Best Humor*, *Esquire Treasury*, *Harper's Reader*, *Prize Articles*, *Great Stories
about Show Business*, *The Silver Treasury of Light Verse*, *Best from
Mademoiselle*, *Golden Treasury of Children's Literature*, *Treasury of Rib-
aldry*, *Britannica Library of Great American Writing*.

It is Bradbury's greatest pride that his fiction is now being selected regularly for high school and college texts such as *New Horizons* and *Modern English Readings*. To date, some fifteen textbooks
have reprinted his stories, and on the contents page his name
stands next to Poe and Thurber and Hemingway and Steinbeck
and Saroyan.

Listed in *Who's Who in America* and in *Twentieth Century Authors*, Ray has soared far beyond the field which nurtured him, and

it is no longer correct to attach the label "science fiction" to his work. Of his 237 published stories, only 100 could legitimately be counted in the SF category; another 43 are pure fantasy and the remaining 94 are "straight" stories set in Ireland or Illinois or Mexico. Of course, these include his crime yarns as well as several off-beat items which all but defy classification.

Bradbury has never claimed to be a science fiction writer in the strict sense of the term, and agrees with Isaac Asimov who stated: "In my opinion, Ray does not write science fiction; he is a writer of social fiction." And, as *Time* magazine put it: "Bradbury's elf of fantasy is obviously only one element in a larger talent that includes passion, irony and wisdom."

In October of 1950, in discussing *The Martian Chronicles*, Bradbury declared: "I've never really called myself a SF writer, *other* people have. In fact, I tried to get Doubleday to take the SF emblem off the book."

However, despite such honest declarations, Ray has always admired and defended the field of science fiction, and feels that it affords a writer the widest possible range in which to deliver serious social commentary. In this respect, Bradbury has utilized the field as a "sounding board," and as a kind of "stage setting" for his parables of the future.

Writing in the *Nation*, regarding science fiction, he stated: "There are few literary fields, it seems to me, that deal so strikingly with themes that vitally concern us all today. There are few more exciting genres, there are none fresher or so full of continually renewed and renewable concepts. It is the field of ideas, where you may set up and knock down your own political and religious states. There are no boundaries, no taboos or restrictions to hold back the science fiction writer. He can function as a moralist of the space age, and show us the dangers and the risks, and possibly help us avoid costly mistakes when we reach new worlds . . ."

Bradbury has been bitterly attacked for the improper use of science in some of his books, and one angry reader protested: "The man is a mechanical moron, an engineering imbecile who knows no practical physics, whose chemistry is an abomination and whose rudimentary notions of electronics are badly short-circuited."

Ray's reply to such criticism: "It is all too easy for an emotionalist to go astray in the eyes of the scientific, and surely my work could never serve as a handbook for mathematicians. Somehow, though, I am compensated by allowing myself to believe that while the scientific expert can tell you the exact size, location, pulse, musculature and color of the heart, we emotionalists can find and touch it quicker."

Emotion has always been the key to Bradbury's work. He writes out of the primary emotions: love, joy, hate, fear, anger. "Find out what excites and delights you, or what angers you most, then get it down on paper," he advises the neophyte writer. "After all, it is your individuality that you want to isolate. Work from the subconscious; store up images, impressions, data—then dip into this 'well of self' for your stories. The characters you choose will be parts of yourself. I am all the people in all my books. They are mirror reflections, three times or a dozen times removed and reversed from myself. So, the trick is: feed the subconscious, fill the well."

Who is the *real* Ray Bradbury? What kind of man has been formed, and from what background, in his forty-two years of life?

"I was born on a Sunday afternoon in August," says Ray, "while my father and brother were attending a baseball game on the other side of town."

The town was Waukegan, Illinois; the year was 1920—and Mrs. Bradbury was having her fourth child. Ray's brother, Leonard, four years his senior, would grow up with him. But Leonard's twin brother, Samuel, had died at the age of two. A sister, Elizabeth, had died at one year. So this new baby, Ray Douglas, was the last child Esther Moberg Bradbury would bear and raise.

"My father, Leonard Spaulding Bradbury, was a power lineman for Public Service," says Ray. "He came from a family of newspaper editors and printers. My grandfather and great-grandfather formed Bradbury & Sons, and published two northern Illinois newspapers at the turn of the century, so you might say that publishing and writing were in my blood. However, as a boy, I felt a much closer kinship to an ancestor of mine, Mary Bradbury, who was tried as a witch in Salem during the seventeenth century."

Indeed, young Ray's hyper-active imagination was whetted by his Aunt Neva, who read to him from the wondrous books of L. Frank Baum when he was seven as he mentally followed the yellow brick road to the enchanting land of Oz. His mother read Poe to him each evening by candlelight when he was eight, and he was soon old enough to discover Tarzan of the Apes and John Carter of Mars as he delightedly perused his Uncle Bion's collection of Edgar Rice Burroughs.

"I loved Tarzan," says Ray, "and began cutting out the Burroughs comic strips and pasting them in a huge scrapbook. I had already started collecting Buck Rogers comics in 1928, continuing this through '37. I also saved Flash Gordon panels, and Prince Valiant was another favorite. I still have all these beautifully-drawn comic adventures down in the cellar carefully packed away in an old trunk. When I want to recapture that era I just tip back the lid."

Magic entered his life in 1931, when the eleven-year-old boy attended a local stage show which featured Blackstone, the famed magician. Ray was invited onstage, where he was duly presented with a live rabbit from the conjurer's tall silk hat. Overwhelmed with such wizardry, young Bradbury announced to his parents that he would soon become the world's greatest magician.

"Our house became a jumble of dice cabinets and ghost boxes," he recalls. "I sent away to Chicago for my magic kit, put on a paper moustache and made a top hat out of cardboard. Then I'd perform at Oddfellows' Halls and American Legion meetings—and, at home, I talked Dad into assisting me in a mental telepathy routine put on for captive relatives. They accepted quietly rather than have me play the violin, my *other* talent!"

Laboriously, each afternoon for a full year, young Ray wrote down the dialogue from Chandu the Magician's radio program. And when a traveling carnival came to town on Labor Day Bradbury made the acquaintance of "Mr. Electrico," an unfrocked minister who sold the boy a trick vase into which flowers vanished.

"Lon Chaney was my idol," says Ray. "I tried to imitate his genius for disguise, dressing as a bat with black-velvet wings which I cut from my grandmother's opera cape, or making use of jute sacking and uncorded rope in turning myself into a gorilla." Bradbury gleefully recalls hanging in night trees "to scare hell out of my little classmates," while drawings of skeletons and cobwebbed castles filled his school notebooks.

The fear of death has been a recurrent theme in Bradbury's work, and this fear took root in Ray's childhood. He admits: "A good part of my young life was spent anticipating a merciless doom that might descend the day before some personal triumph or happiness was fulfilled." When he was seven, playing at the shore of a summer lake, he had seen his cousin almost drown (an experience which he later transferred into fictional terms in "The Lake"). And when his brother failed to return until very late one evening from the dark ravine near their home, Ray was sure that Death had claimed him. (This incident was vividly recreated in "The Night.")

In 1932, the Bradburys moved to Arizona, and the boy fell under the influence of a neighbor's collection of pulp science fiction magazines. Here were *Amazing Stories* and *Wonder Stories* with their lurid covers and incredible prose. Here were giant ants, bug-eyed monsters, scaly Things from another world and daring, raygun-wielding spacemen who calmly rescued terrified maidens from alien clutches.

"Of course I was hooked," admits Ray. "I was creating my own fantasies on brown rolls of butcher paper by then, writing in pencil—until, on my twelfth birthday, I was given a toy-dial typewriter. I then switched over to this machine, which typed only capitals, and began writing sequels to the stories I'd read. It was then I determined to become a writer because I couldn't imagine a more wonderful life. In fact, I *still* can't!"

Bradbury's amateur stage appearances in Illinois as a purveyor of magic had revealed an aptitude for acting, and although he'd now given up the idea of becoming a professional magician he was fascinated by radio performers. He began to hang around the local Arizona station, KGAR, in the hope that he would be hired, bragging to school chums that they'd soon be hearing his voice on their radios.

"Eventually KGAR's resistance crumbled," says Ray, "and I was assigned the job of reading the comic section over the air to the kids each Saturday night." The boy put in five months at this job, and attempted to change his voice for each character from Tailspin Tommy to Jiggs and Maggie. ("I even assumed a thick German accent for the Katzenjammer Kids.") After the comic-reading stint had ended Bradbury became sound-effects man and bit player on other programs, frustrated only because he could not write the scripts for each show.

In 1934, when Ray was fourteen, he left his budding radio career and moved with his family to California. Upon discovering that the girl next door owned "an honest-to-god typewriter," Ray began dictating stories to her at a furious rate.

Attending Los Angeles High, Bradbury began to see his budding literary efforts printed in the school paper, *The Blue & White*, and two of his poems were published in student pamphlets. He also wrote several plays in which, as he says, "I made darn sure I got juicy lead roles. These parts were always tailor-made for a five-foot, ten-inch, slightly fat, bespectacled youth!"

Under Jennet Johnson, he took a class in creative writing, and began to read the work of Hemingway and Thomas Wolfe, both of whom were to prove strong influences on his style. By skipping lunch twice a week for several months he managed to save enough to buy his first genuine typewriter, and began shooting off stories to the *Saturday Evening Post* and *Harper's*. ("They shot them right back, which seemed insane to me. How, I wondered, could they possibly turn down the work of a mature seventeen-year-old author?")

In September of 1937, Bradbury attended his first meeting of the Los Angeles Science Fiction League, and this proved to be a decisive step toward his professional writing career. Here were other young men and women infected with the same fantasy virus; here was understanding and instant social acceptance. T. Bruce Yerke, who had invited Ray to the club, described him as "a wild-haired, enthusiastic individual who endeared himself to all of us, though he was often the recipient of assaults with trays and hammers by infuriated victims of his endless pranks."

Forrest J Ackerman, who was one of the club's pioneer members, characterizes the teenage Bradbury as "well-nigh impossible . . . a noisy kid with a broad sense of humor, who did endless imitations of Adolf Hitler, W. C. Fields and FDR . . . The calluses on the knees of us oldtimers in the club come from kneeling every night and saying 'Thank God we didn't drown him!'"

It was Ackerman who encouraged Ray to submit a short SF story, "Hollerbochen's Dilemma," for the club's mimeo-magazine, *Imagination*. This appeared in the January 1938 issue and offered no hint whatever of Bradbury's original talent. Nor did the majority of the other short pieces which Ray feverishly penned for a handful of local fanzines (those earnestly edited amateur publications which a columnist for the *New Republic* astutely termed "a peculiar blend of *Screen Romances* and *Partisan Review*").

"During this period I began haunting the doorsteps of the local professionals, many of whom belonged to the club," says Ray. "I was desperate to learn the secrets of the pros, and would pop up with a new story nearly every week which I passed around for criticism and advice from Hank Kuttner to Leigh Brackett to Ed Hamilton to Bob Heinlein to Ross Rocklynne to Jack Williamson to Henry Hasse, all of whom were incredibly kind and patient with me and with these dreadful early efforts. In fact, the above-named authors grew lean and rangy from countless flights through the rear exits of walk-up apartments when Bradbury would suddenly appear at the front door with a new manuscript in his teeth."

Ray graduated from L.A. High in '38, and immediately took a job hawking newspapers from the corner of Olympic and Norton, which netted him a bare $10 a week. Out of this meager sum, and what he could winnow out of his parents, he rented an empty room in a local office building, installed a table and chair, and carted in his typewriter.

"I spent the hours between the morning and evening editions pounding away at that machine," he says. "I also kept my hand in acting, having joined Laraine Day's little theatre group. But the writing took up most of my time; I just filled the pages—with descriptions, images, bits of narrative, character sketches, impressions, dialogue and stories. I was getting rid of a lot of dead weight, learning as I went, trying to clear the deck for professional work."

By the summer of '39, as an outlet for some of this material, Bradbury launched his own fanzine, *Futuria Fantasia*. Here, under his own name and three pseudonyms (Guy Amory, Ron Reynolds, and Doug Rogers), he filled the pages with articles, poetry, satires, and half-a-dozen short stories. Heinlein, Kuttner, Rocklynne, Hannes Bok, Ackerman, Yerke, Hasse, and Damon Knight also contributed brief items to "FuFa," but despite editor Bradbury's plea for financial aid to continue the publication ("Contributions will be happily fondled and sewed up in a green velvet sack.") FuFa died after four issues.

Emerging from the protective womb of SF fandom, Bradbury achieved definite, if somewhat shaky, professional status in November of 1940 with "It's Not the Heat, It's the Hu—," a satirical slap at clichés which appeared in *Script*, a West Coast slick which also gave other talented but unknown writers (among them William Saroyan) their first break. The fact that the magazine was unable to pay for material at that point in its uncertain existence in no way diminished Bradbury's immense joy at seeing his name at last set in professional type.

"However," says Ray, "when several more months passed with no checks in the mail I began to doubt my ability to actually crack a paying market. By June of 1941 I had told myself that if I hadn't made a sale by my twenty-first birthday I'd quit beating my head against the wall."

Just a month before he turned twenty-one, in late July, a check arrived for $27.50 from *Super Science Stories* in payment for a story Ray had plucked from the pages of FuFa and rewritten with Henry Hasse. This was "Pendulum," and it appeared that November under the double byline.

"My end of the check came to $13.75," says Ray, "and it seemed like a million to me! I walked away from the little theatre group for good; acting was behind me. By God, I was a *writer!* When 1941 ended I had written 52 stories in 52 weeks, and had made three sales with the help of my agent Julius Schwartz."

In 1942, on the basis of another half-dozen story sales, Ray left his newspaper job to apply himself to full-time production. He'd invaded the pages of *Weird Tales,* and it was here that his unique talent would flourish. With his second story for this magazine, "The Wind," printed early in '43, he began to examine his own fears and childhood memories in order to fashion emotionally real fantasies. And by December of that year his first quality science fiction story appeared, "King of the Gray Spaces," a warm, moving account of a boy who left friends and family behind to become a rocket pilot. Ray Bradbury was already making his mark as a highly original creator within the SF-fantasy field, but his course was still uncertain.

Confused and directionless, Bradbury was simultaneously producing very good and very bad work. The type of non-gimmick, non-scientific SF he wanted to write met stiff resistance among editors. The only editorial encouragement and help he ever received came from the detective pulps. SF editors advised him to "conform," to write a more standardized formula story if he wished to sell. Bowing to pressure, he produced three painfully obvious imitations of Leigh Brackett for *Planet,* and plunged into the detective magazines with trite, conventional tales of crime and murder. Only in *Weird Tales* did his work prove to be fresh and original, and he was gaining an early following, with stories such as "The Sea Shell," "The Lake," and "The Jar."

Unfit for military service because of eye trouble, Bradbury contributed to the war effort in the forties by writing advertising and radio plays for the Red Cross and the Blood Bank.

"In late 1945 I needed $500 to finance a trip into Mexico," relates Bradbury. "With Grant Beach, who was a good friend as well as an excellent ceramic artist, I planned to make a collection of Mexican masks which would be taken over by the L.A. County Museum. I knew that I would have to make some slick-paper sales, to the higher-paying markets, in order to earn the extra money. Since I had been appearing regularly in the pulps I was afraid that the slick magazine editors would be prejudiced against using my real name. So I bundled off three new stories as 'William Elliott'—and, on three successive days, I got checks from *Collier's*, *Mademoiselle* and *Charm!* Which gave me more than enough for our trip. I immediately wrote each editor, telling him my real name, and it turned out none of them had ever heard of Ray Bradbury, and that they'd be delighted to restore my byline. That was my breakthrough; the wall was down. It was a tremendous week!"

That same year saw the publication of Bradbury's powerful treatment of racial conflict, set in the realistic atmosphere of a baseball park, "The Big Black and White Game." Appearing in the *American Mercury*, the story was selected by Martha Foley for *Best American Short Stories of 1946*—fulfilling a boyhood dream and moving the young author into the exclusive ranks of America's top short storyists.

The trip into Mexico was both terrifying and rewarding. Bradbury and Beach ended up at Guanajuato, and Ray's initial shock at viewing the underground standing mummies in that city was reflected in a superb novelette, "The Next in Line," written (along with several other Mexico-based stories) back in California. "This had been my first trip outside the States," says Ray. "The country was strange and lonely, and we kept going in deeper, to the small, alien towns and villages. For a while, it seemed we'd never get back—and I put this fear into the novelette."

Marriage was "the next fearful step" in Bradbury's life, and his courtship of Marguerite Susan McClure, a UCLA graduate, began in a most unusual fashion.

"Maggie worked in a downtown bookstore," relates Bradbury. "Each afternoon she'd watch this fellow come in, carrying a briefcase. He'd nose around, pick up several books, discard them, then leave. When a number of volumes were reported missing Maggie was convinced she'd found the thief: the suspicious-looking guy with the briefcase—which was me! That's how we met. Luckily, the missing books were recovered, and I ended up stealing Maggie."

They were married in September of 1947, just a month before Ray's first book, *Dark Carnival,* was released by Arkham House. On the evening prior to his wedding day, Bradbury stacked up thousands of pages of manuscript, totaling some two million words, and made a giant bonfire of them. ("It was all bad writing, stuff that needed burning, and I've never regretted destroying it.")

A week after his first daughter was born Ray wrote a poetic tale, "Switch On the Night," in order, he says, "to teach her not to fear the dark as I did as a boy." (This story was published as an award-winning children's book in 1955.)

The next major step in Bradbury's rapidly ascending career had to do with Mars, and a series of delicately wrought, poetic tales of the Red Planet.

"During the summer of '44, on into the fall, I'd been reading a lot of wonderful fiction by Wolfe, Steinbeck, Hemingway, Sinclair Lewis, Sherwood Anderson, Jessamyn West, Katherine Anne Porter and Eudora Welty, and the idea came to me: Do a series of stories about Mars, about the people there, and the coming of the Earthmen, and about the loneliness and terror of space. Over the years the stories formed themselves, inspired sometimes by poetry which Mag would read aloud to me on summer evenings—such as 'And the Moon Be Still as Bright'—sometimes by essays or long conversations. In 1948 the whole thing took abrupt shape for me, due entirely to a rejection."

The rejection had come from Farrar, Straus on a "mixed bag" of fiction which Bradbury had submitted through his New York agent. It was sent back with the comment: "Too pulpish."

Since some of the stories *had* appeared in pulp magazines, Ray was sure that the decision reeked of snobbery and, in a fury, he packed his bags for New York. His intention was to "meet a publisher face to face" and settle the issue of quality.

"I ended up at Doubleday," he says, "and although they liked my work, they wanted a more unified kind of book, with a single theme, and right away the Martian tales sprang to mind. Six months later I turned in the final manuscript."

Overnight, with the release of *The Martian Chronicles*, Bradbury became a major literary figure, and renowned critics such as Christopher Isherwood, Clifton Fadiman, and Gilbert Highet were hailing his talent.

When the book was published in England, as *The Silver Locusts*, critic Angus Wilson declared: "For those who care about the future of fiction in the English language this book is, I believe, one of the most hopeful signs of the last twenty years . . ."

And the venerable British journal *Punch* said of his work: "To take the paraphernalia of 'science fiction'—the rocket ships, the robots and galactic explorations . . . and fashion from them stories as delicate as Farre's songs or Cézanne's watercolors, is a very considerable achievement. It is hard to speak with restraint of these extraordinary tales."

Ray Russell, who was later to buy several of Bradbury's stories for *Playboy*, summed up the impact of the *Chronicles*: "Debate as we will the flaws in Bradbury's work (what Kingsley Amis called, with cutting precision, 'that particular kind of sub-whimsical, would-be poetical badness that goes straight to the corny old heart of the Sunday reviewer'), it is impossible to deny the uniqueness of his position among SF writers: Bradbury alone has achieved 'mainstream eminence' without ever really leaving the genre of his beginnings. Instead of deserting science fiction, he has *elevated* it, along with himself."

In 1952 director John Huston indicated, in a letter to Bradbury, that he hoped to interest a studio in financing a film version of the *Chronicles*—and this was very exciting news to Ray, since Huston was one of his "personal gods," a director with whom he had dreamed of working. As it turned out, this deal never materialized, but Huston did contact Bradbury in the fall of 1953, calmly offering him the chance to do the screenplay on *Moby Dick*.

"I was staggered," says Ray. "As a boy, I had attempted to read the book, but had given up. I told Huston I'd give him a yes or no in the morning—and then plunged into Melville, reading all night. By dawn I knew I could do the screenplay and that September, with Maggie, I headed for Ireland on what was to become a pretty wild adventure."

Bradbury's only real film experience involved an original story he had worked on that year for Universal, "The Meteor," which the studio called *It Came from Outer Space*, and on which he had done a long treatment used as the basis for the Harry Essex screenplay. *Moby Dick* was a far more complex assignment, and involved transferring the essence of Melville to cinema terms. Naturally apprehensive on such a project, Bradbury was unprepared for Huston's aggressive, wild personality.

Ray spent six months in Ireland working on the screenplay, writing and rewriting some 1500 pages to arrive at a final 134. *Moby Dick*, with minor script revisions by Huston, was released in 1956, and although this saga of the Great White Whale was not the critical success Ray had hoped for (due, in large part, to Gregory Peck's weak, inept performance as Captain Ahab), the $5,000,000 film enhanced Bradbury's reputation, paving the way for other script work.

"I was called into one of the big studios to rework a fantasy script," says Ray, "and the producer asked me how I liked it after I'd read the last page. 'Fine,' I said, 'I *ought* to like it, because it's *mine*.' The guy had stolen one of my short stories, given the idea to another writer, then called me in to do the final version, failing to realize that *I* was the author of the original story he'd stolen! He ended up paying for the rights, and I got the hell out of there. This anecdote, it seems to me, is typical of Hollywood."

Bradbury's experience with Huston had supplied material for a basket of Irish stories and plays, in addition to providing him with the chance to see some of the world's great cities: Venice, Rome, Florence, Milan, and Paris. In the summer of 1957 London was added to this list when Sir Carol Reed, the noted British director, sent for Bradbury in order to have him adapt his "And the Rock Cried Out" into a full-length screenplay.

"This has yet to be filmed," says Ray, "but eventually it may be done, since Reed loved the script. He ran into problems getting the financial go-ahead. I had the same kind of bad luck with the *Chronicles* at MGM in 1961 when I worked for several months on a 158-page screenplay based on the book. Now, in '63, this may be activated. Jean-Louis Barrault plans a stage version of the *Chronicles* in Paris—and the French 'New Wave' director, François Truffaut, is presently in the midst of bringing *Fahrenheit 451* to the screen in '63. We'll have to see what develops out of all this."

Bradbury always has several literary irons in the fire, and even the projects which fail to materialize often pay him handsome dividends. (He got $10,000 from the Shirley Temple TV show for an adaptation of "The Rocket," and another $10,000 option money on "The Wonderful Ice Cream Suit" as a projected film. Neither story was produced.)

In addition to his books, poems (he has a file drawer of these which he is polishing for eventual release), short stories, TV and film scripts, plays and articles, Bradbury "keeps in mental trim" by lecturing at least twice a month. He has spoken to PTA groups, luncheon clubs, college classes, and writers' conferences coast-to-coast. In his "spare time" he paints in oil and serves on Guild committees. ("If there were three of me I could keep *all* of us busy!")

As early as 1951 Ray was making 100 reprint sales each year, and his total is now in the thousands, with his work appearing in over a dozen languages in many foreign publications such as *Perspektev, Europa, Crespi, Temps Modernes, Nuovi, Vitalino,* and *Hjemmet.* (One of his stories, "Mars Is Heaven!" has seen over 25 reprintings around the world.)

Bradbury is a strong defender of Los Angeles, and nothing annoys him more than a New Yorker who speaks darkly of the "perils" of living near Hollywood. ("I can attest that a New York writer, afraid for his virginity, can live in Los Angeles and rarely, if ever, go to a wild cocktail party, be thrown into a swimming pool with a blonde starlet wearing nothing but her Fruit-of-the-Loom undies, or be compromised by a Salton Sea real estate promoter.")

Ray hopes to finish his latest novel, *Leviathan '99,* which he calls "*Moby Dick* in the future," by the end of '63, and a new collection of his short stories will also be issued about that time. He has another 100,000 words of Illinois material which will eventually form another book, and more of his plays may later be collected between hard covers.

Bradbury is indeed a prose poet in the age of space, a man possessed by the beauty of the written word; his work reflects a passion for the shape and sound and precise rhythms of the language—and he has been able to translate this passion into imaginative literature of a very high order. Having averaged one new story or article in print each month over the past twenty-three years, he expects to do at least that well over the *next* two decades.

"Success is a continuing process," he says. "Failure is a stoppage. The man who keeps moving and working does not fail."

Ray Douglas Bradbury is still moving—and succeeding.

—*Magazine of Fantasy and Science Fiction* (May 1963)

The Great White Whale

When Ray Bradbury's *The Martian Chronicles* was published by Doubleday, in 1950, the author sent John Huston an inscribed copy. Just out of his twenties, Bradbury was rapidly gaining a reputation for high-quality science fiction, and this book solidified his leading position in the field; it offered an imaginative, bitter-poetic look at man's life on Mars some hundred years in the future. Huston liked the book and expressed interest in bringing it to the screen. The two men exchanged letters over the next three years, and Bradbury continued to send Huston his latest stories as they were published.

"I'd seen and admired every John Huston film," says Bradbury, "and had told him that I felt we were destined to work together. Sure enough, in late August of 1953, when Huston was in Hollywood editing *Beat the Devil,* he phoned from his hotel asking me to drop by. I was naturally excited, thinking that perhaps he was ready to talk about doing the *Chronicles.*"

At the hotel Huston studied Bradbury with deliberate care, as a potential buyer studies a new car. "You ever been overseas?" he asked.

"No," said Bradbury.

"Ever written a screenplay?"

Bradbury said he hadn't.

"Well, how would you like to come to Ireland and write *Moby Dick?*"

The author was stunned. "I—I don't know. I'd have to think about it."

"Take your time. Make a decision and let me hear from you in the morning."

Bradbury walked out to the nearest bookstore and bought a copy of Melville's classic.

"I'd never read the novel," he admits. "As a boy, I'd tried it and given up. Now, as a man, I wondered how Melville would affect me. I couldn't work on a book to which I didn't respond emotionally. Going to Europe as a script writer for Huston would be tremendous, but not unless I possessed the self-confidence needed for so huge a project."

In Melville, who worked a century behind him, Bradbury found a kindred spirit.

"By sheer luck, I opened the book at Melville's chapter on the great spout of the White Whale that fountained on the mysterious sea at night . . . then I came upon the chapter which details the ghost color of the whale . . . then to Ahab's monologue on its being a mild day with the wind smelling as if it blew from the shadow of the Andes . . . I read all night—in a fever of excitement—and called Huston the next morning to accept his offer."

Melville had been tried before; two other screen versions of *Moby Dick* had been released, both starring John Barrymore as the mad Captain Ahab. (In 1926, as a silent, it was called *The Sea Beast,* but when the book was dramatized again in 1930 Melville's title was restored.)

Huston had originally envisioned his father in the pivotal role, but now he had to find a substitute Ahab. The film would cost a great deal of money, and Warner Brothers had agreed to finance it providing a star name headed the cast. They were worried about the fact that no women were involved in the action, and wanted to make certain that at least one major star would be on hand as box-office insurance. Huston settled on Gregory Peck.

"Greg has colossal dignity and great masculinity," John says. "Yet he had never tackled anything like Ahab, which offers a substantial challenge to any actor. Melville's character is a complex man, at war with God. He sees the mask of the whale as the mask which the deity wears—and he sees the deity as a malignant being, out to torment the race of men as well as all other creatures. Captain Ahab is the world's dark champion who grapples with this enslaving force."

Playing Ahab, Peck would bear a long, jagged scar on his bearded face and stump about on a peg leg. His costumes would duplicate those worn by sea captains in the mid-1800s, and the ship he sailed would be authentic to the last detail.

Bradbury left for Europe that September on the S.S. *United States* with his wife and children. ("I finished reading *Moby Dick* at 4 A.M. one morning on the afterdeck in mid-Atlantic during a 100-mph hurricane—which I felt was most appropriate!") He met Huston in Paris, and they discussed Melville at the Longchamp track. In a letter to a friend, Bradbury wrote: "Huston says he is out to corrupt me; he looks forward to putting me on a horse, riding me to hounds, jetting me in a speed plane, and burying me in dope, drink and dames!"

Arriving in Dublin, where he would work at Courtown on the script, Ray was invited to walk the Irish countryside with Huston.

"It was a fine crisp afternoon, and we took off across the hills," says Bradbury. "As we were crossing an open field John spotted a huge black bull nearby, glowering at us. Before I could stop him, he'd whipped off his coat and was waving it like a bullfighter's cape in the brute's face, shouting, 'Ho-oh, *Toro*, ho-oh!' My God, I was paralyzed. Finally, the bull snorted, shook his head, and trotted away. John was actually disappointed because he hadn't charged!"

Huston's cast was truly international, a colorful group of professionals and amateurs gathered from many countries: Peck as Ahab; Britisher Leo Genn as Starbuck; Orson Welles as Father Mapple; the Dublin drama critic Seamus Kelly as Flask; Count Frederick Ledebur, the celebrated Austrian sportsman, as Queequeg; Edric

Connor, a Calypso singer from Trinidad, as Daggoo. For a time, it seemed that John Godley, Lord Kilbracken, would portray the book's narrator, Ishmael, but Huston felt he needed an actor of experience for this key role, and eventually chose Richard Basehart.

The script kept Bradbury and Huston busy for six months, and proved extremely difficult, since the mystical essence of Melville had to be caught on the screen. Ahab's frenzied quest had many levels of meaning, and this film had to offer far more than the usual sea adventure.

"It was exhausting," says Bradbury. "I read the book at least nine times, and rewrote some of the scenes up to thirty times. In all, I did 1,500 pages to get a final 150. Through the early weeks in Ireland I found myself plagued with a vast depression. I felt that I had the weight, the burden of Melville on my back. When I gave Huston the first 60 pages I was ready to quit if he felt they were not right. But he liked what he read, and that gave me the confidence to continue."

They worked closely together scene by scene—with Huston shaping and correcting Bradbury's pages, scribbling changes in pencil, pacing as Ray typed, discussing and dissecting each line of dialogue.

"One of our big problems," says Huston, "was to turn Melville's expositional passages into characteristic dialogue. We decided at the outset that the picture was going to be as close to the original novel as we could possibly make it. But while the book had some tremendous action sequences, it had little actual plot. For screen purposes, we had to make some changes in Melville's construction—like transposing the scene in which Starbuck attempts to kill Ahab to the sequence that begins, 'It's a mild, mild day . . .' Or combining a number of scenes from the book into the one we call 'the chart scene' in which Ahab reveals to Starbuck his plan and purpose in following the white whale.

"Another major problem was putting into dialogue the basic conflict between Starbuck and Ahab, the concept that a century ago whaling was actually considered a holy mission, bringing back oil for the lamps of the world. Starbuck registers shock and horror at Ahab's plan of vengeance against the whale as 'something un-natural.' Then, too, we had to get across the hypnotic effect Ahab exerts on his crew. He carried them to their doom, and it had to be logical that they would follow such a fanatic. Ray and I tried to be as faithful to the meaning of the novel as our own understand-ing and the special demands of the screen medium would allow."

Often when Bradbury worked at Courtown, Huston was out jumping Irish hedges.

"John had several bad falls," says Bradbury, "and would come limping in on canes. Every time he went out again, the rest of us at the house murmured a little prayer for his safety, because all of our jobs hung on that damned horse he was on."

The halfway point had been reached in the script when Huston came in one afternoon looking grave; he handed Bradbury a tele-gram which read: CANNOT PROCEED WITH FILM UNLESS SEXY FEMALE ROLE ADDED. It was signed: JACK WARNER.

"Has the man gone *insane?*" Bradbury shouted. "This is terrible! We can't stick a woman on board! My God, he can't be serious!"

Huston shook his head. "That's Hollywood, Ray. Warner is paying the bill, and if they want love interest, we'll just have to get it in somehow. Maybe Ahab could have an affair with Gina Lollo-brigida as a disguised stowaway . . ."

Furiously, Bradbury crumpled up the telegram and threw it to the floor; then he looked over at Huston.

"John was doubled up on the couch, laughing like a big mon-key," he says. "That's when I knew *he'd* sent the thing. I was so re-lieved I couldn't get sore."

However, Bradbury managed to turn the tables neatly on a later occasion. "John had invited a group of 100% Lords and Ladies out to his Irish estate for dinner. He kept needling me to stay for the evening and I kept telling him I had nothing formal to wear. Well, he just kept needling me in front of Pete Viertel. Finally, when John had stepped out of the room, Pete hustled me upstairs. 'Let's show the bastard!' he chuckled, and dug up an old plaid skirt, some black leggings, a fringed purse, and a dinner jacket. 'Don't you see?' he asked. 'Kilts!' When the ultra-distinguished guests had arrived and John was in their midst playing the casual host, I came down the stairs. From the doorway, in a ringing voice, Pete announced me as 'Laird McBradbury.' All the Lords and Ladies turned in my direction. I saw Huston's jaw drop three feet; it was a lovely moment."

While the script moved slowly toward completion, Captain Ahab's ship was being just as painstakingly prepared.

The whaling vessel, *Pequod,* was graphically described by Melville in his novel, and Huston had his scouts ranging the seas through Norway, Holland, and Denmark in an effort to find a similar craft. After a lengthy search for the wooden-hulled three-master, Huston's crew located a ship called the *Rylands,* floating off Scarborough, England. Launched nearly a hundred years ago, it had run cargo in the British Isles. When Huston purchased the ship it was serving as a tourist attraction, and housed a sea-going aquarium.

Art director Ralph Brinton and his team of experts set to work refitting the 104-foot craft to match Melville's *Pequod.* They stripped the *Rylands* down to her wooden hull and built a new deck some five feet above the old one, continuing the hull lines up to meet it. A new stem and transom were added, together with a quarter deck—and a false bow gave the ship the appearance of an early nineteenth-century whaler. Five whaleboats were built to original specifications, along with a carpenter's bench and a try-works on the main deck (for boiling down whale blubber into oil).

For the ship's figurehead, special Obechi wood was obtained—
and the head of an Indian from an extinct Massachusetts Pequod
tribe was carved to Huston's satisfaction.

The *Rylands* had become the *Pequod,* a three-masted, square-
rigged whaler, as tough and seaworthy as any ship of the line.

"We played a little trick on the viewer," says Brinton. "The crew
of actors only seem to sail the *Pequod.* We had another wheel below decks connected to the real tiller. Six sailors, plus a boatswain,
a mate, and a skipper kept her from yawing or broaching to. You
didn't see them on film, but they were there."

The false tiller, visible on the screen, was exactly as Melville had
described it: made from the skull of a killer whale and the jawbone
of a sperm whale.

Huston extended his mania for authenticity to the smallest details of dress and make-up.

"What a fiend he was for realism," says Peck. "We were all set
on an old seafaring leg called a 'Chelsea peg' for Ahab. It has a cup
into which the knee fits, with a wooden peg from there to the
ground. But that didn't satisfy John. He pointed out that Ahab
had lost the leg in the South Pacific and that Melville described
the peg as being carved out of whalebone by the ship's carpenter.
He wanted the one I wore to look as if it had been made at sea
under rough conditions. He even showed me how to walk with it."

Frederick Ledebur was also forced to submit to Huston's realism, for it was Queequeg of whom Melville had written: "His chest
and arms were checkered with the same squares as his face; his
back too . . . and his legs were marked, as if a parcel of dark green
frogs were running up the trunks of young palms. . . . For all his
tattooings, he was on the whole a clean, comely-looking cannibal."

Huston had Ledebur's head completely shaved. Then a make-
up man covered the actor's entire face and most of his body with
an intricate Maori-like tattoo. Finally, a topknot of hair was fas-

tened to Ledebur's bald head. (This process took over two hours each morning during the long months of shooting.)

Tensions were developing as the weeks passed.

In March of '54, with the main writing done, Bradbury and Huston clashed over a joke gone sour. They were due in England for final script work, and Huston (knowing Bradbury's fear of flight) told Ray that he'd reserved two seats for them on a night plane to London. Bradbury refused to be baited; he'd go by boat and train, and meet the director in London the next morning. Huston, suddenly angry, said this was ridiculous, but Bradbury was adamant. John's secretary was a friend of Ray's, and Huston threatened to cancel her vacation if Bradbury refused to fly with him. The two men exchanged heated words—and Huston took off for London, leaving Bradbury to his slower method of travel.

Huston was obviously under pressure; he'd been dreaming of bringing Melville to the screen for over a decade, and the mass of complex problems he now faced as producer-director were beginning to fray his nerves. He knew he had more to gain—or to lose—with *Moby Dick* than with any other film in which he had been involved.

Shooting was due to begin in July, and while Huston conferred with associates at the Elstree studios in London, his camera crew was off the Azores on a whaling expedition, gathering background action. And in Youghal, at the foot of the Knockmealdown Mountains on the estuary of the Blackwater, in County Cork, Huston's set workers were busily transforming this small Irish seaport village into a replica of New Bedford, Massachusetts. Power lines were removed, as well as all modern signs and street names; false fronts were built on the houses along the quayside; the dock was outfitted to duplicate New Bedford in 1840; the townspeople were dressed in costumes of the period. Even the harbor was deepened to accommodate Ahab's three-master.

Color was an equally important consideration, and Huston again worked with Oswald Morris, his director of photography on *Moulin Rouge*.

"I wanted the final print to have the strength found in steel engravings of sailing ships," says Huston. "Ozzie was able to give it to me."

Morris' main contribution was in the use of four negatives instead of the usual three. Over the color he superimposed a black-and-white negative, lending a hard, textured look to the print.

"This effect could never have been obtained by color alone," says Huston. "It required months of experimentation, because the balance between the negatives demanded infinitely precise adjustment.

"We also evolved a technique—for other scenes in the film—of muting the colors, giving us the grayed tones of a New England winter and the washed blues of sea weather. We'd deliberately pick overcast days in which to shoot such sequences, to heighten this effect."

By mid-April Bradbury had completed his final pages in London and was headed back for the States; his seven-month struggle with the White Whale had ended. Now it was Huston's job to bring the script to life—and for this the director had arranged a shooting schedule that would take *Moby Dick's* crew halfway around the world.

Of the star players, Orson Welles had the smallest part, as a New Bedford preacher. He appeared in just one sequence speaking from a pulpit shaped like the bow of a ship in a seacoast whaler's church, reading a sermon which recounts the story of Jonah and the whale. Yet this sermon, balanced against Ahab's obsession with Moby Dick as an evil force, was vital—and Welles delivered his lines with fierce conviction.

The departure of the *Pequod*, filmed in revamped Youghal, featured the only women in the film. They stood gaunt and black against the sky, on high widow's walks, waving goodbye to their sailing men—and Huston's camera work in this scene expertly set the mood for the sea adventures which lay ahead.

After shooting in Ireland Huston took the *Pequod* to Madeira, where Portuguese whalers still pursued the mammoths of the sea from open longboats.

"In a single day we killed twenty whales," says Huston. "Killed 'em the old way, with harpoons. This can be incredibly exciting—and unless you've harpooned a whale in a rough sea you haven't really hunted!"

The sea was a little rougher than Huston expected, and the giant model he was using for Moby Dick broke its towline and was soon lost among the waves. The RAF sent out search planes. Skippers were alerted throughout the area. The 92-foot monster weighed several tons due to the steel frame beneath its rubberized skin and posed a very real threat to small craft. (A second model broke away with Huston aboard, but was caught again before it could join its mechanical brother.)

While filming at sea Huston always managed to inject his own brand of horseplay into the day's activities—and one of his gags thoroughly startled the passengers on a passing steamer.

"John had everyone play dead on deck," says Basehart. "When the other ship passed us we were all sprawled about as if the hand of God had struck us down. It was really pretty funny."

On another occasion an actor's agent insisted on boarding the *Pequod* to watch the action. Annoyed, Huston told him where to stand, "so you won't get wet." He had been strategically placed by the director, and within moments a giant wave drenched him to the skin.

More problems arose with the costumes; they could not be kept dry on the *Pequod*'s spray-washed decks—and an entire wicker factory in Ireland was put to work making 200 oversize wardrobe hampers, lined with canvas, for transportation at sea. The extra costumes were kept dry in these portable hampers. Also, Huston found that he needed some sperm-oil vats—and the Guinness' Stout brewery rushed 150 hogsheads to him from Dublin.

"There was always something to worry us," says Peck, who put in twenty-seven exhausting weeks in place of his originally scheduled twelve. "When John told us he was going to shoot the Typhoon scenes right on the ship during an actual storm at sea we told him such a thing had never been done and that it was impossible. But it's a mistake to tell John that something is impossible. Then he's bound to do it."

In the script Ahab insists on keeping all sail flying while the storm rages—and this is the way Huston insisted on filming it.

"We began to think of John as a real-life Ahab," says Peck. "Three times we were sure we'd lost the *Pequod*—and three times she was de-masted. It's a miracle we survived."

Huston allowed salt water to break over the camera lens, which he then dried with an air hose; he swung his cameras on elastic ropes in the wind—and shot footage on the tilting, storm-washed deck as his crew battled mountainous waves.

"Sure, we could have done most of it in a studio," Huston admits. "Yet there's nothing that compares with the fury of a real storm at sea. I wanted to capture as much of that on film as I could."

The waters off Fishguard, Wales, offered the next shooting site on Huston's agenda, and it was here that he worked with Lord Kilbracken on the script's final polish.

"I certainly never expected to be adapting Melville," says Kilbracken (who was still disappointed that he had not been able to land the part of Ishmael), "but John wanted some things done to the last third of the script and asked me to step in and help. I inserted three original scenes from Melville, which pleased me—but working with Huston was something of a trial.

"On a Monday, for example, we would be precisely on the same wavelength, thinking in precisely the same way and fully understanding one another. On Tuesday, inexplicably, there would be no point of contact between us, and collaboration was impossible. On Wednesday he would suddenly speak with violent enthusiasm of what I had written—then the next day, tear the same scene to pieces. I was liable to be called any time from 7:30 in the morning to midnight. Working with Huston was exasperating, degrading, and inspiring."

Costs rose swiftly on *Moby Dick*. The three-months planned location ran to eight, and damage to the *Pequod*, plus cast casualties, ate up time and money.

"There are always casualties on any picture John directs," says an associate who was working with Huston. "In this one Dick Basehart broke three bones in his foot jumping into a whaleboat; Leo Genn slipped a disc in his back and got pneumonia; Peck hurt his kneecap; a dozen men in the crew were injured at sea. And it could have been a lot worse."

In February of 1955, some thirty-five weeks after filming had begun, the final location shots were obtained in the Canary Islands—and Huston sailed the *Pequod* back to London.

Much remained to be done, particularly in the use of models representing the White Whale. In a gigantic concrete marine tank at the Elstree studios, made to hold several boatloads of harpooners, Ahab's enemy had been cunningly fashioned from latex and steel by Robert Clark, the British oceanographer and whale expert. Clark had divided his creation into three parts: head, tail, and midsection. To cover these he used a mica-like plastic coated with white latex. A substance of aniline dye mixed with an oily chemical was added just beneath the false skin, and would "bleed" when harpooned. The three sections were mounted on metal frames in the 80,000-gallon tank, and activated by a special mechanism, which allowed the beast to swim, leap, dive, chew up men and boats, and shoot streams of water into the air. Smaller versions were also used in certain scenes. (In all, twenty electronic whales were constructed.)

Shooting the final scene, in which Moby Dick carries Ahab to a watery death, Huston arranged to have Peck lashed to the back of the huge mechanical beast so that he seemed caught there in a tangle of harpoon lines.

"By then I had a severe head cold," says Peck. "The wind machines were roaring and I was half drowned by torrents of water. Huston told me, 'I want you with your eyes staring open as you slowly come out of the sea on that whale's back—with your dead hand beckoning the men to their doom . . .' What I didn't know was that the winch they were using to rotate the section I was tied to was hand-operated. Later I learned that when they'd first tried it out the damn thing jammed! I could have *really* come up dead, which I think would have secretly pleased John—providing the last touch of realism he was after."

Before the edited print of *Moby Dick* was ready for viewing, costs had mounted to over $4,500,000. It had taken two years to film, but Huston was boyishly happy with the result. At the preview he kept exclaiming: "It's good, isn't it!"

The critics did not wholly agree. Reviews were mixed, and although most of them praised the film's color and technical brilliance, they faulted Huston for his selection of Gregory Peck.

"Peck's make-up for his role is expert," said Hollis Alpert, in the *Saturday Review*, "but the force needed for conviction is seldom present." And Eugene Archer elaborates: "Ahab, a role almost as difficult as Lear, is played by Gregory Peck in a deliberate, ranting style which . . . robs him of tragic stature. Huston's technique makes no apology for the actor's weakness, but places him as the focal point of the action in a manner which emphasizes the inadequacies of performance and crucially damages the center of the film . . . Peck struggles futilely with a role which demands the classical authority of a Ralph Richardson."

However, both critics found much to admire in the film, and Alpert stated: "Huston's re-creation of perhaps this most monumental of American novels is a kind of monumental work in itself." Archer comments: "If *Moby Dick* does not capture the full force of Melville, it conveys more depth than any American film of recent years. . . . It is probably as distinguished an adaptation of a great novel as the contemporary screen is capable of producing . . . a technical masterpiece, impressive in conception, formidable in execution—but emotionless at the core, a film for critics rather than patrons, difficult not to admire, impossible to enjoy."

Holiday magazine summed up: "*Moby Dick* is ultimately an intellectual achievement of considerable stature and power."

The Motion Picture National Board of Review cited Huston for "the year's best direction." He also won the New York Film Critics Award for Best Direction that same year with *Moby Dick*.

If he had not actually conquered the great White Whale, he had fought it with courage and high purpose. For Huston, the battle had been reward enough.

–John Huston: King Rebel (1965)

The Best of Ray Bradbury

Twice 22 by Ray Bradbury (Doubleday: $4.95).

California's celebrated prose-poet, Ray Bradbury, is a man in love with words, with their weight, shape, music, and texture, and he joyously clashes them together, seeds them, and plays their intricate rhythms across a page. This love is on abundant display in his current volume, a two-in-one collection of earlier work (*The Golden Apples of the Sun*, 1953, and *A Medicine for Melancholy*, 1959). Here are many of the stories which helped win Bradbury his reputation as the nation's most respected science-fictionist—but at least half of the 44 tales fall into mainstream genres: stories of murder, of ancient China, of Mexico, of the Irish, etc. Each reader will discover his own favorites, and the range extends from the author's pulp period in the mid-40s, when he was selling to *Weird Tales* and *Startling Stories*, into his *Harper's-Esquire–New Yorker–Playboy* period.

Sometimes, it must be admitted, the style becomes overly rich, to a self-conscious, cloying degree—but these occasional excesses are to be forgiven a writer of courage and zest who is always far out on the literary limb. At his best, Ray Bradbury is able to deeply stir us; he probes at our collective, sensitive skin, and we react with fear, anger, tears, joy. He is the puppet-master with a sure grasp on the strings of our emotion.

With Bradbury, we tremble in the shadow of glittering monster-flesh in "A Sound of Thunder"—drift the world in the delicate shell of a lonely witch girl who seeks human love in "The April Witch"—remain young forever in the eternal twelve-year-old of "Hail and Farewell"—taste the wine-tart balloon winds with "Icarus Montgolfier Wright"—return to the quiet of a lazy brick-street yesterday in "A Scent of Sarsaparilla"—spin drunkenly across the green of Ireland in "The First Night of Lent"—discover a wondrous, jeweled mermaid in "The Shore Line at Sunset"—receive the impossible gift of yellow sunlight on an alien world in "All Summer in a Day"—and share the police-state fear of frosted night walks in "The Pedestrian."

Here is a poetic, hugely imaginative book, whose best stories haunt the mind long after the last page is turned.

—*Los Angeles Times* (April 3, 1966)

Ray Bradbury

Much has been written about him, just as he has written often of his own beginnings. We know he grew up in Waukegan, Illinois, as Ray Douglas Bradbury, a bespectacled, darkly imaginative boy, fascinated by the many-shelved town library, fearful of the ravine near his house, happy with his Aunt Neva (who read Poe to him) and his Uncle Einar (the man he fictionally transformed into a winged vampire), in love with Oz and Tarzan and Buck Rogers and summer night porches and Saturday matinees. We know about the lake near his town and of the black-tented October carnivals on the shore, about the top-hatted magicians who intrigued him, about his amateur magic acts and radio readings—and about his formative days as a frantic science fiction enthusiast in California, when he contributed to a dozen fan magazines and dreamed of rockets. It is well known, also, that he wrote his first story at twelve, as a sequel to Burroughs, on a toy typewriter, that he sold newspapers on a corner for three years to support his fumbling, ill-starred early efforts at the short story, that he made his first sale just a month short of his twenty-first birthday, that he burned over a million bad words before beginning to write the good ones.

He exists today, a vitally alive man of forty-seven, straddling past and future, a spaceman in a straw hat with bicycle clips on his legs. The vanilla summers of a green, tree-shaded boyhood haunt his work; the red flare of a yet-uncharted Mars fires his mind. His stories—poetic, symbolic, passionate, evocative—reflect this double self: parables of the future echoing his own yesterdays.

"Quite often," Ray admits, "the people in my Illinois stories cross-pollinate the people in my Martian stories, and I find whole families from 1928 showing up in the year 2000 and helping to colonize Mars."

Thus, the initial entry in his Martian series, "The Million Year Picnic" (published in 1946), finds a typical Midwestern family having their "outing" on Mars. In "The Strawberry Window," a homesick colonist imports stained glass windows and porch rockers from Earth. In the startling, much-reprinted "Mars Is Heaven!" the spacemen of a rocket age land to confront a Victorian town. And Poe's House of Usher is re-burned on the Red Planet, horrors and all, in Bradbury's "Usher II."

He sees no basic conflict here. "A man cannot possibly speak futures unless he has a strong sense of the past," Bradbury declares. "Thirty-some years ago, at L.A. High, I was the only boy in my class who really believed in the Space Age, who believed we'd go off someday in rockets and land on Mars."

The genesis of Bradbury's Martian series can be traced directly back to this period, to 1940, when he printed his own fan magazine and included in it his story "The Piper." Here, clearly, we find the roots of the mature fiction he would later write and collect into book form as *The Martian Chronicles*, and which would finally extend into 1967 and "The Lost City of Mars."

A few lines from this early effort reflect the mood and tone later adopted for the *Chronicles*: "Mars is a dying world . . ." [the old one said. "We] were once a brilliant race. Now, out there beyond the mountains, beyond the dead sea bottoms . . . the men from Earth . . . rip open the bowels of our planet, dig out our precious life blood . . . no culture, no art, no purpose . . . greedy, hopeless Earthlings . . . despoilers . . . Death for the men of Earth!"

In 1963, when Time, Inc. published a special Reading Program edition of *The Martian Chronicles*, they dubbed it "the finest creation of the best contemporary writer of science fiction." This Time, Inc. volume contained seventeen stories from the series, plus "bridge passages," with Bradbury's addition of "The Wilderness" and "The Fire Balloons," neither of which was in the original 1950 Doubleday book. (In all, Ray has penned thirty Martian tales, including "Christmas on Mars," sold to *Esquire,* but never printed.)

"Science fiction is the ideal literary form in which to express the demands of our age," Bradbury says. "We are a science-fictional people living in a science-fictional culture. . . . In this time of the rocket, man has a chance to be immortal. Man can seed the universe and live forever! People often say, 'How great it would have been to be alive when Columbus sailed!' But this is just that kind of time, with our sailing ships poised on the rim of a vast star wilderness. Our exciting, awesome voyage into space, to the moon and Mars and beyond, makes this the greatest age in all of man's history."

With more than four hundred stories, articles, essays, plays, and poems to his credit, Ray Bradbury is unique. He is not a technical man. Science baffles him (even as *Life* sends him chasing after astronauts and radar eyes); he can over emotionalize; he writes, more often than not, of symbols in place of flesh-and-blood characters. Yet with all his flaws he has combined his very considerable strengths, and has become (as Kingsley Amis calls him) "the Louis Armstrong of science fiction, the most widely-known, widely-read writer in the field." At its best, Bradbury's work glitters on a page; his prose touches the core of loneliness, of wonder and warmth. He communicates on a basic level, using subtle skills acquired over long years. It is impossible to overemphasize the humanizing influence his work has exerted on science fiction. Had he done nothing more than *The Martian Chronicles* his place would be secure.

I've known Ray since 1950, and whenever we meet he is invariably excited about something. Angry, delighted, or disturbed, he is seldom placid; life holds great fascination and constant challenge for him. He fights for rapid transit, for the downtown library, for more open park areas within the city; he organizes classic film showings, serves on Writers' Guild committees, produces his own plays; he lectures at U.C.L.A., at the Cal Tech, at L.A. State, at PTA meetings ("I'm the purest kind of hambone. In my teens I did a great deal of amateur acting and this is still an important part of my psyche."); he fires off letters to magazines and newspapers, prowls downtown bookshops, rides his bike in Venice, collects modern art, is involved in oil painting and animation and old radio shows (lovingly gathering discs of *Vic and Sade*); he vigorously defends Southern California against cultural attack; he writes poetry and light opera, delights in Disneyland, and stands shaken to watch 200,000-pound-thrust rockets fire up from Rocketdyne test pads. He loves his family, holds fast to his friends, works happily in his cellar, surrounded by jammed filing cabinets, his collection of Mexican masks, trunks of old comic strips from his childhood. He is the fulfilled man-boy, loved and loving.

Critic Gilbert Highet credits this talent and energy which "have transformed him from an eager, self-taught tale spinner into a distinguished American author."

Indeed, accolades and awards, medals and grants have come his way steadily since 1946 when his uniquely styled fiction began to gain solid recognition. (That year marked his first appearance in *Best American Short Stories*.)

Ray has written in several fields: crime and suspense, stories of Hollywood and of Europe, tales of Ireland (based on his six-month screen writing stint there with John Huston on *Moby Dick*), but he always returns to science fiction, since his visionary imagination is best served by the field which nurtured him.

"I want to sell people on the inevitability and the beauty and the distinction of the Space Age," he says. "The real job of a writer is to measure the difference between things as they are and things as they should be. That's the measuring stick imaginative writers over five thousand years have used: the dream of man, the disillusionment, the reality, these things that are constantly moving in a circle through our consciousness. . . . The future rushes upon us. To read the symbols it writes on space with some prescience is our everlasting, frightening, and exhilarating job."

"The Lost City of Mars" is the first new piece of Martian fiction Bradbury has published since 1954; it is also one of his most sustained efforts—since the majority of Ray's stories are well below novelette length. It is part of the basic fabric of *The Martian Chronicles* and was written in conjunction with a projected screen version of the book.

Ray Bradbury may take us to Illinois, 1928, or to Mexico for the Day of the Dead, or to an Irish pub in Dublin—but his final drive is to the stars, to red Mars floating in a dark sea of space. Now, after fourteen years, he revisits it.

The return trip is well worth taking.

—3 *to the Highest Power* (1968)

Leigh Brackett and Ray Bradbury

In 1940 *Planet Stories* was shakily emerging as an action pulp magazine with a particular slant: its editors were looking for writers in the Haggard-Burroughs-Merritt tradition who could supply romantic space sagas on a grand scale for readers seeking wide-open action-adventure. In its fifth issue (Winter 1940) *Planet* presented a story called "The Stellar Legion" by a brand new writer, Leigh Brackett. (Her first published story had appeared in *Astounding* in February of that year.)

Reader response was direct and enthusiastic: "Give us more Brackett!" By the following summer she was back in *Planet* with "The Dragon-Queen of Jupiter," a thunderous space yarn which established her bent for poetic, swashbuckling adventure, starring iron-muscled heroes, equally adept with sword or blaster, and beautifully evil women who ruled jeweled kingdoms with cruel intensity.

Leigh Brackett soon became the brightest star among *Planet's* writers, and twenty of her rousing space sagas appeared in the magazine over a fifteen-year period. (Fittingly, a Brackett tale was featured in the final issue of *Planet* in the summer of 1955.)

Between *Planet* tales she wrote major screenplays for director Howard Hawks, turned out expert mystery and suspense fiction, much of it in the hardboiled Hammett style, and wrote award-winning westerns. (Nine of her sixteen books are science fiction; five are mysteries; two are westerns.) She's written for *Argosy* and *Cosmopolitan*—and her credits also include the Hitchcock TV show. Yet Leigh Brackett's fame rests with the fabled space epics she concocted for *Planet* and other SF markets during the '40s and '50s when the gory, glorious pulps flourished. Here, under the Brackett byline, readers were held in thrall by "The Beast-Jewel of Mars," "Citadel of Lost Ships," "The Last Days of Shandakor," and dozens more.

Editor Donald Wollheim, in selecting one of Leigh Brackett's tales for his *Prize Science Fiction* anthology in 1953, best described her position in the genre: "The mantle of the singer of sagas that pluck the heart strings and entangle the listeners in webs of suspense originally belonged, in science fiction, to H. Rider Haggard and was later inherited by Edgar Rice Burroughs. Today it rests securely upon the feminine shoulders of Leigh Brackett."

A native of California, with Mohawk and Sioux blood in her family line, Leigh Douglas Brackett was born in Los Angeles and claims that she "grew up on the sand, a book worm and a beach-comber. When I wasn't swimming or fishing I was reading. By the time I was into my teens I knew I'd be a writer. It was just a matter of selling what I wrote. That took me ten years!"

Teaching engaged Leigh's interest for a time, and she taught classes in swimming, speech, and dramatics—but the steady desire to write remained with her.

There are major turning points in each career, pivotal years in which the course of life turns in a completely new direction. For Leigh Brackett 1940 was such a year. Not only did she make her debut as a pro in *Astounding* and begin her long association with *Planet*, but 1940 is also the year she first encountered Edmond Hamilton.

A published SF writer since 1926, "world-wrecker" Hamilton specialized in stories dealing with the destruction of alien planets and was, during the 1930s, one of the more prolific purveyors of rocketing space opera. He was thirty-six when he was introduced by his agent Julius Schwartz to a slim and handsome girl of twenty-five who told him her name was Leigh.

"Ed and I had a lot in common," she says. "We'd both read Edgar Rice Burroughs from early childhood and we both shared a passion for Eddison's *Worm Ouroboros*. But it took six years for us to realize we wanted to spend the rest of our lives together."

Hamilton, who lived in Ohio, did not return to Los Angeles until 1941. By then Leigh was attending a weekly writing salon being informally conducted by Robert Heinlein. Young Ray Bradbury was also in the group. He was just on the edge of his professional career, but had yet to sell a science fiction story. He'd come to Southern California in 1934, had joined the Los Angeles Science Fantasy Society in 1937, and had completed high school with the class of '38. A frustrated fictioneer, he'd submitted twenty short stories to the class annual during his senior year. All were rejected. (But some of his poetry had been accepted.)

When Leigh met him Ray was peddling newspapers on Los Angeles street corners in order to finance his writing efforts, and looked to professionals such as Heinlein for critical aid and inspiration.

Bradbury—also an early Burroughs enthusiast—and Brackett became close friends. "I was looking for a way to break into the SF markets," he recalls. "Leigh's poetic style and dramatic content appealed to me and I modeled several of my earliest SF stories on her work. A lot of my stuff (which later appeared in *Planet*) directly reflected her influence. I hadn't found my own individual voice in science fiction and it was a clear case—in stories such as 'Lazarus Come Forth,' 'The Monster Maker,' and 'Morgue Ship'—of Bradbury imitating Brackett!"

By the following summer, Hamilton was back in town, renting an apartment for an extended stay. Bradbury was a frequent drop-in. He'd regularly appear with several fresh manuscripts for Hamilton to read and criticize.

"In those days," Bradbury declares, "I jumped all over Los Angeles with my stories. Hank Kuttner taught me to stop writing purple passages; Henry Hasse cut my stories to the bone; Ross Rocklynne was on hand with plot ideas. Bob Heinlein and his wife got some of my humor material into *Script*, a local California magazine. Then there was Jack Williamson, issuing forth with gentle praise when I needed it to keep going, and patient Ed Hamilton constantly in there with his solid professional advice. And always, of course, during those frantic years, Leigh was on tap to show me the way. They were a grand lot and I'll never be able to repay them for their help."

In 1942 Ray moved from central Los Angeles to Venice, near the ocean. "It was Leigh's habit to spend each Sunday morning playing volleyball with the weight lifters at Muscle Beach not far from Venice," says Bradbury. "I'd finish a new short story late Saturday and rush over there with it for Leigh to read on Sunday after her sessions with the muscle men. She'd light into it, make suggestions for cuts and changes—and I'd revise the story that night and send it off to market on Monday. This continued, week to week, for four years. Leigh would often have a new manuscript for *me* to read, and we'd discuss her work too. We were a pair of odd beach birds, the two of us, dreaming our deep space dreams on a strip of sunny California sand . . ."

Ray claims that he learned a great deal about action and pacing from Leigh. "She had a marvelous ability for moving a narrative along, and she knew how to begin stories properly. Her 'hooks' always worked. I remember one story of mine, 'Tomorrow and Tomorrow,' which had me frozen; I just couldn't get the right start for it. She took over and wrote the first thousand words—and it was published that way. Same thing happened with Hank Kuttner, only this time I couldn't *end* a story. He wrote the last 200 words of 'The Candle,' which was my first sale to *Weird Tales*. Writers are really very generous with one another. I've helped many young writers myself over the years and they'll go on, I'm sure, to help others."

Leigh Brackett has her own sharp memories of those long-ago Sundays on the sand. "Working with young Bradbury was a joy and a pleasure. Ray had talent fairly bursting him at the seams; he was eager, full of enthusiasm, and hungry for criticism. He never got hurt or angry at what was said about his work. And it was fine for me, having a kindred soul at the beach."

During the summer of 1944, slightly more than halfway into an action novella for *Planet*, Leigh received a phone call from Warner Brothers Studio. Could she come in and work with William Faulkner and director Howard Hawks on a screen adaptation of Raymond Chandler's detective novel, *The Big Sleep?* It would star Bogart and Bacall.

Here was literally a dream assignment. As a dedicated fan of the Hammett-Chandler school, Leigh had published her first detective novel that year, *No Good from a Corpse*. It was this book which had attracted Howard Hawks.

She gave the studio a dazed yes, phoned Ray and arranged to meet him at the beach.

"I handed him approximately 12,000 words of manuscript," says Leigh, "with absolutely no outline or instructions as to where to take the plot, and asked him to finish it. He was strictly on his own."

The idea of completing a major novella by Leigh Brackett delighted Bradbury. He now trusted his talent. The twenty-four-year-old was moving along rapidly in his career, with more than two dozen stories in print under his byline in *Weird Tales, Thrilling Wonder, Super Science, Astounding, Famous Fantastic Mysteries, Amazing,* and *Planet*. Plus sales to various detective pulps. He had already written "The Wind," "The Crowd," "King of the Gray Spaces," "I,

Rocket," and "The Lake"—all classic examples of what would later be termed "the Bradbury style."

He took "Lorelei of the Red Mist" home to Venice and tackled the second half. "I attempted to match Leigh's style and mood," says Ray, "since the parts had to meld. It took me two weeks to write the final half—and during that time I visited Leigh at the studio, got to meet Hawks and Bogart and Bacall and Faulkner. Which was a rare treat."

Working on *The Big Sleep* with the legendary Faulkner was also a rare treat for Leigh Brackett. She recalls Faulkner as "rather a small spare man, fiercely erect, with bristly iron-gray hair and moustache, a hawk nose and unusually piercing eyes."

Hawks had put a third writer, Jules Furthman, on the Chandler script for "back-up." (Furthman was a seasoned Hollywood veteran who could be relied upon to dig the script out of any holes along the way.) All three writers were instructed by Hawks to "keep the story moving fast."

Leigh spent three months on the script with Faulkner. The two worked from separate offices at opposite ends of a long hall. "He was very reserved," she remembers. "He'd come walking down the hall, straight as a soldier into my office, hand me a batch of typed pages and stride out silently. I doubt that we spoke a dozen words to one another. They changed a lot of his dialogue on the set, but kept his story construction. Faulkner was a master at screen construction."

Bradbury had meanwhile completed the full version of "Lorelei" and was anxious for Brackett's opinion.

"I was delighted with it," says Leigh. "I'm convinced to this day that Bradbury did a better job with the last half than I would have done. And it's *all* Ray's work. I didn't touch his half. It didn't need a thing, and I told him so."

Ray verifies her reaction. "I could see that Leigh was quite pleased with what I'd done with her horde of 'living dead men' and since this was my first major space epic *I* was pleased about bringing it off properly. It had been a real change of pace for me, writing a wild, Conan-inspired action-adventure. And great fun, naturally."

Brackett's use of the name "Conan" in this story was drawn from the swordsman-hero created by Robert E. Howard. When Hugh Starke, the Brackett space bandit, finds himself inhabiting Conan's massive body the plot really begins—and few space sagas offer more sheer storytelling enjoyment. This one-time Brackett/Bradbury collaboration proved to be an unqualified success in its genre and years later critics were still discussing it. In 1965, Richard Lupoff (in a book on Edgar Rice Burroughs) described "Lorelei" as "a strange combination of Burroughs-type swordplay and misty, moody fantasy. It is well worth reading."

As a personal joke, directly related to their collaboration, Leigh sold a story that year entitled "Murder Is Bigamy" to *Thrilling Detective*—in which the killer was named Bradbury and another of the main characters was named Starke. (The action was set in Venice, California.) Bradbury still has the issue, tucked away in the depths of his basement.

"Lorelei of the Red Mist" finally appeared in *Planet* during the summer of 1946, two years after its completion. Bradbury was bylined twice on the contents page—since that same issue carried his short story "The Million Year Picnic," first in his modern series of moralistic Martian tales. Thus, *two* Bradburys were side by side in *Planet* that summer: the young man just finishing his literary apprenticeship with "Lorelei"—and the maturing artist capable of creating the first in a series which would result, just four years later, in the superb *Martian Chronicles*.

For Leigh Brackett, 1946 was another pivotal year. *The Big Sleep* was released by Warner—and she married Ed Hamilton that December. Over the decades since *Big Sleep* Leigh has written several other films for Hawks, including the popular John Wayne vehicles *Rio Bravo* and *Hatari!* And her development as a creative novelist is reflected in such works as her suspense thriller *The Tiger Among Us* and in her SF triumph *The Long Tomorrow* (which Tony Boucher cited as "a quiet, persuasive, realistic story of the future, with the focus on people and believable human problems"). In 1963 she received the Silver Spur Award from the Western Writers of America for her frontier epic *Follow the Free Wind*—and capping her career in SF Leigh was invited (along with her husband Ed Hamilton) to be a Guest of Honor at the 1964 World Science Fiction Convention.

The heroic, fanciful, darkly poetic space adventures splashed in full color on the gaudy covers of *Planet Stories* are no longer with us. Brackett and Bradbury have progressed far beyond them, and *Planet* is dead. But the story these two writers produced during a warm California summer in 1944 remains very much alive on a printed page.

Take off your coat, lean back in your chair, and settle into the glorious saga of Starke-Called-Conan as he tangles with Beudag, warrior-goddess of Crom Dhu, blind Faolan of the Ships, Rann of the Red Sea, and the death-hordes of Venus.

Swords up!

On, Conan!

—The Human Equation (1971)

Ray Bradbury: Space Age Moralist

The world knows his work. Ray Bradbury is one of the major international names in the genre of science fiction. His words are translated into nearly every language; his books have become important films (such as *Fahrenheit 451* and *The Illustrated Man*); his stories are dramatized on the BBC in London, on radio in Canada, on the stage in New York; he is an in-demand speaker on university campuses. A master of the short story, poet, playwright, essayist, and philosopher, Bradbury is a space-age prophet who is not afraid to speak out boldly regarding man's destiny in the universe. The body of his work represents a study of morality set against the backdrop of the future.

"We are now into the greatest age in human history," he says, "and, sooner than any of us suspect, man will be leaving his home-planet Earth and voyaging into space on a tremendous new wilderness trek."

How will man react to this ultimate challenge? What values will he bring into space with him? How will he deal with what he finds in the vastness of our universe?

Since 1941, over the course of three busy decades, Ray Bradbury has been examining such fascinating questions within the commercial framework of science fiction. He has confronted his fictional heroes with tomorrow's unique conflicts, then has resolved these conflicts in humanistic and moralistic terms, blending drama with artistic dedication. As a result, Bradbury has become a vital and respected spokesman for the future; his books (particularly *The Martian Chronicles* and *The Golden Apples of the Sun*) are space-age classics.

At fifty-one, Ray retains the fire and joy and enthusiasm of his youth. A man of immense zest, he refuses to "settle down," refuses to allow his ideas to congeal; he remains vital, flexible, splendidly opinionated, a smiling, happy fellow who treats each day as a fresh adventure. He speaks of moon travel and space stations with the easy familiarity of a man-boy who grew up fired by the inner vision of man's leap into space—an apostle of the rocket at home among the stars.

His *physical* home is in West Los Angeles, a pleasant white up-stairs-downstairs house with a garage (for his bicycle; he has never driven a car) and a basement workroom (for his typewriter, books, and files). When I talked to him recently, in the living room of this California home, we tackled the subject of God and space. Ray had much to say.

"I believe that space travel will give us a new image of God," he declared. "Man must stand as God."

"You mean, represent Him in space?"

Ray shook his head. "No, no—not represent Him. *Be* Him. Man is a fusion of the human and the divine. I believe that the flesh of man contains the very soul of God, that we are, finally, irrevocably and responsibly, God Himself incarnate, that we shall carry this seed of God into space."

"What about other forms of alien life?" I wanted to know. "Are you saying that God is with man alone and not with the creatures we'll meet in space?"

In answer, he walked over to a shelf, pulled out one of his books. "I have two stories in this collection relating to priests who must face what they think of as 'godless' aliens on Mars. They come to realize that they are wrong, that all forms of life in God's universe partake of Him." Bradbury's eyes flashed. "How *dare* we consider ourselves God's only true children? In this era of deep-space exploration we have no room for blind ego. A giant spider on Venus may be born of God, as we are, and contain the same sensitivity." Ray laughed. "The missionary of tomorrow is going to have a few surprises in store for him!"

"Ray, do you really believe we'll ever come upon such creatures—or is it just an extension of your science-fictional imagination?"

Bradbury put away his book and settled into the couch; he tented his hands, eyes thoughtful and serious. "We'll meet them out there. Not in our lifetime, perhaps, but in the lifetime of our children. We *are* going out into space. It's our final frontier, and man has always been driven to explore his frontiers. The far horizon is no longer a mountain range; it is now a star cluster. And somewhere out there, amid all the billions of worlds, we'll run into creatures of vast intelligence, alien in shape and attitude but who share the God in man. I surely believe that. This belief is as solid to me as the couch I'm sitting on."

"But how will we be able to communicate with them?"

"The same way we're beginning, even now, to communicate with dolphins. It may take a thousand years, but the gap between man and alien *will* be crossed. We'll find, once we're able to reach other galaxies, that we are far from alone in the universe. And this is not my particular fancy; most of our leading scientists share my views."

I switched from aliens to origins in asking him my next question: "Did you deliberately choose science fiction as a field in which to express your personal philosophy?"

"My functioning in this field is a happy accident," he told me. "As a boy of nine I became an avid fan of Buck Rogers, and I soon devoured all of Burroughs' Martian tales. I was captivated by the world of rockets and space travel. And, instead of growing out of it, I grew *into* it. I matured into manhood reading and writing and relating to science fiction. The first sale I made, in July of 1941, was a science-fiction tale to *Super Science Stories*, a pulp magazine of that period. When I moved into the bigger magazines I took my science-fiction ideas with me."

"But you've written in several fields," I pointed out. "Irish stories, mystery-suspense, terror tales, nostalgic trips into your Illinois boyhood . . . yet you always seem to come back to science fiction. What lures you back?"

"I keep coming back to the field because science fiction is the fiction of *ideas*," he said, "of sociology, psychology, and history, compounded and squared by time. Many people still tend to think of it as comic-strip material, without roots, yet most of our greatest writers have added to the genre—from Plato to Lucian to Sir Thomas More and Francis Rabelais, on down through Jonathan Swift, Kepler, and Edward Bellamy. We all know the work of Wells, Huxley, and Orwell, as well as the 'father' of the field of modern science fiction, Jules Verne—a writer I still read and enjoy immensely. My work follows on a direct line from such men as these, and I'm very proud of my literary ancestors."

Bradbury went on to project some startling ideas of man in relation to a universal image. "A human being is not a shape at all, in the ultimate sense—not a thing of torso, head, arms, not a color, nor does it have to do with a particular place of habitat. Humanity is an *idea*, a concept, a way of doing, a motion toward light and away from darkness. We must never wear a label, not even the label of human being, for in space, we transcend all labels. So we must constantly seek new ways to know and encourage the will toward light in each of us; we must never go back into darkness. We must not, *cannot*, repeat the mistakes of our immediate past in our future. Man must rise up to meet the alien on foreign shores for we are, in reality, taking God out to meet God."

"A lot of science-fiction writers are negative with regard to the future," I reminded him. "They foresee the destruction of man by his own hand. How do you feel about this?"

"I'm an optimist," said Bradbury. "I discard all such dark to-morrows. I have faith in man as God and God as man; I believe we'll be immortal, seed the stars and live forever in the flesh of our children. That's my job as a writer—to show man his basic goodness, to dramatize his struggle up and away from this planet. I reject the doomsayers!"

We got into the area of science fiction as a prophetic form of literature, and Bradbury enthusiastically expanded this view.

"Look," he said, "there's hardly a subject that hasn't appeared in the science-fiction magazines twenty years before it came into public notice in the large-circulation popular publications. In the fields of politics and philosophy, science fiction predates all the mouthings of our present politicos and space philosophers by many years. In fact, it seems to be that every time a government official opens his mouth these days something from a 1928 issue of *Amazing Stories* falls out! Most of today's astronomical theories, printed in learned scientific bulletins, were dramatized in *Wonder Stories* back in 1931!"

Bradbury and I discussed the "death of God" idea current in some segments of our society.

Ray laughed. "If some think we showed God out the front door, they may be startled to find He has quietly infiltrated the basement." Then he got serious again. "If all the universe is God, then are we not extrusions of miraculous matter put in motion to combat darkness, to cherish Being and, with our own extrusions, our metal rockets begot in testpit and factory, to go off in search of yet finer miracles basking under far suns? Man, the ant, will yet build the mountain. We are busy now with the first sand grains that will fill the vast hourglass of our billion-year endeavor."

Then he summed up our conversation.

"Science fiction offers us the quickest route between these two points, a way of shorthand, to educate ourselves to our basic scientific and moral problems without resorting to pomp, preachment, or pushing, and remain entertaining withal. You can't reach people, and deal with fundamental issues of life and morality, without entertaining along the way." Ray walked over to a table in the room on which one of his daughters had placed a small toy rocket. He picked it up, turning it in his fingers. "Today we're still playing at space," he said softly. "Even our moon landings are little more than a halting step at the rim of space. But, with future vision, I look beyond our moon and see man, a Godform, lifted in thunder to seed space and live forever."

The poet, the moralist, the optimist had set me to thinking. I walked away from the quiet, tree-shaded home of Ray Douglas Bradbury and paused for a long moment on the walk outside, shading my eyes to peer into the vault of blue sky.

I heard his words again, echoing inside my head: ". . . not in our lifetime, but in the lifetime of our children . . . we *are* going out into space . . . to the stars."

Far above me, the stars waited, and are waiting . . . for me, for us, for man.

—*Unity* (April 1972)

Bradbury in the Pulps

For the first full decade of his professional career, the bulk of Ray Bradbury's fiction first appeared in the pulps.*

In all, nearly a hundred of his short stories (roughly a third of his lifetime published output of 300-plus) were sold to and were first printed in pulp magazines—beginning in 1941 and extending through 1950, when the success of *The Martian Chronicles* as well as a variety of sales to slick-paper markets allowed him to leave the pulps behind.

Critics outside the SF-fantasy genre have been quick to dismiss the pulp work of any author who later achieves world fame. They refer to "crude beginnings in the lurid pulp markets," and then proceed to discuss the author's "serious" work.

But just how "crude" was this early pulp work of Ray Bradbury? How much of it remains lost and unreprinted? Are the critics correct in their statements that a writer's early pulp work can be put aside as "inferior" to his more mature fiction?

These are the basic questions I'd like to examine in this article— the first to separate Bradbury's pulp work from the main body of his fiction.

Ray Bradbury was twenty-one when his first pulp story, "Pendulum," was printed in the November 1941 issue of *Super Science Stories*. A collaboration with Henry Hasse (based on an earlier Bradbury fanzine tale), it *was* crude and pulpish—a story Bradbury wisely never reprinted in any of his collections.

---

*As I use the word in this article, "pulps" refers strictly to the full-size, rough-paper publications, with their gaudy covers and untrimmed pages; I exclude the semi-pulp, digest-size magazines, such as *Galaxy* and *F&SF*.

He followed it, a year later, with his first sale to *Weird Tales*, "The Candle." This story was also crude and unmemorable, and was never collected or anthologized. His third pulp appearance, "The Piper" (in a 1943 issue of *Thrilling Wonder Stories*), was equally bad—an overwritten, never-collected dud.*

Looking at this trio of early Bradbury tales, one would tend to agree with the critics and dismiss the work as "trashy." Yet with his fourth pulp entry, "The Wind" (in a 1943 issue of *Weird Tales*), Bradbury exhibited the first strong evidence of an original talent for off-beat fiction. "The Wind" was the first Bradbury "classic"—and has been reprinted many, many times since its revised version appeared in Bradbury's first book, *Dark Carnival*, in late 1947.

How many other "classic" Bradbury stories appeared originally in the pulps? The answer: more than two dozen. A listing of their titles alone is enough to stir wondrous memories in any Bradbury reader:

> "The Crowd" (1943)
> "The Scythe" (1943)
> "King of the Gray Spaces" (1943)
> "The Lake" (1944)
> "There Was an Old Woman" (1944)
> "The Jar" (1944)
> "Skeleton" (1945)
> "The Night" (1946)
> "The Million Year Picnic" (1946—first tale of *The Martian Chronicles*)
> "The Small Assassin" (1946)
> "Zero Hour" (1947)
> "The October Game" (1948)
> "And the Moon Be Still as Bright" (1948)

---

* "The Piper" was later anthologized in England.

"The Earth Men" (1948)
"Pillar of Fire" (1948)
"Mars Is Heaven!" (1948)
"The Women" (1948)
"Touch and Go" (1948)
"The Off-Season" (1948)
"The Man" (1949)
"Marionettes, Inc." (1949)
"The Naming of Names" (1949)
"Kaleidoscope" (1949)
"Dwellers in Silence" (1949)
"Outcast of the Stars" (1950)
"Carnival of Madness" (1950)
"Forever and the Earth" (1950)
"Death Wish" (1950)

More could be added, depending on personal favorites. Do these stories represent the "crude beginnings" of a career? Indeed, they do not! On the contrary, these marvelous tales are the work of a writer in his prime—an outpouring of literary richness unsurpassed in Bradbury's "mature" years. (Admittedly, his work in other non-pulp markets in this same period contains many fine tales, but none finer than the best of these pulp classics.)

Today, in the 1970s, these same pulp stories are being regularly selected by college professors for use in textbooks—sharing space with Hemingway, Steinbeck, Fitzgerald, and Faulkner.

Bradbury wrote all of them when he was a "hungry" young man in his twenties. (The last was printed just as he turned thirty.) He was in desperate need of sales to pay the rent (in contrast to the 1970s, when his lecture fees alone approach $100,000 annually). His income during these productive pulp years was below the "poverty level" by today's standards, and each small pulp check was vital to Ray's survival. He has elsewhere revealed his writing income for this period, and the low figures are shocking:

1941–$75 (3 sales)
1942–$104 (4 sales)
1943–$503 (12 sales)
1944–$1,064 (23 sales)
1945–$2,100 (15 sales)
1946–$2,900 (18 sales)
1947–$3,174 (27 sales)
1948–$3,184 (number of sales not revealed)
1949–$4,410 (number of sales not revealed)
1950–The "breakthrough" year, with many sales to major markets. (No figures given.)

By the close of 1950, his income increased greatly, as it has each year since—yet this low 1940s income had beneficial effects on Bradbury's career: he was *forced* to produce a large amount of fiction, forced to use all his talents and imagination to survive. Example: 24 of his stories—pulp and slick—were printed in 1950; in the 1970s his printed total, in eight years, reaches only 11!*

Looking at the other side of the coin, not all of Ray's stories printed in the '41-50 period are classics—and 32 of them remain unknown and unreprinted. Many of these were unsuccessful and deserve their obscure fate: they are not to be found in any Bradbury collection, nor were they ever anthologized. They remain "lost" in the pulps that printed them.

Ray is well-known for his fantasy, horror, and SF tales, but it is interesting to note that he had 17 stories printed in the detective pulps of the '40s, and that his byline appeared rather often in the

---

*Although a sizable amount of verse, plays, and nonfiction pieces balance this small amount of fiction in overall wordage.

pages of *Dime Mystery.* Bradbury claims that these detective tales were failures, with three exceptions: "The Small Assassin," "Touch and Go" ("The Fruit at the Bottom of the Bowl"), and "Wake for the Living" ("The Coffin"). He has allowed these three to be collected in his books. Three others have been anthologized over his objections ("The Candy Skull," "It Burns Me Up!," and "The Trunk Lady"). The remaining 11 exist only in their original pulp format.*

Beyond the three exceptions, Bradbury is correct as to the value of these detective efforts—although at least one other tale, "A Careful Man Dies," is effective enough to merit book publication. (As the editor of *Gamma,* in the early 1960s, I reprinted this story.)

In the same basic period, beginning in 1945 with "The Big Black and White Game," Ray was also selling his fiction to slick markets—but his prime creative work over these formative years appeared in the pulp magazines, particularly in *Weird Tales,* where he established his early reputation as a modern master of fantasy, and in *Planet Stories* and *Thrilling Wonder* where major portions of *The Martian Chronicles* first appeared. In all, he had original work printed in 16 pulp titles through 1950—with his biggest year being 1948, when 17 of his stories were printed in these markets.

Beyond 1950, Ray had only reprints in the pulps—the last of these in *Planet Stories* for November 1953: "The Golden Apples of the Sun." By the mid-1950s the grand and gaudy pulp magazines were gone—but not before a young writer named Ray Douglas Bradbury had made a large and lasting contribution to literature in their perishable pulpwood pages.

—*Xenophile* (November 1977)

---

*Bradbury later allowed Dell to collect 15 of his crime/detective tales as *A Memory of Murder* in 1984, but he was never happy with these early stories.

Introduction to *The Last Circus and The Electrocution*

Tom Mix on Tony the Wonder Horse, at full gallop, firing a target pistol from each hand . . . a trained-cat act, with felines in tiny red helmets climbing fire ladders . . . Mr. Electrico, blue flames dancing from his fingers . . . Blackstone the Magician, white rabbits hopping merrily and magically from his glossy top hat . . . dwarfs, clowns, sword swallowers, tattooed men, and spangled ladies . . . leopards and trained lions, leaping to the crack of the ringmaster's whip . . .

All these and more came to Waukegan, the quiet little Illinois town close to Chicago in the 1920s and early '30s—and were met, full-tilt, by a wide-eyed, bedazzled boy named Ray Douglas Bradbury who would write about all of them, who would transform his lifelong fascination with carnivals and circuses, stage shows and magic acts, into books and stories uniquely his own, celebrating the joys and excitements of sideshow tents and circus wagons, Ferris wheels and steam calliopes . . .

"From a very early age, growing up in Waukegan, I was madly in love with carnivals and circuses," declares Bradbury. "At ten, one summer, having encountered a gigantic red-and-yellow circus banner on our main street, I backed up, awestruck, lost my balance and fell through an ungrated window pit into a cellar barber shop, severely upsetting the patrons."

This mesmerizing banner announced the arrival of the fabled Ringling Brothers, Barnum and Bailey Circus, which visited Waukegan each summer for a weekend stopover on its way to Chicago.

Bradbury vividly remembers "the five-o'clock-in-the-morning circus train that pulled in down by the wide lake shore. My brother Skip and I up early, shouting in whispers, dressing as we

98

ran across town—to stand and watch the circus elephants unloaded in the cold dark . . . all the animals in their night-barred cages shivering their hides, horses jingling their black-and-silver equipment, men cursing, lions roaring . . . camels, zebras, llamas passing in a dawn line—the mighty burden of Barnum's entertainments opening out and unfolding from the mile-long freights . . ."

Ray also recalls working hard to see the show. "We were very poor in those days," he says. "Skip and I had no money for tickets. So we earned our tickets by coiling tent ropes, lugging soda-pop bottles, watering the animals . . . As payment, we got in free for the weekend."

Later, as a professional, Bradbury recreated these magic days in such stories as "Time in Thy Flight" (1953), dealing with a visit via time machine by a group of futuristic schoolchildren, none of whom had ever seen a circus. Here, Bradbury describes the pre-dawn arrival of the circus train: "From it stepped gigantic gray elephants, and cumbersome red-and-gold wagons rolled from the long freight flats, as lions paced in boxed darkness . . . They saw candy-pink trapeze people whirling while baking powder clowns shrieked and bounded."

The carnival/circus world exerted a strong influence on young Bradbury. "The shrill tooting and wheezing of calliopes and the up and down going-nowhere-in-a-circle of those bright carnival horses fascinated me," he says.

But this world had its dark side. Many of society's physical outcasts, billed as "freaks," traveled with these shows—and in his mood-murder story, "Corpse Carnival" (*Dime Mystery*, 1945), Ray dealt with these unhappy misfits: "The tall circus banners fluttered somber and high in the night wind . . . and the tent canvas sagged like a melancholy gray belly . . . Beneath the stomaching canvas, in a rectangle, stood the flake-painted platforms, bearing their freak burdens of fat, thin, armless, legless, eyeless misery: The Tattooed Man,

Blimp, Popeye . . . The naked electric bulbs buzzed in the air, large fat Mazda beetles shedding light on all the numbed, sullen faces."

Bradbury was particularly drawn to the freaks. As a boy, he had felt equally out of touch with the world around him, experiencing a strong sense of his own lack of conformity: "I could see that I was an orange monkey in a society of brown monkeys!"

Anita Sullivan, writing in the *English Journal*, declares: "Bradbury's brand of fantasy came to birth in the world of the carnival . . . a subconscious touchstone for a whole system of moods and images which emerged later in his writings. The carnival was . . . a clearinghouse for his imagination . . . and many of his tales contain skeletons, dwarfs, magicians, and carnival freaks."

The title of Ray's first book, published in 1947, reflected this absorption: *Dark Carnival.*

Analyzing what he termed "Bradbury's carnival concept," the late Henry Kuttner (Ray's friend and early critic) found this same "alien" element echoed in many of the stories. "His protagonists are most often outsiders. They are children, or they are old, or they are circus freaks—or baroque in some other way. They have been ejected, or have ejected themselves, from the materialistic culture which is Bradbury's prime target."

Indeed, the characters Bradbury created were often misfits, attempting to cope with a hostile outside world. In "The Dwarf" (1954), the protagonist is destroyed when the illusion of normalcy shaped by a carnival mirror is cruelly reversed, and his freakish condition becomes unbearable.

Bradbury's carnival horror tale, "The Illustrated Man" (*Esquire*, 1950), offers another example of a tortured individual existing outside the norm, whose "body paintings" assume a sinister life of their own, predicting murder and destruction. (Bradbury later used this story, rewritten, as a framing device for his second collection of stories, under the same title.) The story's ill-fated protagonist was based on a combination of tattooed men, whose grandly illustrated bodies had held him in thrall on the high, summer-night platforms. His description of The Illustrated Man is classic: "Dinosaurs, trolls, and half-women-half-snakes writhed on his skin in the stark light . . . The roses on his fingers seemed to expel a sweet pink bouquet. The Tyrannosaurus rex reared up along his leg . . . and rockets burned across spaces of muscle and flesh . . . In so many accordion pleats of fat, numerous small scorpions, beetles, and mice were crushed, held, hid, darting into view, vanishing, as he raised or lowered his chins . . . He was a crowd unto himself . . . an entire civilization."

In "The Black Ferris" (*Weird Tales*, 1948), Bradbury created a melancholy atmosphere for this fantastic tale of a Ferris wheel which had the power, as it turned against the sky, of moving its passengers through time, into old age or youth. He uses "increasing storms and leaden skies" to establish his mood, then takes us to the carnival: "It lay by the sounding lake with nobody buying tickets from the flaky black booths, nobody hoping to get the salted hams from the whining roulette wheels, and none of the thin-fat freaks on the big platforms. The midway was silent, all the gray tents hissing on the wind like prehistoric wings."

Although "The Jar" (1944) is set in Louisiana swamp country, this is another dark tale from his own childhood, based directly on the shivery experience of seeing a floating embryo, which he described in the story as "one of those things they keep in a jar in the tent of a sideshow on the outskirts of a little, drowsy town." This weird carnival object becomes the basis for power and murder as the tale progresses.

The circus and the carnival often assumed separate identities in Bradbury's writing—as the two stories in this book clearly demonstrate. The circus represents lost innocence, the carnival corruption and evil.

Previously unpublished, "The Last Circus" is an elegiac tale of sad warmth and nostalgia, a celebration of the rite of passage from childhood to adulthood. The boy in this story feels that he has seen the last circus. In actual fact, Bradbury's family moved away from Waukegan in 1934, when he was thirteen, leaving the summer big-tent shows behind forever.

"The Electrocution" reflects the dark side of Bradbury's carnival concept. And while the circus came to Waukegan in bright summer, the carnival always arrived in the chill of autumn, for Bradbury a time symbolizing the end of growth and the beginning of decay.

"Each September, over Labor Day, the Dill Brothers Combined Traveling Show would assemble near the lake," says Bradbury. "It was a seedy affair of patched canvas and paint-blistered sideshow platforms, arriving in run-down rusted trucks. The carnival smelled of cabbage, and the carny men reeked of cheap whiskey. The magic was there, of course, but it was a different kind of magic."

The word "carnival" derives from the Latin *carnem levare*, meaning the "putting away or removal of flesh." Thus, the carnival assumes its own dark reality, independent from the flesh-and-blood world beyond its tents. It offers a seed ground of illusion ideal to the purposes of a fantasist. Here, the impossible becomes ordinary; that which is alien is the accepted norm, and miracles are promised. As critic Steven Dimeo has observed: "The carnival becomes Bradbury's catch-all image for those persistent conflicts between dream and reality, youth and adulthood, the past and the future . . . signifying the madness of life itself, as well as death, which looms large in the metaphor of the carnival."

One very real character from Dill's Traveling Show stands out sharply in Bradbury's memory—an unfrocked minister-turned-performer, the man billed as "Mr. Electrico."

"He sat, caped in black velvet, on a platform in an electric chair," says Bradbury. "A man in his sixties, thin, pale, ascetic, fierce-eyed, with a great white shock of hair that flamed on his head. The barker would shout, 'Watch him, folks! Here comes ten thousand volts!' A switch was thrown and blue sparks hissed from Mr. Electrico's fingertips. He quivered in the surge of raw electricity, his face burning like white phosphor as the current sizzled his frail body. Fire squirmed in his ears. Flames danced in his nostrils. Blue light ran along his tongue and jittered his teeth."

Mr. Electrico, with a showman's flourish, picked up a sword dripping hot sparks, touching the arms, necks, shoulders of the stunned crowd members below his chair—among them twelve-year-old Ray Bradbury, who remembers "standing there with balls of fire tufting my earlobes and frying my lashes. It was beautiful, like being knighted by God. I shut my eyes and cupped the grand lightning to gather it in."

After the act had ended, the crowd moved on to other miracles, but young Ray lingered at the tent entrance behind Mr. Electrico's platform—until the regal showman himself noticed the wide-eyed youngster. What could he do for him? He could let him see the chair, that's what!

"And he did. He let me touch it, sit in it—and after that took me under-wing to walk me around the grounds and introduce me to all the stars: the dwarf, the skeleton, the giant, the trapeze people, the tattooed man . . . and he gifted me with a trick vase which vanished black balls in an instant."

Bradbury sheepishly returned the following noon, bringing back his vase, which had broken. "Mr. Electrico gave me another— and we walked along the lake shore, talking of magic and life. I told him I wanted to become a great magician, and he nodded seriously. Then he looked at me deeply and told me a very remarkable thing. He said he'd met me before, long years ago, that he had seen my eyes, my look, in the face of a young man who had died in his arms, on the battlefields of France in the Argonne during the First World War."

Young Ray was, of course, greatly impressed and felt himself, at twelve, part of a much larger world. "I felt quite immortal, gifted with a part of someone from the past."

Bradbury never forgot those meetings with the incredible man in the carnival electric chair—and much later, in 1962, he used him again in his novel, *Something Wicked This Way Comes*: ". . . the Electric Chair was a hearth and on it the old man blazed like a blue autumn tree . . . as electricity sheathed over him . . . a slam and sizzle of power which prowled in around over under about man and prisoning chair . . . The old man's hair stood up in prickling fumes. Sparks, bled from his fingernails, dripped seething spatters on pine planks."

This novel is Bradbury's full and final tribute to the dark carnivals of his youth, described with intensity and passion. It deals with a carnival of deadly evil which descends on a small Illinois town, in the dark of October, to threaten the lives of two young boys ("myself and Skip, in fictional guise!") who, with the help of their father, finally triumph over it.

"The Last Circus" and "The Electrocution," presented in tandem, represent the light and dark sides of Bradbury's circus/carnival theme. Collected here in book format for the first time, they reflect, like carnival mirrors, the youth who woke in an Illinois dawn, listening to the steam calliope whistle off by the lake shore, calling him to its painted tents, to its bright illusions and fresh magics.

"There goes the whistle, the trumpet, the drum," writes Bradbury. "The circus moves and, moving, takes us with it—from some mysterious beginning to some unknowable end."

—*The Last Circus and The Electrocution* (Lord John Press, 1980)

Afterword to "The Fireman"

"The day came when I set myself a task larger than any before," recalls Ray Bradbury. "I wanted to write a short novel and have it as 'truthful' as my stories . . . about a fireman named Montag, a book-burner in some future year who suddenly discovers that books are flesh-and-blood ideas and cry out, silently, when put to the torch."

Ray Douglas Bradbury was thirty, and already famous in science fiction for *The Martian Chronicles*, when "The Fireman" was printed in the February 1951 issue of *Galaxy*. He was at the peak of his writing power, and was in the final phase of his move from the lower-paying pulps into the large-circulation, slick-paper markets which would bring him world acclaim. Despite his brilliance in the short-story form, Bradbury had yet to prove himself with a major piece of longer fiction. Could his intensely poetic, symbolistic style be maintained at short-novel length?

The idea of a regimented, book-burning society had been fictionally examined by Bradbury as early as 1947, when he wrote the short "Bright Phoenix." (The story had failed to sell.) In 1948 his novelette "Pillar of Fire" was printed (a story he later called "a rehearsal for *Fahrenheit 451*"). Ray explored other variations of the idea in "The Exiles" (1949) and in "Usher II." By the middle of 1950, when *The Martian Chronicles* was published, Bradbury had drafted, in nine days, a story he called "Long After Midnight." (He changed its title to "The Fireman" soon thereafter, and used the "Midnight" title on a collection of short stories in 1976.)

In his introduction to a 1967 special edition of *Fahrenheit 451*, Bradbury recalled the process from idea to novel: "Its real root-system goes back to my great and abiding love of libraries. From the time I was nine, up through my early teens, I spent at least two nights a week in the town library at Waukegan, Illinois. In the summer months, with no school, there was hardly a day I could not be found lurking about the stacks, smelling the books like imported spices, drunk on them even before I read them. . . . It followed then that when Hitler burned a book I felt it keenly. . . . I'd pass the firehouse often, coming and going to the library . . . and I find among my file notes many pages written to describe the red trucks and coiled hoses and clump-footed firemen."

Bradbury also recalled the night he awoke to fire at his grandmother's house. "There, climbing the wall, was a bright monster . . . . it made a great oven-roaring sound . . . as it ate the wallpaper and devoured the ceiling . . . I never forgot it. . . . Perhaps it was all these memories . . . of a thousand nights in lamplit libraries, the fire station, and the fiendish fire itself . . . that caused *Fahrenheit 451* to grow—from notes to paragraphs to story to novel."

Another stimulus to the eventual expansion of the novella into the novel-length version was an attempt at library censorship imposed by Senator Joseph McCarthy in his fanatical pursuit of Americanism. Bradbury was greatly disturbed at the idea of being told which books he could or could not read. "So I wrote about a totalitarian," he says. "A stupid man . . . a prejudiced man . . . who, in the midst of this nightmare, wakes himself up and begins to look around and realize he's burning the ideas of the world."

When Bradbury expanded his 25,000-word novella into a 50,000-word novel (published in October 1953) he followed the same basic plot sequences. Many brief references in the novella became full scenes in the novel; characters were fleshed out and expanded; story elements were rearranged and developed in greater depth. Bradbury added to the story's fire-and-sun symbolism, and deepened the character of Montag's wife. All to the good. But, inevitably, certain original passages, dialogues, descriptions, mood-bits, were sacrificed in transition.

Fahrenheit 451 has become a best-selling classic. Over three million copies have sold in U.S. paperbacks alone, and it won Bradbury an Award in Literature from the National Institute of Arts and Letters in 1954. But the superb, pioneering novella that inspired it has been unjustly neglected for almost three decades, never collected or anthologized anywhere. It is proper to have it back in print—a classic in its own right, proving that Ray Bradbury, at novella length, could achieve the same impact and power of language and ideas exhibited in his shorter fiction.

—*Science Fiction Origins* (1980)

Introduction to *Ray Bradbury Review* (1988 Edition)

For me, this book is a time machine. Its 1988 reincarnation, in hardcover, whirls me back three dozen years—to the fall of 1951 when I lived in San Diego, California, and worked for Convair Aircraft as a packing sheets inspector on B-36 bombers. At a raw twenty-three, I was a recently transplanted Missourian, just four years out of Kansas City, and disturbingly uncertain of my place in life. Having attended the Kansas City Art Institute, I seemed to be headed in the direction of commercial art, but I had no real faith in my ultimate ability to sustain a career in this field.

I was desperately in love. Not with a woman; not then (I didn't marry until 1970); I was in love with words. With books and stories. With plots and ideas. Somewhere in the back of my mind a goal was forming, the pearl within the oyster: I wanted to be a writer. A professional. A man able to live entirely by the written word.

That previous year, in the summer of 1950, I'd met twenty-nine-year-old Ray Bradbury, who seemed to be living exactly the life I hungered for. Here was a young man with two successful books and a sizable group of stories to his credit, with his byline featured in an impressive variety of magazines, and who had been writing professionally for a full decade, earning more money and acclaim each year.

Ray thus became a tangible role model for me. We were on the same wavelength. I found emotional resonance in his fiction and personality. And we had both grown up in the Midwest.

I began to analyze his style and technique; in longhand, I copied out descriptive passages from his work, trying to get the "feel" of how he handled words and phrases. I'd been reading him for six years, having discovered Ray's fiction in the pages of *Weird Tales* when I was in high school.

Of course, I enjoyed the works of many other writers during this period, from H. G. Wells to Jack London (and had been writing stories of my own since the age of ten), but Bradbury was special. After we met, talked, corresponded, the idea of becoming a published writer seemed far less remote. Bradbury had done it; he'd taken the plunge into that dark and uncertain sea of words and was very much afloat. Why not Nolan?

But I needed a major project, a work that would fully engage me, test my writing mettle, and possess an intrinsic value beyond the usual amateur effort. I decided on a book-length coverage of Ray's first decade as a professional writer. By living inside his skin for a few months, as it were, I'd be functioning as both writer and observer. This profile of Ray would serve as a possible future profile of my own life as a writer. A blueprint for success. A road map leading to the kind of life *he* was living.

This book is the result.

It was an obvious labor of love. I paid its publication costs, illustrated its pages, and had it photocopied by one of San Diego's top litho firms. Actually, I couldn't really afford to do it. But, emotionally, I couldn't afford *not* to do it. Ray was very cooperative, happy to have his life and work examined in depth at this relatively early stage of his career. He provided manuscripts, and much personal information.

I worked on the *Review* during the entire summer of 1951, completing it in the fall. That was a pivotal year for Bradbury. His second daughter, Ramona, was born in May, joining her older sister, Susan, born in 1949. (Eventually, Bettina and Alexandra would be added to the family.) In June 1951 Ray's first paperback appeared (a Bantam edition of *The Martian Chronicles*) and, after

100 stories, he had moved from the pulps into the higher-paying, higher-prestige slick paper magazine markets. He was also going into nonfiction, and had his first major essay printed in *Charm* that year. Already established in radio (on *Dimension X*, *Suspense*, etc.), he entered the TV arena in '51 on *Tales of Tomorrow*.

By year's end, at thirty-one, he achieved a major breakthrough, being interviewed in the *New York Times Book Review*. Critics were now becoming aware of this dynamic young Californian. The *Review*, therefore, seemed ideally timed to mark Bradbury's transition from a science fiction cult favorite to a writer of national importance.

On January 7, 1952, having just received his first copy of the *Review*, Ray sent me a letter from his home in Los Angeles: "I write with humility and gratitude. It is a beautiful job, a fine job, a job that I will remember for a long time."

Greatly cheered by these words, I awaited the verdict of others. The critical reception quite literally stunned me:

"A very handsome and scholarly piece of work."
                                                    Robert A. Heinlein

"Without a peer in its field, and illustrated with some of the finest and most imaginative artwork we've yet encountered."
                                        Don Fabun, in *Rhodomagnetic Digest*

"About as nifty an item as we've seen, well-styled, capably illustrated, beautifully printed."
                                        Jerome Bixby, in *Startling Stories*

"To the scholar and collector . . . this mass of material on the first ten years of Bradbury's career will prove fascinating. A welcome reference work now—and a valuable collector's item in the future."
                    Anthony Boucher, in the *Magazine of Fantasy and Science Fiction*

Tony Boucher was right: Copies of the original printing seldom appear in catalogues, but I recently saw one listed at fifty dollars. (I sold it, at publication, for fifty *cents!*)

This book began my writing career, and within two years of its publication I had sold my first professional story. Two years beyond that saw me quit my job and set sail on that dreamed-of life as a full-time professional writer. Now, in 1988, with a thousand sales behind me, with forty-seven books published, having been a full-time pro for thirty-two years, I look back to the *Ray Bradbury Review* as the launching platform that helped make it all possible.

Appropriately, I dedicated my first published collection of short stories to Ray Bradbury.

The *Review* was forerunner to a dozen books and pamphlets on Bradbury's life and career, including my own *Ray Bradbury Companion* in 1975. Yet the *Review* retains importance as the first extensive treatment of his work—and its rebirth gives today's readers a chance to examine pioneering, autobiographical, and critical material that has been previously unavailable. For example, Ray's lengthy and sensitive essay "Magic, Magicians, Carnival and Fantasy" has never been reprinted. It provides a revealing, penetrating look at his early years. His other work for the book, two articles and an off-beat short story, also retain power and value—and can be found only in these pages.

Additionally, the *Review* is notable for the contributions of two major talents who are no longer with us today: Henry Kuttner and Anthony Boucher. (Kuttner died in 1958, Boucher in 1968.) Their commentary on Bradbury and his early work is sharp and insightful.

I still happily maintain friendship with a third major contributor to the *Review*, Chad Oliver (who was then at the beginning of his own highly respected career as writer and anthropologist). Chad discovered Bradbury in the pulps and immediately recognized Ray's unique gifts. From his home in Austin, Oliver continues to teach and write—having become head of the Department of Anthropology at the University of Texas.*

Sad to say, I've lost contact with most of the other contributors, but I can tell you what became of Frank Anmar. Several years ago, in a fit of pique, I killed him. (That's right, he was one of my alter egos; I don't use pseudonyms these days.)

The book's Bradbury Index has its own fascination. Ray has come a long, long way from this listing of his first published decade of work. Consider the statement: "To date, all of Bradbury's movie deals have fallen through." This about the man who went on to write the screenplay for John Huston's classic *Moby Dick*, and who has seen dozens of his books and stories on the big screen and on television since 1952: *Fahrenheit 451*, *The Martian Chronicles*, *The Illustrated Man*, and *Something Wicked This Way Comes*. To name a few. Currently, Ray is writing for his own syndicated *Ray Bradbury Theatre*.

The *Review* lists 170 Bradbury stories; his output now exceeds 300. And his three-book total has mounted to 70-plus, including limited editions. He has seen 200 of his poems in print, along with hundreds of articles, essays, reviews, and introductions. He's written countless stage plays, TV scripts, and screenplays—and his work has been selected for more than 1,300 anthologies and textbooks around the world.

But it's time to let the *Review* speak for itself—time to climb aboard my personal time machine and travel back to January of 1952 . . . Here, then, in its first hardcover edition, is the *Ray Bradbury Review*, reproduced in facsimile exactly as it appeared thirty-six years ago.

---

*[Oliver died in August of 1993, at the age of 65.—WFN.]

I wish to thank my friends, Craig and Patti Graham, for this literary rebirth. Due to their loving and enthusiastic efforts, the *Review* has attained a new life in the 1980s.

–*Ray Bradbury Review* (Graham Press, 1988)

A Half-Century of Creativity

Welcome to the party! That's what this is, a celebration.

All of us, all the authors in this book, are here to celebrate Ray Bradbury's fifty years of professional writing. From 1941, when he appeared in the pulp pages of *Super Science Stories* (shortly after his twenty-first birthday), into 1991, he has produced an unbroken flow of books, stage works, television shows, and magazine stories.

Ray's ubiquitous output includes six novels, several hundred stories (printed in over a thousand anthologies and textbooks and in two dozen Bradbury collections), as well as a countless array of poems, essays, plays, articles, scripts, and reviews. Some 350 editions of his books have been translated in thirty countries around the world.

Bradbury's influence on other writers has been enormous and steadfast, particularly in the fields of science fiction, horror, and fantasy. His name comes up again and again when professional writers are asked which authors influenced them in the formative stages of their careers. (My first published story was a Bradbury pastiche.)

We all grew up reading his books, and just listing those early titles stirs a host of memories: . . . *The Martian Chronicles* . . . *Fahrenheit 451* . . . *The Illustrated Man* . . . *The Golden Apples of the Sun* . . . *Dandelion Wine* . . . *Something Wicked This Way Comes* . . . and, of course, *The October Country*, where, according to Bradbury, "it is always turning late in the year . . . where the hills are fog and the rivers are mist . . . where noons go quickly . . . twilights linger, and midnights stay."

He is October's friend. Ray's favorite holiday is Halloween and, in testimony, his basement studio is awash in monsters and skeletons.

More expansively, he is Imagination's friend—and he has never limited himself to any one area of storytelling. Ray has set his tales in California, Ireland, New York, Mexico, Mars, and Deep Space, while becoming poet laureate of the American heartland—the bard of Green Town, Illinois.

He's written of dwarfs and dinosaurs, mummies and Martians, of dark carnivals and dandelion wine, boyhood lakes and book burners, of fire balloons and flying machines, marionettes and million-year picnics, kaleidoscopes and magical kitchens, of ice cream suits and invisible boys, Irish ghosts and robot grandmas, mermaids and mechanical hounds, fever dreams and farewell summers, of astronauts and small assassins, drummer boys and Dublin beggars, trolleys and time travel, sea shells and star rockets . . .

All of which are represented, at least in spirit, in this anthology celebrating Ray Douglas Bradbury's fifty years of creativity.

Among a stellar cast of contributors, Gregory Benford explores a theme linked to *Fahrenheit 451*; Charles L. Grant delves into the grim territory of Mr. Dark, from *Something Wicked This Way Comes*; Ed Gorman takes us into Bradbury's seedy carnival world in an affecting sequel to "The Dwarf"; Chelsea Quinn Yarbro and William Relling deal with Bradbury's vampire family from *Dark Carnival*; Cameron Nolan writes of the emerging sexuality of *Dandelion Wine*'s Douglas Spaulding, and Orson Scott Card takes us into the autumn of Doug's life, when he is a grandfather with a family of his own; Robert Sheckley, James Kisner, and Roberta Lannes rocket to the sandy deserts of the Red Planet in their own *Martian Chronicles*; F. Paul Wilson offers a chilling sequel to "The October Game"; Chad Oliver journeys into Bradbury's nostalgic summer-lake Midwest, and John Maclay picks up on a scene from *Death Is a Lonely Business*.

There's more! J. N. Williamson sends several Bradbury characters on a bizarre journey into immortality, and Norman Corwin gleefully introduces us to Ray's feisty Muse. Richard Christian

Matheson conjures up a deft little mood piece reminiscent of "The Invisible Boy," and from the files of the late Charles Beaumont comes a tale strongly linked to Bradbury's "The Meadow."

Here, too, exploring Bradbury country, are Christopher Beaumont (with his first prose story), Richard Matheson, Bruce Francis, and Isaac Asimov (with a Bradbury tribute).

Bradbury himself joins the celebration with "The Troll," a wickedly delightful new fantasy tale, and caps the book with a special "Afterword," in which he looks back on a half-century of remarkable creativity.

A toast, then, to the Maestro of Imagination, whose enduring works have affected us all, entertained us, enriched our lives, and illuminated our collective humanity.

Here's to *you*, Ray!

—*The Bradbury Chronicles* (1991)

Behind the Illustrations:
The Real Ray Bradbury

I was sixteen, still attending high school in Kansas City, Missouri, when I bought a copy of the November 1944 issue of *Weird Tales* and read "The Jar" by Ray Bradbury.

It literally stunned me. In those long-ago Missouri days I was a dedicated horror buff, familiar with an impressive amount of material in the genre—but I had never encountered a story with the poetic power and dark originality of "The Jar." Who *was* this Bradbury fellow, and how much of his stuff had I been missing?

I began buying *Weird Tales* on a regular basis, hoping for more Bradbury, and sure enough there he was with five stories in 1945, another four in '46, and two more in '47.

By then I had moved to San Diego, California, where I discovered Ray's first book of tales, *Dark Carnival*. The quality level in the book was astonishing, and I was happy to find that he had included "The Jar." The book's dust jacket told me that he had been born in 1920, hailed from the Midwest, had been writing since the age of twelve, and now lived in California. I obtained his address (in the Los Angeles area) and we began exchanging letters. He seemed very pleased with my interest in his work.

I was soon tracking down Ray's stories in a variety of magazines, and in May of 1950 I happily acquired a first edition of *The Martian Chronicles* when the book was published by Doubleday. Ray had switched from horror to science fiction and was praised as a new master of the genre. In making this book-to-book switch, he took me with him; my extensive interest in SF dates directly from that period. (There would never have been a *Logan's Run* had I not read *The Martian Chronicles*.)

Two months later, in July of that year, we met for the first time at his home in Venice, California. Ray was still under thirty, boyish and ebullient, in a bow tie and crewcut, bouncing his eight-month-old daughter Susan on his knee as we talked. I recall a long discussion about creativity and about the importance of finding and following the correct path in life . . . "working at what you really love."

Ray had grown up in the small-town atmosphere of Waukegan, Illinois, and from a very early age had known that he was destined to become a writer. He had never wavered from that course, tapping out his earliest stories at twelve on a toy-dial typewriter.

I, too, had written stories as a young boy, continuing the practice through high school, but had veered away from writing in the direction of cartooning and commercial art. In Missouri, I'd worked as an artist for Hallmark Cards and had attended the Kansas City Art Institute. Now, in San Diego, I painted outdoor murals and had my own art studio in Balboa Park. After my talk with Ray I realized that I was in the wrong profession: what I *really* wanted to do was write. He had convinced me that if I possessed genuine talent and worked hard at the craft, I could follow in his professional footsteps. I suddenly had a new goal in life.

The year 1951 was pivotal. By February, Ray's third book, *The Illustrated Man,* had been issued by Doubleday, garnering raves from readers and critics across the nation. *Galaxy's* reviewer declared that

> Bradbury is writing some of the best short stories being turned out in America today. . . . He is original, he is moving, he is colorful, he is rich in ideas. I don't know what more to ask of a writer of science fiction or anything else.

And the *New York Times* stated: "There is no writer quite like Ray Bradbury."

We became fast friends and Ray stoutly encouraged me in my

creative efforts. When he was living in Ireland late in 1953, work-ing on the screenplay of *Moby Dick* for John Huston, I sent him the manuscript of a story I felt was good enough for professional print, "The Joy of Living."

He wrote back to say that it was indeed excellent and *would* sell, but that it needed a different, more upbeat ending. He outlined that new ending in detail: I incorporated it into the manuscript and "The Joy of Living" became my first story sale—to *If: Worlds of SF* in February of 1954. I was off and running on a career of my own, thanks in large part to the faith and encouragement of a unique gentleman I'd discovered in *Weird Tales* ten years earlier.

There is much that has been written about Ray Douglas Bradbury. At last count there were no less than fifteen published books and pamphlets devoted to his work (including my own 1975 *Ray Bradbury Companion*). He has been interviewed in scores of magazines and has published countless essays and autobiographical pieces dealing with his life and career.

By 1934 he had left Illinois and was living with his parents in Los Angeles, where he eventually graduated from L.A. High after writing for the school paper.

"I survived on ten dollars a week in 1939," he recalls, "peddling the Los Angeles *Daily News* from a downtown street corner. When I wasn't selling papers I was hunched over my ten-dollar typewriter, banging away at stories nobody wanted to buy."

But a breakthrough was inevitable. In 1941, at the age of twenty-one, Ray made his first professional sale to a science fiction pulp magazine, *Super Science Stories*—"But I didn't publish anything at all worthwhile for another two years, until 'The Wind,' which appeared in the March 1943 issue of *Weird Tales*."

Bradbury's assault on the pulp markets lasted through 1950, with more than 100 stories printed in *Thrilling Wonder, Startling, Planet Stories*, etc. Beyond 1950 he began selling steadily to the higher-paying, higher-prestige "slick" markets, from *Collier's* to the *Saturday Evening Post*. He had left the pulps behind, but they had served him well.

Which brings us back to *The Illustrated Man*. This book reflects the full span of Ray's work during the 1947–1950 period. Nine of the eighteen stories originally appeared in pulp magazines, two were in literary journals, five in slick magazines, and two were first printed in the collection itself.

At the time that Ray assembled these stories for Doubleday in 1950 the book had no title. His editors told him that they did not want to publish a random selection of his stories without a connecting link. The colonization of Mars had been the connecting link for the stories in *The Martian Chronicles*, and they asked Ray if he could provide another one for this follow-up book.

At first he had no solution to the problem. But then he thought about a story of his that had been printed in *Esquire* that year, "The Illustrated Man." It dealt with a lonely individual named William Phelps who becomes the victim of the illustrations tattooed across his flesh by an eccentric old woman. These "pictures" predict his future—as well as his violent death.

Now, seeking a framing device for the new collection, Ray decided to utilize basic elements from this *Esquire* story. He wrote a new "Prologue" and an "Epilogue" in which the tattoos on the body of his illustrated protagonist come to life, forming an entry into each of the tales. And, of course, this gave him his title, *The Illustrated Man*.

The book is one of Bradbury's classic volumes and has remained in print, edition after edition, since its debut in early '51; it has sold millions of copies and is a solid world favorite (having been translated into many languages), but until now has never been published in a special small-press, limited, signed edition. Providing this introduction for it is a personal pleasure.

What can I say about the stories? They are all superb and each retains its individual power and punch after more than four decades. Readers will naturally pick favorites; mine are "The Veldt," "The Exiles," "The Other Foot," and "The Rocket Man." However, I'm not going to discuss them here. I leave their delicious discovery to you, the new generation. Or perhaps, if you are part of an older generation and have read them in the past, I leave you with the joy of rediscovery.

Bradbury has turned out more than 400 stories over the span of his long career but none superior, in my opinion, to the selections in this book. He was writing at the height of his powers in the late-40s/early-50s period when these tales sprang from his expansive imagination. Here, in the pages before you, his awesome talents are on full display—vintage fiction from one of this century's outstanding storytellers.

Ray and I have now been good pals for some forty-five years and people want to know, "What about the real Ray Bradbury? What kind of a guy is he?" They are asking me to tell them about the individual, not the public persona; they want to know about the man "behind the illustrations."

Well, for one thing, I cannot recall a single time down the years when Ray wasn't a bundle of enthusiasm. He is excitedly involved in a dozen projects on any given day—stories, plays, poems, scripts, essays, lectures, and at least one new novel constantly in progress. He has strong ideas and opinions on writing, creativity, politics, science, space travel, the national economy, movies, modern theatre, and life in general—and he's quick to state such opinions loudly and clearly. Whether you agree or disagree, you can't help but respect his passion.

Ray loves to laugh. He has a wild sense of humor, sometimes ribald and irreverent, always forceful. Married for some fifty years, he's proud of his wife, Maggie, his four daughters, and his growing brood of grandchildren. He loves his "home away from home" in Palm Springs (having bought a second house there in 1980). He loves cats. He loves Paris. He loves theatre. He loves dinosaurs. He loves bookshops. He loves Old Radio, particularly the shows that were written by his mentor and longtime friend Norman Corwin. He loves to take the stage in front of a crowd, roll up his sleeves, and with the zeal of a tent-show preacher tell them about life and literature. He's a committed advocate of NASA's space program. He's a canny design consultant for the Walt Disney people and helped them put together EPCOT. And, as he has been for nearly all of his life, he remains a dedicated film buff.

Wasn't there a movie version of *The Illustrated Man?*

Yes, and there's nothing very positive that can be said about it. Based on the book's "Prologue/ Epilogue," plus three of the stories ("The Veldt," "The Long Rain," and "The Last Night of the World"), the 1969 film was muddled and fragmented.

Although his name was placed above the title, Bradbury was not consulted on the screenplay (written by the film's co-producer Howard Kreitsek), and the film suffers greatly from this. Tone and content are badly mangled, and Rod Steiger's wild-eyed, scenery-chewing star turn does not help matters. Claire Bloom is excellent in her small role as the witch—a sadly wasted effort in an otherwise lackluster production.

As a futuristic science fiction writer, Ray has always been vitally concerned with the past. In his fiction, yesterday and tomorrow are fused as he straddles past and future—an astronaut in a straw hat. The vanilla summers of a green, tree-shaded boyhood haunt his work, and the themes and images of these early years have dominated the bulk of his creative output for more than half a century. He defends this position by declaring: "A writer cannot possibly speak futures unless that writer has a strong sense of the past."

For many years Ray refused to fly. He firmly believed that, if he did finally board a plane, it would surely crash. However, Fate, in the form of a railroad line being eliminated by Amtrak, forced Ray to buy a one-way flight on Delta, asking only that the Disney people, whom he was celebrating with at the Grand Opening of EPCOT in Florida, feed him three double martinis and then pour him on the jet. Thus poured, he made the air journey home without running up and down the aisles shouting to get off, and in a few years his fears vanished, and he was booking flights on the Concorde to Paris.

He never learned to drive and has often publicly condemned the huge loss of life caused by auto accidents each year. Yet he moves continually around greater Los Angeles by limo (with a chauffeur who drives just for him). I kid Ray about this, telling him that despite his refusal to get behind the wheel he knows every entry and exit ramp on the entire L.A. freeway system. (He has long since abandoned the bicycle he used to pedal through Beverly Hills.)

He chuckles: "As a teenager, I went everywhere on roller skates. From Venice to MGM in Culver City, and on to Paramount in Hollywood—collecting celebrity autographs. I've still got my book of them packed away in the basement."

A note about one of the stories in *The Illustrated Man*: "The Fire Balloons" properly belongs with Ray's chronicles of Mars and was indeed added to the contents when Rupert Hart-Davis originally published the book in England as *The Silver Locusts*. Later, "The Fire Balloons" became part of an expanded edition of *The Martian Chronicles* published by Doubleday in 1973. (I was also responsible for the introduction to that one.)

In all, Ray has written some three dozen stories set on Mars, half of which have never been incorporated into his *Chronicles*. These include three stories from *The Illustrated Man*:

The Other Foot," "The Visitor," and "The Exiles." The reader is invited to speculate as to how and where they might be fitted into the earlier book. Perhaps Bradbury will someday authorize a further expanded edition to include such tales.

What about the Ray Bradbury of the 1990s, the seventy-five-year-old white-haired elder statesman of science fiction? Does he still write every day? Yes. Does he still lecture at least once a week? Yes. Does he still work on new novels and stories? Yes. Is he still the ebullient, self-confident, smiling fellow from earlier decades? Yes.

Every few months (and this has been going on for several years now) Ray phones me: "Hi, pal! Ready for the *Queen Mary?*" To which I reply: "Absolutely!"

Then a familiar and happy ritual begins. Ray assembles his buddies: me, satirist Stan Freberg, publisher Herb Yellin, writer Dennis Etchison, and artist Donn Albright (who owns the definitive collection of Bradbury's work in all media). Jabbering away, we all pile into Ray's hired stretch limo for a trip to the *Queen Mary* in Long Beach, with an inevitable stop-off en route to a bookshop or two.

The shipboard dinner is superb; the conversation is loud and spirited; and the occasion is always memorable.

This is the relaxed, offstage, private Bradbury, out for an evening of jolly good fun with his special friends.

I look forward to his hearty voice over the wire: "Hi, pal! Ready for the *Queen Mary?*"

Absolutely, Ray . . . Absolutely!

—*The Illustrated Man* (Gauntlet, 1996)

Fifty Years with Bradbury:
A Birthday Tribute

So now, as of August 2000, the grand master is eighty. For half a century we've been good pals. And, ah, how those years have rushed past.

When we met in July of 1950, Ray was still a young man, just shy of his thirtieth birthday. *The Martian Chronicles* had been published by Doubleday two months earlier, and Bradbury was suddenly (as one ad claimed) "the biggest name in science fiction."

Although he was soon to move into his own home (as a settled Californian transplanted from Illinois), at that time he was still renting a small house near the beach, at 33 South Venice Boulevard. (Originally modeled after the elegant Italian city, California's Venice was in sad decline—its black-water, trash-strewn canals cracked and abandoned reminders of a once-colorful turn-of-the-century past.)

When I arrived that summer afternoon in 1950, Ray's wife, Maggie, was wheeling their first daughter (nine-month-old Susan) along the front walk in a pink-and-blue baby carriage. Where was Ray? Mag gestured toward the rear of their one-story bungalow. "He's back in his office, writing."

Ray's "office" was in one corner of what looked like an oversized tool shed at the end of a long, graveled driveway. Inside were two chairs, a typewriter, a small table, stacks of paper—and Bradbury. Lean and fit. Crewcut. Glasses. Open-collar sport shirt and slacks. Smiling. Approachable. Welcoming.

We shook hands and began talking. God, how we talked! I had a hundred things I wanted to say to him, and Bradbury accepted my wild enthusiasm with patience and humor.

His prose had exploded into my life from the pulp pages of *Weird Tales* six years earlier, when I was sixteen and still attending high school in my home town of Kansas City, Missouri. Ray's work, which stunned me with its poetic intensity, was unlike anything I'd ever encountered, head and shoulders above all the other fiction in the magazine (and I was an avid *Weird Tales* reader). Who could forget such gems as "The Jar," "The Lake," "Skeleton," and "The Wind"?

With feverish dedication I began to seek out the Bradbury byline in other magazines and, over the next three years, savored the rare delights of "'King of the Gray Spaces." "The Big Black and White Game," "Invisible Boy," "One Timeless Spring," "The Million Year Picnic," "Homecoming," "The Small Assassin," "Zero Hour," and "The Next in Line" (this novelette from his first book, *Dark Carnival*).

And in the 1948–1950 period: "The October Game," "Powerhouse," "The Black Ferris," "And the Moon Be Still as Bright," "Mars Is Heaven!," "The Naming of Names," "Kaleidoscope," "There Will Come Soft Rains," "Way in the Middle of the Air," and "The Veldt"—to name only my top favorites.

I had the pleasure of encountering these magical tales as they appeared in their first magazine printings, well before they were gathered together into book collections. Thus, by the time I had moved to Southern California and contacted Ray, I was one of his most enthusiastic readers.

Indeed, we had much to talk about.

In that summer of '51, I had gathered together half-a-hundred of Ray's pulp tales, clipped them from their original magazines, and had them bound by a local bookbinder as *Fifty Fantasies*. Ray not only inscribed the book, he contributed an original introductory essay, "The Beginnings of Imagination."

Our friendship became a pivotal part of my life and has endured—and flourished—to this day.

When I became the managing editor of *Gamma*, a new digest-size SF magazine in the early '60s, I included Ray's work and, of the twenty-five anthologies I've edited over the years, Bradbury's fiction is represented in a dozen of them. I've watched Ray turn into a global public figure, a world icon, delivering weekly lectures, appearing on radio and television and in news magazines, being feted in Paris and London, signing his books by the thousands in stores from Los Angeles to New York. He's even had a crater on the moon named after one of his books.

A long way from the murky canals of Venice!

He savors it all. What he fantasized about, as a boy in Waukegan, has become a glittering reality. And his success with books and stories has allowed him to indulge his love of play writing. "I write plays because I can afford to lose money on 'em," he declares. "I love putting my work on the stage, producing, sitting in on rehearsals, mingling with the actors. It's all magic!"

At Ray's invitation I have attended many of these plays, beginning in 1964 with *The World of Ray Bradbury* and extending into the 1990s with *The Wonderful Ice Cream Suit*.

Of course, many of Ray's stories have been successfully produced for radio, and he has written originals for *Suspense* and other shows. In fact, his original drama *The Meadow* was selected for the *Best Radio Plays of the Year*, and this is only one of an impressive number of "best" anthologies that have featured his work. Additionally, a multitude of school textbooks have included Bradbury alongside Hemingway, Steinbeck, Faulkner, and other modern masters. I can think of no other writer who has progressed from the pulp pages of *Weird Tales* to the literary heights achieved by Bradbury.

His poetic, emotionally charged work has influenced many thousands of young writers and has generated a lasting affection around the world. I've watched his listeners as he talks to them from the lecture stage, and their faces glow. Ray's warmth and deep sense of humanity always creates a special bond with each audience.

When my first novel, *Logan's Run*, was published in 1967, Ray generously provided solid words of praise for an ad in the *New York Times*. And when MGM filmed the book in 1975, I invited Bradbury to be on the set with me in Culver City. Conversely, I was his on-set guest in 1981, at the Disney studios, when they were filming *Something Wicked This Way Comes*.

In 1985, I invited Ray to a special preview screening of my Movie of the Week, *Terror at London Bridge*, at the at the Director's Guild Theatre, while he made sure I was in attendance for his Emmy-winning animated version of *The Halloween Tree* when it screened at the Academy of Motion Picture Arts and Sciences Theatre.

In 1991, I paid him a career tribute with my book, *The Bradbury Chronicles* (following my 1975 biography/bibliography, *The Ray Bradbury Companion*), and in the 1990s Ray was a central part of my anthology of West Coast writers, *California Sorcery*.

A very personal Bradbury highlight, for me, was being part of Ray and Maggie's fiftieth wedding anniversary, in 1997, at the Four Seasons Hotel in Beverly Hills. A wonderful night of friendship and nostalgia.

So many years, so many warm Bradbury memories: experiencing the frights of *Alien* at the Fox Studio Theatre . . . sitting at a candlelit table for a Houdini séance at the Magic Castle in Hollywood . . . tramping around Disneyland with Ray and his kids . . . swimming in the pool at Bradbury's second home in Palm Springs . . . appearing with him at Bowling Green State University in Ohio for the dedication of their Ray Bradbury Collection . . . sharing an evening of mad Frebergian humor at the Museum of Television and Radio . . . celebrating birthdays at Herb Yellin's house in Northridge . . . visiting an art gallery on La Cienega Boulevard for an exhibit of Joe Mugnaini's paintings (Joe having illustrated many of Ray's books) . . . speaking at a dinner in Bradbury's honor at California State College on Halloween night . . . drinking truly excellent champagne at his first daughter's wedding reception . . . signing books together in Hollywood and Burbank and Beverly Hills . . . watching Hammett's *Dain Curse* at my home in Woodland Hills.

Which leads. finally, to this tribute, a celebration of Ray Bradbury's eighty years on Planet Earth.

Knowing him for this last half-century, I can personally attest to the fact that he is a man fulfilled. Since the day we met in 1950, Ray's enthusiasm for writing, for his friends and family, for his countless readers around the globe (who send him a ton of letters each year), and for life itself has increased with each passing year.

He's a national treasure and a dear, beloved pal.

Live forever, Ray!

–*Outré* (August 2000)

Ray Bradbury: Space-Age Legend

During the summer of 1950, the immediate success of Doubleday's newly published collection, *The Martian Chronicles*, prompted one critic to cite Ray Bradbury as "the hottest name in science fiction." Ray was twenty-nine years old at time of the book's publication and had been selling professionally since 1941. Many of his early stories had been printed in pulp magazines from *Weird Tales* to *Planet Stories*. In fact, it was in the wood pulp pages of *Weird Tales*, late in 1944, that I first discovered his work (with a moody chiller I've never forgotten, "The Jar"). He had been active as a writer in three fields, turning out science fiction, horror, and crime tales. Three years earlier, in 1947, his first book, *Dark Carnival*, a fantasy-horror collection, had come out from Arkham House. *Dark Carnival* had been a breakthrough volume in terms of style and content, and it is still unsurpassed for sheer originality and inspired imagination. Then, with *The Martian Chronicles*, his second book, Bradbury had been suddenly catapulted to fame in science fiction. Again unsurpassed in its genre, this collection of Martian tales continues to enchant millions of readers around the world. Now long considered a major SF classic and still appearing in new global editions, it has never been out of print in more than a half century.

So in that late August of 1950, having just turned thirty, Ray Bradbury was already on his way to becoming a space-age legend.

Today, in our new millennium, his distinguished reputation is secure. With more than 400 stories and dozens of books to his credit, and having won numerous awards, Bradbury is widely acknowledged as an icon in world literature. (His books have been printed in thirty countries around the globe.)

Ray will be eighty-one in August [2001], but he retains the mind and spirit of a young man, exhibiting an immense zest for life and writing. Beyond his daily output—novels, stories, plays, essays, and poems—he lectures constantly, energizing audiences around the world. His message is always clear: Assert the best that is in you. Discover what you love most—law, sculpture, acting, science, medicine, writing—and follow that love. Nurture it. Expand it. Let it enhance every day of your life.

Ray has followed his own love of writing from his earliest years in Illinois to the sun-kissed coast of California. A long, happy, and truly remarkable journey for one of America's most influential writers.

Ray Douglas Bradbury was born in Waukegan, Illinois, on August 22, 1920, and claims he has vivid memories of his early infanthood. "I was a ten-month baby," Ray declares. "That means I was born with more fully developed senses. I remember sucking . . . watching my mother through the bars of my crib . . . crawling across the floor. I even remember, as a baby, having nightmares about being born, about being forced to make that fearful journey through the birth canal. You've been warm and comfortable in there all these months and suddenly you're ejected into the cold world. It's a real shock!"

He put all these early memories into his classic story of a killer infant, "The Small Assassin," claiming that *he* was the lethal baby. When astonished readers would ask where he ever thought up such a wild idea, Bradbury would say, "I didn't think it up, I *lived* it."

Ray was the third child of Esther Moberg Bradbury. Earlier, in 1916, she had given birth to twins, Leonard and Samuel. Leonard, known in the family as "Skip," would grow up with Ray, but Samuel died in 1918 at the age of two.

Ray's father, Leonard Spaulding Bradbury, worked as a telephone lineman for the Bureau of Power and Light in Waukegan.

He was descended from an English family that had immigrated to America in 1630. Esther had been born in Sweden and had come to the United States in 1890 with her father, a steelworker.

Raised a Baptist, Ray recalls having to attend Sunday School each week through age thirteen—though in his adult years he has followed no formal religion. But every Bradbury reader is well acquainted with Ray's inherent morality and his deepest beliefs about the transcendence of life. His work abounds with spiritual content.

Ray was introduced to the shivery joys of horror when, at the age of three, his mother took him to see Lon Chaney in the silent horror classic *The Hunchback of Notre Dame*. The film made a deep and lasting impression on the toddler.

Three years later, when he was six, he was taken to another fright classic, *The Phantom of the Opera*. "That did it," Bradbury declares. "My abiding fascination with being frightened took root with those two films. I grew up with a real fear of what 'things' might be lurking in the dark."

Ray attended grade school in Waukegan, but his schooling was temporarily interrupted in 1928 when he was bedridden for three months with whooping cough. "That's when my mother read Poe to me by candlelight," he remembers.

In the same year he discovered the world of science fiction with a pulp issue of *Amazing Stories*. He was awestruck. "This is where I wanted to live," he says. "I wanted to slip into the covers of that magazine and never come out."

The Waukegan terrain played a pivotal part in stimulating Ray's developing imagination. A deep, weed-choked ravine split his hometown in half, becoming a fearsome place by night—and made all the more frightening by the rumored presence of a local killer known as "The Lonely One." Deeply impressed with this real-life specter, Ray would later feature the mysterious ravine as an area of menace in several of his works, placing it thematically center-stage in his *Dandelion Wine.*

At nine, Bradbury's early creativity was fueled by Tarzan and John Carter of Mars as the boy devoured the lurid works of Edgar Rice Burroughs. He also avidly collected the comic-strip adventures of Buck Rogers and Wilma Deering.

"The Waukegan library became my second home," Ray recalls. He spent many hours there each week, prowling the stacks and feeding what was to become a lifelong hunger for books.

It was inevitable that all these grand passions would burst forth in stories. In 1931, at age eleven, Ray began scribbling wildly fanciful tales on a roll of butcher paper. The following year, when he received a toy-dial typewriter for Christmas, he began typing out new adventures of buck and Wilma as "sequels" to his beloved *Buck Rogers* comic strip. I reproduced one of these all-in-caps toy-dial efforts in 1975 for *The Ray Bradbury Companion.* It concerns an alien invasion and reads in part:

> BUCK: QUICK WILMA WE'VE GOT TO GET TO WORK. THIS . . . MEANS AN INTER PLANETARY WAR.
>
> COMMAND: YOU FLY AT ONCE . . . WE'LL COMMUNICATE WITH YOU BY COSMIC-RAY TELEPHONE.
>
> BUCK: SQUADRON ATTENTION . . . ENEMY CRAFT MANEU-VERING OVER AREA IN FORCE . . .
>
> WILMA: STEP LIVELY NOW. GET THE CLOUD GUNS READY.
>
> HELEN: AN IDEAL DAY FOR THE CLOUD GUNS, MISS WILMA.
>
> WILMA: YES, THERE OUGHT TO BE PLENTY OF LIGHTNING IN THOSE PUFFBALLS UP THERE.

Needless to say, Buck and Wilma destroy the alien invaders and save Earth. The seeds of *The Martian Chronicles* had been planted.

"I wrote at least a thousand words a day, every day, from the age of twelve," says Ray. "It was like a fever burning inside me. My stories were all dreadful, of course, but I was learning. I keep telling young writers, you must get rid of all the bad stuff before you can begin to write the good stuff. And the sooner you start, the quicker you'll reach a level of quality. I had a long way to go, but I was on the way."

In the 1930s, the nation was suffering an economic crisis. The Great Depression struck Leonard Bradbury; in 1932, he lost his job with the Bureau of Power and Light in Waukegan. Ray's father decided to move the family to Tucson, Arizona, where he was able to get work selling "chili bricks" to local restaurants.

Now in that pivotal developmental cusp between childhood and adolescence, young Bradbury talked his way into a spot at the microphone reading the comic pages to children over Tucson radio station KGAR each Saturday. He also won the lead role (as Hans) in an operetta staged at the Amphitheater School.

By April 1934, Ray's father was jobless once again. He drove his family 800 miles to Los Angeles in the hope of finding work.

"I became a dedicated Angeleno," says Bradbury. "Fell in love with the city and have stayed here ever since. Wouldn't live anywhere else."

At fourteen and now determined to become a professional writer, Ray discovered that the girl next door owned a typewriter. He immediately began dictating stories to her. "She'd type them for me," he remembers, "and I'd send them out to *The Saturday Evening Post* who sent them right back. But I persisted, convinced that some day I'd appear in their pages."

The many radio and film studios in the Los Angeles area proved to be magnets for young Bradbury. He became "an audience of one" at the George Burns/Gracie Allen radio show and even sent the comic duo gags to use on the air. Each day, after school, he'd strap on his roller skates and head across town to the Paramount gate so he could obtain autographs from famous personalities as they emerged from the studio. To this day, tucked away in the depths of his basement, Bradbury retains his book of autographs containing the signatures of W. C. Fields, Marlene Dietrich, and a host of other film stars from Hollywood's Golden Age.

In September 1935, at fifteen, Ray entered Los Angeles High School. He became active in the drama club and enrolled in special short story and poetry classes. Still determined to write professionally in the future, he was also seriously drawn to the stage. As an adult, he would combine both with his produced stage plays.

Four days prior to his sixteenth birthday, in August 1936, Bradbury had a poem printed in the *Waukegan News-Sun,* a tribute to humorist Will Rogers. It was his first appearance in print. *The Anthology of Student Verse for 1937* also included one of his poems— and he wrote, co-produced, and directed *The 1937 Roman Revue* at L.A. High. Additionally, he began writing for *The Blue and White,* his school paper, after purchasing a used typewriter for $10 out of accumulated lunch money.

In early October of that year, Ray discovered SF fandom, joining the Los Angeles Science Fiction League (which later evolved into The Los Angeles Science-Fantasy Society). He befriended super-fan Forrest Ackerman, writer Henry Kuttner, and future stop-frame animation genius Ray Harryhausen. Soon thereafter, under Ackerman's editorship, Ray's work began appearing in the club's mimeo magazine, *Imagination!*

"I was a kind of freak among the 4,000 students at L.A. High," recalls Bradbury. "They neither knew nor cared whether or not one damned rocket was ever built or pointed toward the Moon, Mars, or the Universe. But *I* cared—a lot—and let everybody know it. I talked of going out to the stars, to new frontiers, of landing on other planets. I was 'Ray the space nut,' but I didn't mind because I *knew* that the visions I had would come true."

Bradbury was a straight-A student during his final high school semester. Beyond his school work, he was busily writing material (stories, poems, letters, movie reviews) for several amateur SF publications known as "fanzines."

"When it came time to graduate," recounts Bradbury, "we were too poor for me to buy a suit coat, so I borrowed one from an uncle. It didn't fit all that well and it had a hole in it, but I wore it anyhow. You don't look a gift horse in the mouth."

Following high school graduation and still living with his family in the heart of Los Angeles, Ray spent the early part of each day pounding out new short stories on his used typewriter. Then, each afternoon, he'd peddle newspapers from a downtown street corner. "I made enough to keep me in postage and typing paper and help out with family expenses. In those days," he says, "you could buy a full meal for 50 cents, including the tip. A dollar went a long way."

The first World Science Fiction Convention was held in New York in July 1939, and Ray managed to borrow enough money to make the trip. By then, he was the editor/publisher of *Futuria Fantasia*, his own fanzine (which ran to four issues), and he was also included in *Who's Who in Fandom*. At the convention, he made important contacts within the SF field, meeting several influential editors.

Bradbury was facing a crisis point in his life. As a member of the Wilshire Players, the drama group headed by actress Laraine Day, he was deeply involved in acting. Perhaps *this* was the direction he should take in life; perhaps he should aim for an acting career. He wasn't sure.

However, by 1940, when a story of his was accepted (without payment) by *Script*, a respected West Coast magazine, his future course became clear. Deciding that he could no longer divide himself between writing and the stage, he resigned from the acting group.

He actively sought the help and advice of seasoned professional writers: Kuttner, Ross Rocklynne, Robert A. Heinlein, Jack Williamson, Leigh Brackett, Edmond Hamilton, and Henry Hasse. In fact, a story he wrote in collaboration with Hasse, "Pendulum," generated Ray's first sale (for $27.50) when it was printed that August in the pulp pages of *Super Science Stories*. At twenty-one, Ray Bradbury had achieved his long-sought goal: he was now a published professional, represented by Julius Schwartz, his friend and literary agent.

Now an adult, Ray moved close to the ocean, to 670 Venice Boulevard, and set up a small office. Working at a feverish pace, he wrote fifty-two stories that year. Schwartz sold three of them. By the end of 1942, with yet more sales under his belt, Ray was making enough (barely) from his fiction to enable him to quit his job hawking newspapers and write full-time. (Eye trouble kept him out of military service during World War II, but he aided the war effort by contributing radio spots for the Red Cross and the Department of Civil Defense.)

His first "quality" year was 1943, when Bradbury began to write the type of fiction that would eventually make him famous: darkly poetic stories of horror such as "The Wind," "The Crowd," and "The Scythe" (all printed in *Weird Tales* within a period of five months in 1943).

Yet, despite the fact that he was beginning to find his own distinctive style, he discovered that most editors were put off by such bold originality; they rejected Bradbury's work in favor of more standard fare. In order to make ends meet, Ray was forced to churn out routine fiction for the crime pulps; his work appeared in *New Detective*, *Detective Tales*, *Dime Mystery*, and *Flynn's Detective Fiction*.

"I was no threat to Hammett and Chandler," he admits. "Unable to sell what I really *wanted* to write, I was going against the grain of my talent, turning out crime stuff that was, for the most part, second-rate. As each month passed, I grew more frustrated."

His frustration was about to end. In writing "The Lake," a story based on a beloved cousin who had almost drowned in Lake Michigan when Ray was seven, Bradbury realized that his boyhood in Waukegan could provide a rich emotional base for his fiction. This was the real turning point in his career. He began producing powerful, deeply personal stories such as "The Jar," "The Dead Man," "The Big Black and White Game," and "Skeleton." No one else was writing stories like these.

Ray Bradbury had found his true direction.

"I had to discover my interior self," says Ray. "Up to then, without realizing it, I'd been imitating, not creating. I had to dig down, into myself, to find the truth of fiction."

Bradbury was now mining his subconscious, opening up the doors into his past and dipping into long-stored memories. He cited his father as an example of this "opening up" process:

"My father and I had never really been close—until very late in his life. His language, from day to day, was not remarkable, but when I said, 'Dad, tell me about Tombstone when you were seventeen,' or 'Tell me about the wheat fields in Minnesota when you were twenty.' And Dad would begin to speak about running away from home when he was sixteen, heading west in the early part of this century, before the last boundaries were fixed—when there were no highways, only horse paths and train tracks and the Gold Rush was on in Nevada. . . .

"After he'd talked for five or six minutes and got his pipe going, quite suddenly the old passion was back, the old days, the old tunes, the weather, the look of the sun, the sound of the voices, the boxcars traveling late at night, the jails, the tracks narrowing behind as the West opened up ahead—all, all of it and the cadence was there and the moments—the moments of truth."

To strengthen the realism within his fantasy tales, Ray shifted his reading from SF pulps to contemporary fiction by Hemingway, Steinbeck, Wolfe, Welty, and Jessamyn West. He was making notes for "a book about people on Mars," and sold the first of his now-classic Martian tales, "The Million Year Picnic," to *Planet Stories* that December.

In 1945, with "The Lake," Ray made his initial anthology sale to August Derleth (for *Who Knocks?*) and he achieved a major career breakthrough when "The Big Black and White Game" was chosen for the annual *Best American Short Stories.*

Several tales to the higher-paying "slick paper" magazines (*Mademoiselle, Charm,* and *Collier's*) financed his two-month trip into Mexico where he collected masks for the Los Angeles County Museum. "Mexico scared me to death," he recalls. "It was a totally alien land." He put that fear into such classic tales as "The Next in Line" and "El Día de Muerte."

Ray sold eighteen short stories in 1946, appeared in three anthologies, and had his first radio dramatization broadcast (for the *Mollé Mystery Theater*).

In 1946 Ray had earned just under $3,000; he was able to better this by only $200 more in 1947. Thus, money was tight for Ray and his new wife, Maggie (Marguerite Susan McClure), as they moved into a small house at 33 South Venice Boulevard. Maggie took a job at Hertz to supplement the family income. When her boss read Ray's collection of terror tales he became alarmed. "This husband of yours is a mentally sick man," he declared. "I'm very worried about your safety, living with such a twisted individual."

When Ray heard, he laughed. "Tell him I haven't decided to cut your throat yet and have no plans in that direction."

On the career front, August Derleth, who had established Arkham House by then, published Ray's first book, *Dark Carnival*, in the spring of 1947.

Ray now had a new agent, Don Congdon, who had replaced Julius Schwartz and would continue to represent Bradbury into the new millennium. Operating out of New York, Congdon concentrated on placing Ray with the better-paying, higher-prestige markets. That year, Bradbury's fiction appeared in both *Harper's* and the *New Yorker*—a huge step up from the pulps.

Bradbury's reputation for quality was enhanced further by appearances in the *O. Henry Prize Stories*. He was also on the radio program *Suspense*, and 1948 saw the first printing of his classic SF tale, "Mars Is Heaven!," a perfect example of Bradbury's nostalgia for the past combined with his fictional projection of the future.

Norman Corwin, radio's outstanding dramatist, admired Ray's work and was sympathetic to Bradbury's frustration over not having books out from a major New York publishing house. Corwin told him the solution lay in personal contact—Ray must meet publishers face-to-face. Bradbury took Corwin's advice and, in 1949, met with Doubleday's chief editor in New York, who agreed to publish the young author's first novel.

"But I've never written one," Bradbury protested.

"Sure you have. All those science fiction stories of yours about the Red Planet. Couldn't they be combined?"

The note that Ray had jotted down in 1944 concerning "a book about people on Mars" suddenly took on reality. That same night, in a New York hotel room, Bradbury pieced together what became *The Martian Chronicles*—for which he received an advance of $500.

That November, Ray became a father when Susan Marguerite, the first of his four daughters, was born. A week later, "to teach her not to fear the dark," Bradbury wrote his initial book for children, *Switch On the Night*.

Twenty-four Bradbury stories were printed in 1950, a record year, enabling Ray and Maggie to purchase a house on Clarkson Road in West Los Angeles for their family.

Bradbury achieved another long-sought triumph when "The Veldt," his classic SF story concerning a deadly children's nursery, was printed (as "The World the Children Made") in the *Saturday Evening Post*. His persistent efforts to break into their pages had finally paid off; the *Post* now welcomed his work.

At thirty, after a full ten years of writing mainly for the pulps, Bradbury had transcended the genre. One hundred of his stories had been printed in pulp publications from *Super Science* to *Weird Tales*, but now, under Don Congdon's guidance, his fiction would sell exclusively to top markets.

Ray also began to appear regularly on the lecture circuit, earning substantial money and fulfilling his desire to perform on the stage. He made yet another breakthrough that year, when literary establishment icon Christopher Isherwood lavishly praised *The Martian Chronicles* in print, conferring mainstream critical acceptance on Bradbury's work. The following year, in February 1951, Doubleday followed *Chronicles* with *The Illustrated Man*.

That same month, Ray had dinner with film director John Huston. Bradbury told Huston of his admiration for Huston's films and that someday he wanted to write a script for the director. The admiration was mutual and Huston promised to contact Bradbury "when the right project comes along."

In the spring, Ramona Anne, Ray's second child, was born. Ray saw his work reach television, and his first mass-market paperback was published by Bantam Books. He received major coverage in the *New York Times Book Review*, strengthening his mainstream credentials, and his first major piece of nonfiction appeared in *Charm*.

The following year, in January 1952, I launched my own writing career by editing and publishing the *Ray Bradbury Review*, a booklet highlighting Ray's initial decade as a professional. This work proved to be the pioneer in a long string of more than twenty books and pamphlets about Bradbury that would appear over the next half-century. (In 1988 the Graham Press reissued the *Review* in a limited-edition hardcover with a new preface by Bradbury.)

As Ray has been for so many other writers, he was a strong role model for me in my career. I would marvel at his use of the exact word to convey a special emotion or to communicate just the right mood or atmosphere. His descriptive powers achieved a high level of prose-poetry and sometimes I would copy out, in longhand, a particularly fine section from one of his stories. One such section was this description of a T-Rex from "A Sound of Thunder":

> It came on oiled, resilient, striding legs. It towered 30 feet above the trees, a great evil god, folding its delicate watchmaker's claws close to its oily reptilian chest. Each lower leg was a piston, a thousand pounds of muscle, sheathed over in a gleam of pebbled skin like the mail of a terrible warrior. Each thigh was a ton of meat, ivory and steel mesh. And from the great breathing cage of the upper body those two delicate arms dangled out front, arms with hands which might pick up and examine men like toys, while the snake neck coiled. And the head itself, a ton of sculptured stone, lifted easily upon the sky. Its mouth gaped, exposing a fence of teeth like daggers. Its eyes rolled, ostrich eggs, empty of all expression save hunger. It closed its mouth in a death grin. It ran, its pelvic bones crushing aside trees and bushes, its taloned feet clawing damp earth, leaving prints six inches deep wherever it settled its weight.
>
> It ran with a gliding ballet step, far too poised and balanced for its ten tons. It moved into a sunlit arena warily, its beautiful reptile hands feeling the air.

Well . . . that was writing. Damn fine writing, and I yearned to match it, to absorb it, to understand its rhythm and force. For me, each Bradbury story was a fresh learning experience.

In the spring of 1952 Ray met a man who would occupy a vital role in his career, artist Joseph Mugnaini. "Joe's paintings were incredible mirror images of my own fantasies," Ray declared. "I'd found the perfect artist to illustrate my books."

Bradbury accepted the first film studio job that September when Universal hired him to create an original SF project, "The Meteor," that would be released as *It Came from Outer Space*. Bradbury's 110-page treatment formed a direct basis for the Harry Essex shooting script, but Ray was frustrated. He wanted to write a screenplay of his own.

He got the chance in August 1953, when John Huston kept his earlier promise and contacted him. Huston was convinced that he had found an "ideal project" to fit Bradbury's talents: the film adaptation of Herman Melville's mystical masterpiece, *Moby Dick*. To tackle the saga of Captain Ahab's search for the Great White Whale, Huston insisted that Ray work in Ireland (near Huston's home). Bradbury hesitated; he had never read the novel, but when he sampled it he responded strongly to the poetic force of its narrative.

"I'd just finished writing *Fahrenheit 451*," says Ray, "and Doubleday published my *Golden Apples of the Sun* with Joe's illustrations, so I felt that I had some space for Melville. Besides, I wanted to see Europe. So that September Maggie and I packed up, left the children with my parents, and headed for Ireland."

Bradbury spent six months overseas, writing a total of 1,500 script pages on *Moby Dick* to get a finished two-hour screenplay. Working with the often sadistic yet brilliant Huston had been part nightmare, part dream-come-true, but "in the end, worth it."

"After finishing the script," Bradbury reported, "Maggie and I toured Europe. Sicily, Paris, Florence, Milan, Rome, Venice. A grand adventure!"

Meanwhile, he was particularly honored to receive the Award for Literature from the National Institute of Arts and Letters.

In 1955, Ray wrote his first produced teleplay for Alfred Hitch-cock. That was also the first year that a Bradbury story appeared in a school textbook. (Eventually, his work would be represented in over 750 of them, sharing space with Hemingway, Faulkner, Steinbeck, and, yes, Melville.)

Ray's third daughter, Bettina Francion, was born in late July, and that fall Ballantine Books published *The October Country* (basi-cally a revised and expanded version of *Dark Carnival*).

Bradbury was becoming quite active in radio, stepping behind the mike to narrate one of his 1956 shows for the *CBS Radio Work-shop*—while another of his original dramas for radio was selected for *Best One-Act Plays*.

With *Moby Dick* now in wide release, he was offered several ma-jor screenplay assignments, but held out for one of his own, *The Rock Cried Out*, which he scripted in London for Carol Reed (who had directed *The Third Man*). "He was very happy with what I'd done," says Ray, "but we couldn't raise enough money to get the script produced."

Bradbury's richly evocative celebration of his Illinois boyhood, *Dandelion Wine,* was published in 1957 (a repeat of *The Martian Chronicles* format, in which a group of theme-related short stories were combined, with new bridge material, to make up a "novel").

Ray's father died in Los Angeles that year, at age sixty-six. (His mother's death occurred nine years later.) However—in the ongo-ing human cycle—life followed death when Bradbury's fourth daughter, Alexandra Allison, was born the following summer. She would be Ray and Maggie's last child.

On Thanksgiving Day, 1958, the Bradburys moved into a new (and permanent) home in the Cheviot Hills section of West Los Angeles. Ray set up his workroom in the basement, surrounded by the many books and artifacts of his burgeoning career.

In 1959 he began what turned out to be an unhappy relationship with television icon Rod Serling. Bradbury wrote two scripts
for Serling's new series, *The Twilight Zone*, but both were rejected.
A third *was* produced later, but Bradbury was unhappy with the
result and with Serling himself. "Serling made promises he didn't
keep," says Bradbury, "and that marked the end of our relationship."

Representing Bradbury's amazing climb from the lowbrow
pulps to the top literary markets, his work was included in the
1960 *Britannica Library of Great American Writing* and his first professionally produced play, *The Meadow*, was staged that year at the
Huntington Hartford Theatre in Hollywood.

Ray was working on a screenplay at MGM—riding his bicycle to
the studio each morning (he has never learned to drive a car)—
when *Life* magazine contacted him; they wanted Bradbury to write
a piece for them. His research and interviews produced the "hard
science" article "A Serious Search for Weird Worlds." Printed in
the October 24, 1960, issue of *Life*, the article generated excellent
reader response and demonstrated that Bradbury was more than a
lyrical fantasist—he could also handle fact-based material.

Ray was gratified to learn that in Russia he was top-ranked in
popularity with Faulkner, Steinbeck, and Hemingway, but the fact
that he would have to travel to the Soviet Union in order to bene-
fit from his royalties became a source of continuing anger. Although a Russian bank account bulging with "blocked rubles" had
been established in his name, he could only redeem and spend the
currency inside the Soviet empire. Were he to travel there, he
would be forbidden to remove any monetary proceeds from the
country.

In 1962 he returned to dark fantasy, marked by the publication
of his novel *Something Wicked This Way Comes*. The book deals with

two young boys who battle an evil carnival that invades their small town and dramatizes the victory of laughter over fear.

During this period, Bradbury received his first Academy Award nomination, for his animated film *Icarus Montgolfier Wright*—and his original teleplay, *The Jail*, won the Writers Guild of America Award for "Best-Written Script of 1962."

Ray's talents extended well beyond writing. In creating *An American Journey*, a special attraction celebrating highlights in United States history, Bradbury was named "interior design consultant" for the U.S. Government Pavilion at the World's Fair. He would also design several attractions for Disney's EPCOT Center in Florida, become instrumental in the creation of a "people-friendly" mall at Santa Monica, and become involved in the attempt to solve the complex problems of L.A.'s rapid transit system.

"But no matter what else I'm doing," he says, "I write every day of my life. Work is the key to continuing creativity. Once the work is done, if good, you learn from it. If bad, you learn even more. Not to work is to cease, tighten up, become nervous—all destructive of the creative process. And you must use *sensory* language. In order to convince the reader, you must assault each of his senses in turn—with color, sound, scent, taste, and texture. Your reader should feel the sun on his flesh, the wind fluttering his shirt sleeves. The logic of events always gives way to the logic of the senses."

In October 1964, at the Coronet Theatre in Los Angeles, Ray became his own producer by staging *The World of Ray Bradbury*, with Charles Rome Smith directing a set of Ray's short plays. The production was a solid success and ran for eleven months. Ray followed it with another successful play, *The Wonderful Ice Cream Suit*, in the same theater.

In 1965 his futuristic tale of racial prejudice, "The Other Foot," was selected for a prestige anthology showcasing the finest short fiction of the past half-century: *Fifty Best American Short Stories, 1915–1965,* adding luster to his growing reputation for quality fiction.

French director François Truffaut's version of *Fahrenheit 451* was released as a major film in 1966. Although Bradbury did not write the screenplay, he was well pleased with this adaptation. "Truffaut was quite successful in translating the spirit of my novel," Ray declares. "Look at the film through the eyes of the French impressionists. See the poetic, romantic vision of Pissarro, Monet, Renoir, that Truffaut evokes and then remember that this method was his metaphor to capture the metaphor in my novel."

Early in 1967, on a new assignment from *Life,* he spent a week at the Manned Space Center in Houston, interviewing astronauts. "They told me they'd all read my stuff in high school," he reported, "and that my future tales made them want to go into space. I was deeply moved. What a wonderful thing to hear!"

Ray's work was now acceptable in the halls of academe; the first university thesis on his life and work was written in 1967 by a student at Harvard. Many more would follow, including several doctoral dissertations. Today his work is taught at every educational stage, from junior high through post-graduate university level. The fact that science fiction, long regarded as the bastard child of literature, came to be considered worthy of serious academic study is due, in large part, to Bradbury's superior talents for reaching mainstream readers with this once-despised genre. As editor Ray Russell put it: "Bradbury didn't simply elevate himself; he elevated the entire field of SF." Just as Dashiell Hammett revolutionized mystery fiction with his hard-boiled realism, so has Ray Bradbury transformed science fiction.

The awards kept coming. In 1968 Ray was selected for the Ball Memorial Award by the Aviation-Space Writers Association for his article in *Life,* "An Impatient Gulliver Above Our Roofs."

Leviathan '99, an original radio drama about a fanatic rocket captain on the trail of a giant white comet (*Moby Dick* in space!), was broadcast over the BBC in London in May, and Ray's final essay for *Life*, on his abiding love for train travel, was printed that summer.

In 1969, Jack Smight's film version of *The Illustrated Man* was released. Bradbury was anything but pleased. He had not been consulted, nor had he been shown the screenplay; he felt that his work had been ill-served in this heavy-handed, overwrought production. "That's when I determined to maintain artistic control over anything I sold to Hollywood in the future," he said. "Too many producers only care about the money and don't give a damn about the quality."

Ray was in London when U.S. astronauts landed on the moon in 1969. (During a 1957 interview in the *Los Angeles Times*, Bradbury had predicted a moon landing by 1967; he'd missed by just two years.) Ray appeared on British television, jubilant and energized by this momentous event, speaking of "our first step into immortality." He was now convinced, as he had been since boyhood, that humankind would indeed go out into space to conquer "the last frontier."

In addition to all his other activities, Bradbury was now serving, with Norman Corwin, on the Documentary Awards Committee for the Motion Picture Academy of Arts and Sciences, a position I always envied because he was able to view most of the good documentaries produced in a given year. (Documentaries had become the hidden creative works of the entertainment industry. Mainstream theaters didn't show them any more and neither did television, which meant that superb works of high creativity were nearly invisible to all except those lucky few Academy members who served on the Documentary Awards Committee.)

Ray was also becoming active in the world of music. That winter his first "space cantata," *Christus Apollo,* was performed in Royce Hall at UCLA. He also wrote the published lyrics to *Madrigals for the Space Age* and eight of his stories were adapted into "narrative songs" for an LP record album. "I want to explore every aspect of creativity," Ray declared. "There should be no limits to the imagination."

The first book devoted entirely to Bradbury's life and career was published in 1971. And, in further recognition, a section of the moon was named "Dandelion Crater" by the rocket crew of Apollo 15 in honor of Ray's contributions to space travel.

His musical stage version of *Dandelion Wine* was produced at California State College in Fullerton in 1972 (where Bradbury served as writer-in-residence). He also created his own comic-strip version of *The Martian Chronicles,* which ran in *West* magazine. "Nothing has gone to waste in my life," Ray told me. "I had no idea, when I collected *Buck Rogers,* that many decades later I would be creating my *own* comic strip. Never turn your back on early loves. Use them. Make them work for you. They're all grist for your creative mill."

That same year (1972) saw publication of his first book of plays, along with a new novella for children, *The Halloween Tree.*

In February of 1973 his *Madrigals* were performed at the Los Angeles Music Center while Ray was working with composer Leonard Rosenman on an opera, *The Lost City of Mars.*

He completed his initial book of collected verse for Knopf that year, closing a full circle in his life which extended back to 1936 when his first poem was printed. "I've always wanted to write good poetry," Ray declares. "Most of it, for thirty or forty years, was pretty bad. Then, in my late forties, my poems began to get better. Poetry is an old love of mine, one which is central to my life. And that will never change."

In 1974, for "contributions to the motion picture community which have brought dignity and honor to writers everywhere," Ray was presented with the prestigious Valentine Davies Award by the Writers Guild of America.

Long After Midnight, which Ray dedicated to me, was published in 1976. The book's title (which I had suggested) came from his early draft of "The Fireman," a novella Ray had expanded into *Fahrenheit 451*.

The World Fantasy Convention recognized his work in 1977 when it presented him with its Life Achievement Award. Bradbury also functioned as a co-writer on Hollywood's Academy Awards show that year. He was feted in Paris as guest of honor at a Jules Verne anniversary celebration by the French Government in 1978 and—back home—Mayor Tom Bradley declared "Ray Bradbury Day" in Los Angeles at a dinner in Ray's honor at California State College in Northridge, highlighted by a letter of congratulations from the governor.

His income was rising in proportion to his awards. In 1979, Ray was paid handsomely for TV rights to a three-night, six-hour telecast of *The Martian Chronicles*, and Kirk Douglas, via the Disney Studios, purchased the film rights to *Something Wicked This Way Comes*. Ray wrote the screenplay for this picture, which was re-leased in 1983, but was shocked when shown the director's cut.

"The first preview was a total disaster," he recalls. Bradbury felt that he knew exactly what was wrong and took his case to Disney studios head Ron Miller. "We worked for two months redoing a large part of the picture. In a way, the head of the studio and I re-directed *Something Wicked*, putting back the things that the original director [Jack Clayton] had changed or taken out. I think we saved the film. Now it *works*—and I'm very proud of it."

In 1980 Ray and Maggie's daughter, Ramona, gave birth to her own daughter, Julia, making Ray and Maggie grandparents.

Also in 1980, Knopf published a massive retrospective volume, *The Stories of Ray Bradbury*, containing 100 of his best short works of fiction. And on the honors front, he was named a "Grand Master" of science fiction at the Hugo Awards.

The Bradburys purchased a second home in Palm Springs in 1980, where Ray now does a lot of his writing. ("I like to get out to the desert where it's quiet and I can work without interruptions," he says.) He was also written up in *Time* magazine that same year as "a million-dollar earner." The boy from Waukegan, who had graduated from L.A. High wearing a borrowed coat with a hole in it, had indeed come a long way.

Two years later, in the spring of 1982, Bradbury appeared with me at Ohio's Bowling Green State University for the official dedication of my extensive collection of his work (which is now a permanent part of the university's Popular Culture Center). Rather than risk losing any of this material during shipping, I drove my collection of 28 cartons from Los Angeles to northern Ohio in a rented station wagon. Inside one of the boxes was the original, ribbon-copy, hand-corrected manuscript of *Fahrenheit 451*. (You don't put such an item in the mail!)

The Complete Poems of Ray Bradbury was issued that year, containing the full texts of his three Knopf collections. (Ray's verse has received mixed responses from critics and readers, but he continues vigorously to defend it, often beginning his day at the typewriter by writing a new poem.)

By the early 1980s, 18,000,000 copies of Bradbury's Bantam Book editions had been sold, with *The Martian Chronicles* topping the list at 4,000,000. But, ironically, there were no "best-sellers."

"I've never had a book of mine make the current best-seller lists," Ray says, "but my stuff stays in print and continues to sell steadily, year after year. So the totals keep adding up and that's what counts in the long run."

Following six years of work (and many drafts), Ray's first mystery novel, *Death Is a Lonely Business*, was published in 1985. Peopled with characters he'd known when he lived with his family in downtown Los Angeles, the book dealt with his early days in the California beach community of Venice. Its sequel, *A Graveyard for Lunatics*, came out five years later, and today Ray is working on a third. A mystery fan, he had read Hammett and Chandler for many years and now he was able to enjoy writing in their genre. ("Not hardboiled, God knows, but in the same mood and texture.")

The big news for Ray's ever-expanding audience in the 1980s was *The Ray Bradbury Theatre*. This prize-winning television show (six ACE awards in its first season) was co-produced by Bradbury for HBO; Ray hosted the show and also wrote all 65 of the teleplays (based on his published stories). "I found that I wasn't afraid to make changes in adapting my early stuff," he says. "I'd learned a lot about script writing and I said to myself, 'Well, why don't we turn a corner here instead of there and see what happens?' And that's what I did. There are many variations between my teleplays and the original stories. And that was all to the good!"

Ever since he had worked on *Moby Dick* in the 1950s, Ray had been planning a book about his experiences in Ireland, including his often-abrasive relationship with John Huston. By 1992 the book was a reality. *Green Shadows, White Whale* was actually an autobiographical account of this period, disguised as a novel.

"I'll always be grateful to Huston," says Ray. "In giving me the chance to write *Moby Dick* he changed my life. It was a great experience. But John was a very difficult, self-destructive man who was often quite cruel to those around him. He enjoyed sadistic jokes, seeing people squirm. He'd find your weak points, then go after you. We almost came to blows in London."

The 1990s proved to be another successful decade for Bradbury, with his script for the animated (by Hanna-Barbara) TV version of *The Halloween Tree* winning him an Emmy. ("It's really a study of Halloween done as a short novel. I wrote it to teach children what Halloween is all about, its traditions and history. Joe Mugnaini illustrated the book version and did a marvelous job.")

Of his many plays, Bradbury's lyrical stage production of *The Wonderful Ice Cream Suit* has been his most successful. For many years he sought to have it filmed. In the late 1990s, his friends at Disney took on the task of bringing it to the screen. Unfortunately, the studio did not feel that the finished film would command a strong enough commercial market; as a result, they released it directly to video. "I think they were wrong," says Ray, "but at least it got made. And they did a fine job with it."

Ray's chief collector and bibliographer, Donn Albright, has been given free access to Bradbury's files over the years and, as a result, has unearthed many completed manuscripts that had never been submitted anywhere. Ray explains: "Back when they were written I was doing a new story every week, far too many for the markets that existed at the time, so I ended up putting a number of stories away; I forgot all about them. Along comes Donn Albright, these long years later, to dig them out and suddenly I am rediscovering my lost children!"

These "lost children" have formed the heart of Bradbury's recent collections (*Quicker Than the Eye, Driving Blind,* and *One More for the Road*). Others are forthcoming.

In March of 2000, Ray was summoned to New York for what became his finest hour—walking onstage to receive the acclaimed National Book Award for Literature. He was presented with a Gold Medal signifying his lifelong contribution to American letters.

This honor capped a truly astonishing career stretching over six decades in which Ray Douglas Bradbury has met every creative challenge and explored every possible avenue of imagination in his hundreds of novels, short stories, poems, stage plays, radio dramas, articles, reviews, essays, comic strips, commentary, song lyrics, screenplays, television scripts, musical productions, and design projects.

Indeed, the poet of the space age has done it all.

One would assume that the most valuable item in a Bradbury collection would be a fine, jacketed copy of Ray's first book, the 1947 Arkham House edition of *Dark Carnival.* And, indeed, this is much sought after. But the key collectible is a special edition of *Fahrenheit 451.* Just 200 of the 4,500-copy 1953 first edition were signed, numbered, and bound in white asbestos. The binding was quite brittle and most copies have splits or cracks at the top of the spine. Thus, really fine copies command high prices. I saw one offered in a dealer's catalogue for $5,000—and that was nine years ago!*

Another scarce Bradbury volume is the illustrated 1955 first edition from Pantheon of *Switch On the Night,* Ray's initial book for children. Copies of this title rarely surface.

Almost all the many Bradbury pamphlets are difficult to locate. Not being primary items, most of them have been excluded from the Albright checklist, but the completist collector will want them all. The 24-page 1957 pamphlet version of Ray's short story *Sun and Shadow,* from the Quenian Press in Berkeley, California, is seldom seen in the market. Only 90 copies were printed and dealers were asking $900 for it as long ago as 1980. Other hard-to-find pamphlets: *The Essence of Creative Writing,* a selection of three of Ray's letters issued from the San Antonio (Texas) Public Library in 1962, and *No Man Is an Island,* a 12-page speech privately printed by the Los Angeles Chapter of the National Women's Committee of Brandeis University.

---

*[In 2012, copies of this book were being offered on the Internet for close to $15,000—each.—WFN.]

Additionally, all the pamphlets published by the late Roy Squires, each of them hand-set on his home press in Glendale, California, are scarce and highly valued—particularly *The Pedestrian* (1964) and *The Aqueduct* (1974). The same holds true for the beautifully printed and bound Lord John Press limited editions (most in hardcover) from publisher Herb Yellin in Northridge, California.

Naturally, a fine Doubleday first of *The Martian Chronicles* is essential, as are firsts of such early Bradbury classics as *The Illustrated Man* and *The Golden Apples of the Sun*.

Several other limited editions, some from book clubs and lavishly illustrated by Joe Mugnaini, have been published. Variants of listed titles, they form an attractive addition to any Ray Bradbury collection, but are not primary items.

—*Firsts* (June 2001)

Ray, Ray, and Ray

Among the seventy-plus books of mine, three of them deal with Ray Bradbury: *Ray Bradbury Review*, *The Ray Bradbury Companion*, and *The Bradbury Chronicles*. In addition to these, over the past half century I have written a sizable number of shorter items about Ray (profiles, articles, introductions, reviews, bibliographies, and story headings). At last count the total had reached sixty-five.

Have I exhausted my subject? Not at all. Why? Because there are so many Bradburys to write about.

There is Bradbury the poet (who saw his first piece of verse in print at age fifteen), Bradbury the artist and painter (who has executed the dust jackets for several of his books), Bradbury the designer (providing creative input on projects from Disneyland to EPCOT), Bradbury the playwright (with new dramas staged each year), Bradbury the public speaker (with lectures delivered to public audiences, libraries, business groups, universities, and high schools across the nation), Bradbury the film and television scriptwriter (with a multitude of credits from *Moby Dick* to *The Ray Bradbury Theater*), Bradbury the critic (with multimedia book reviews), and Bradbury the essayist (with pertinent messages for the space age).

This book celebrates Bradbury the "fictioneer"—the creative powerhouse whose massive output of stories has inspired literally thousands of other writers over the past six decades. I think it is safe to say that no other modern author, with the possible exception of Ernest Hemingway, has exerted a wider literary influence.

As clear proof of his presence in the field of education over the past half century, more than one hundred of his stories have been selected for a multitude of school textbooks. The most often reprinted titles include "There Will Come Soft Rains" and "All Summer in a Day," each of which has achieved over seventy textbook appearances since the mid-1950s.

In the pages that follow, Jonathan Eller and William Touponce trace, dissect, analyze, and list all of Bradbury's fiction, from short stories to full-length novels. The effort involved in this remarkable under-taking boggles the mind.

Late in 1973, I completed *The Ray Bradbury Companion* (published in 1975), containing what was up to then the most comprehensive printed record of Ray's work extant. I listed his poems, essays, articles, reviews, published speeches, stage works, radio/television/film projects, and printed letters—and, of course, his stories and novels. My total for his fictional works by late 1973 ran to just under 300. More than 100 others have been printed in the decades since. They are all fully catalogued here by Eller and Touponce—some 400 published stories and another 230-plus titles of (as yet) unprinted works.

Fiction is never created out of a vacuum. All professional writers have read, admired, and been influenced by a host of others. The influences on Bradbury's fiction can be classified into several groups.

First—during his earliest years—he was inspired by Charles Dickens, Edgar Allan Poe, H. G. Wells, Jules Verne, L. Frank Baum, and Edgar Rice Burroughs.

Then—as he moved from amateur to professional—he became deeply involved in the world of science fiction, writing fan letters to *Astounding*, *Thrilling Wonder Stories*, *Fantastic Adventures*, and *Amazing Stories*. During this science fiction period, he was aided and encouraged by several then-current genre writers: Leigh Brackett, Edmond Hamilton, Henry Kuttner, Jack Williamson, and Robert A. Heinlein. (And Ray has also acknowledged the strong influence of Theodore Sturgeon.)

When he began selling his science fiction, he quit reading in the genre, turning to such mainstream literary masters as Hemingway, John Steinbeck, Thomas Wolfe, F. Scott Fitzgerald, Franz Kafka, Shirley Jackson, John Collier, Jessamyn West, and John Cheever. Along the way he was introduced to the crime novels of Dashiell Hammett, Raymond Chandler, and Ross Macdonald.

During the 1950s—when he was hired to write the script for *Moby Dick*—he became a disciple of Herman Melville, William Shakespeare, and George Bernard Shaw. In recent years—as a playwright—Bradbury's stage works strongly reflect these classic influences.

I have mentioned only his major sources of inspiration, but there were others who shaped Bradbury's thinking—essayists (such as Loren Eiseley) as well as a host of philosophers and poets. In fact, decades ago, Ray all but abandoned the reading of fiction in favor of verse, plays, and essays.

In tracing the progression of Bradbury's work, we can discern the influence of all these writers. In his stories and poems, Ray has paid open tribute to several of them: Nathaniel Hawthorne, Hemingway, Wolfe, Verne, Dickens, Poe, Melville, Shaw, Fitzgerald, and Emily Dickinson.

This study lists eighty-seven Bradbury books and pamphlets (novels, collections, single-story volumes, and such) containing fiction in which Ray's stories are cycled and recycled. The reader is guided through the complex creative history of each fictional work. Drawing from hitherto unavailable correspondence, the authors trace the often-lengthy interaction between Bradbury and his agents, editors, friends, and publishers in shaping the stories and novels from manuscript to printed text.

These pages provide detailed textual and thematic analysis for all Ray's major fictional works. If—in this writer's opinion—the criticism is tipped too heavily in favor of a Nietzschean interpretation (Bradbury claims never to have read Nietzsche), Eller and Touponce have every right to interpret Bradbury's work as they see it. Their judgment is obviously based on an in-depth reading of the Bradbury canon, and their critical conclusions are of unquestioned value. Without doubt, future scholars will be compelled to take into full account the groundbreaking analysis revealed in this carefully considered study.

The book is in no way a Bradbury biography, yet many biographical facts emerge via the history of Ray's work, echoing the book's title, *The Life of Fiction.*

Of particular interest and value, the authors include a detailed examination of two unfinished Bradbury novels, *The Masks* and *Summer Morning, Summer Night.* The former supports their ongoing "carnivalization" theory—that all Bradbury's work fall into the category of "masks, myths, and metaphors" and is rooted in the carnival aspects of life. They show us that the carnival has formed—both literally and symbolically—the centerpiece of Bradbury's work. Citing the bold theatricality of Ray's fiction, and using *The Masks* as their starting point, Eller and Touponce expand this theory with each succeeding chapter.

The notion of carnivalization is itself well founded in the history of Bradbury criticism, of which I have made several surveys. Bradbury himself acknowledged this source for his work when he declared that "the carnival . . . along with magicians and magic . . . has shaped much of my thinking and my existence." *The Masks,* as the authors of this study tell us, "is infused with carnival ideas and concepts."

In Ray Bradbury's world, what he terms "the intolerable truths of life" must be masked in order for us to confront them. ("The dramatic play of masking/unmasking is at the heart of Bradbury's major fiction.") One mask, when removed, uncovers another and—

with that one removed—reveals yet another in Bradbury's metaphorical prose.

In the case of *Summer Morning, Summer Night* (initially projected as a sequel to *Dandelion Wine*), Eller and Touponce explore the author's intention to dramatize a war between youth and age in which the passage of time itself is seen as a deadly adversary.

Of course, Ray's fictional children ultimately discover that time cannot be stopped and that their battle is hopeless. In truth, Ray himself never wanted to grow up, and this unfinished novel is testimony to the fact that the child in Bradbury is enemy to the man.

The Life of Fiction is enhanced by an impressive variety of graphic charts, tables, and manuscript pages that supplement and clarify the main text. The appendixes alone—an amazing job of research and compilation—are worth the price of the book. In them, all Bradbury's more than 400 items are listed, showing their progression through first printings, reprints, anthology and textbook appearances, and media adaptations (radio, films, television, and stage).

A full decade of painstaking effort is represented in the pages that follow. This book will take you on a compelling journey through Bradbury Country.

It is a trip you will never forget.

—Jon Eller and William Touponce, *Ray Bradbury: The Life of Fiction* (Kent State University Press, 2004

William F. Nolan Interviews Ray Bradbury

Note: The following interview was conducted in the home of the late Ray Bradbury. It was during a visit with Bradbury, William F. Nolan, and Jason & Sunni Brock in 2010, and is a part of the extensive Brock video archive of great authors, artists, and filmmakers discussing their lives, professional experiences, and friendships. Portions of some of these exclusive interviews have appeared in the JaSunni Productions feature-length documentaries *The AckerMonster Chronicles!* and *Charles Beaumont: The Twilight Zone's Magic Man.*

William F. Nolan: I know you've said a lot about Chuck [the late author Charles Beaumont, friend to Nolan and Bradbury], but I want to ask you something nobody's ever asked you before.

Ray Bradbury: OK.

Nolan: If Chuck Beaumont were alive today, what do you think he'd be doing?

Bradbury: He would be equal to me. He would be equal. He would. . . . People would know him all around the world, because he was on his way there. He followed the advice I gave him when he was twenty-one years old. I said, "Write a short story a week for the next year, and at the end of the year you'll be a short story writer." I said, "Come to my house every Tuesday night, 8 o'clock, and scratch at the door. I'll look out and if you've got a manuscript in your mouth, like a dog begging [wags his head], to come in, I'll let you come in." [laughs] So he showed up with my friend [Sid], another writer, and I let them in every Tuesday night, and he followed my advice. He did fifty short stories that first year, including "Miss Gentilbelle," and so I was his friend, and I helped sell "Miss Gentilbelle." I think I sent it to somebody . . . I can't remember.

Nolan: Yeah, you sent several of his stories out to people.

Bradbury: That's right.

Nolan: You acted as his agent for a while. You were his agent.

Bradbury: Yes.

Nolan: He didn't ask you to do it, you just wanted to do it. You said, "I want to send these stories out."

Bradbury: Yeah. They were . . .

Nolan: "They were too good not to be printed," you said.

Bradbury: So he finally followed my advice. And you did too [points at Nolan].

Nolan: Yeah.

Bradbury: I told Bill, do a story a week for a year. You can't go wrong.

Nolan: I did it!

Bradbury: You begin to write quality.

Nolan: Yeah, yeah. Maybe fifty-one of them are lousy, but the fifty-second is gonna be a damn good story.

Bradbury: HA HA! [laughs heartily]

Nolan: But if you'd never had written the first fifty-one, you'd never get to that good story.

Bradbury: That's right.

Nolan: You said that, and I remembered that you said it, and then in the first year after I quit my job, I wrote fifty-one. Every week . . .

Jason V Brock: [off camera] Bad stories?

Bradbury: [chuckles]

Nolan: Let me ask you this: When I asked you what do you think Chuck would be doing now, what I meant was, do you think he'd be doing novels? Do you think he'd be writing novels?

Bradbury: He'd be doing everything. He's like . . . He was a hybrid, like me. I'm a hybrid. I'm one-third movies, I'm one-third stage, and one-third writer. I was a hybrid writer and he was a hybrid writer. He loved movies and he loved short stories, and he loved novels. He didn't love stage, but that's OK. The rest is all right. [laughs]

Nolan: [laughs] The rest is all right. You forgive him for the stage, right?

Bradbury: [nods]

Nolan: No, no. He never got around to it. He might have done plays later.

Bradbury: Oh God, yeah.

Nolan: Yeah, he might have.

Brock: [off camera] How did he meet Forry [agent and editor Forrest J Ackerman]? How did Chuck get hooked up with Forry?

Nolan: [to Bradbury] How did Chuck meet Forry Ackerman? Do you remember?

Bradbury: I introduced him to Forry.

Nolan: You introduced him?

Bradbury: Forry became his agent.

Nolan: Yeah, that's right. He was Chuck's first agent, right.

Bradbury: That's right.

Brock: [off camera] You introduced him to Don Congdon, too, right? [meaning Beaumont]

Bradbury: Years later.

Brock: [off camera] What about Rich Matheson? Did you introduce him to Congdon?

Nolan: [to Bradbury] Yeah, Richard Matheson. Did you introduce him to Don Congdon?

Bradbury: That's right, I did.

Brock: [off camera] What about you and Rich? How did you meet? Rich wrote you a letter? Rich Matheson wrote you a letter?

Nolan: [to Bradbury] Oh, Richard Matheson. How did you . . .

Bradbury: Yes, and I wrote back. You've seen the reply I gave him, haven't you?

Nolan: [nods] Yeah, I saw it. I saw the letter that you wrote to him.

Bradbury: He's got it framed in his house. I wrote back and said, "If your other stories are as good as this one, you going to be doing very well."

Nolan: [to Brock] That's right. He had sent Ray a story and Ray replied to that. You know, Ray has helped a lot of writers. [to Bradbury] You helped a lot of young writers. You've gone out of your way. You've written to them. You've sent their stories out. You've encouraged them. You've really done a lot. You haven't just sat back, you give of yourself. You've helped a lot of people. And that's important, I think, to know. People should know that.

Bradbury: Yeah, back in 1951 I went to a party one night, and this young woman came up to me and said, "I've got a short story here by my brother, will you read it?" I said, "Oh, gee. I don't know . . ." So I took the short story and I read it, and I called her, and I said, "My God, this is beautiful. I can sell this to a magazine overnight. I'm not an agent, but I'll send it to some contacts and they'll buy it." So I had him come to the house, and he gave me two more short stories, and I sent them out and they sold. Just like that. He was brilliant. He was twenty-one years old. Beautiful young man.

Nolan: He was Irish, wasn't he? Irish?

Bradbury: No, no. He lived in Santa Barbara. But anyway, he showed up at the house a year later, and he was wearing a sailor outfit with the Korean War. He had joined the Navy, and went off around the world. And fifty years went by. . . . He had a chance to be famous, because everything he wrote I sold just like that! I've got some of his short stories down in the basement right now, I never sold them fifty years ago. And fifty years went by, and I went and did a lecture in Santa Barbara about ten years ago, and an old man came up to me, laughing and drunk or on dope or something, and saying "Geesh, Ray!" and going like this [shakes hands in air], you know. And I said "Who are you?" He gave me his name, and it was that young man. I said, "You son-of-a-bitch! You get out of here . . . and go write!"

[everyone laughs]

A Bradbury Top Ten, Plus Fifty:
My Personal Evaluation of
Ray's Finest Stories

I began writing about Ray Bradbury as a fan in the spring of 1951, and I close my commentary as a seasoned professional in the summer of 2012, more than six decades later. Reading his work through the years, I naturally gravitated toward certain favorite tales. In this piece, I celebrate these favorites; starting with an in-depth look at my top ten and adding another fifty that I feel richly deserve to be cited. Over the course of his long career Ray wrote some 600 stories (including many not yet printed), and I listed several of his early best (into 1953) in my essay "The Bradbury Years." In this current piece, I rate his extended output, covering many of the early titles as well as a host of newer ones. My selections are purely subjective, and readers may well name Bradbury titles not included here as personal favorites. Fine. To each his own.

In selecting these sixty stories, I have relied upon his two seminal collections: *The Stories of Ray Bradbury* (Knopf, 1980) and *Bradbury Stories* (Morrow, 2003). I began by jotting down favorite titles among the 100 in each volume. Out of these, I selected my top ten. Why these? What makes them special? How do they relate to Bradbury's life? I answer with in-depth commentary on each. Lacking space here to comment on each of the remaining fifty, I leave it to the reader to seek them out. They are well worth the effort.

I begin my top ten with what many consider to be Ray's most memorable story, "Mars Is Heaven." Here is "capsule" Bradbury, as he blends past and future—along with his abiding fear of death—into a seamless whole. When Earthmen land on Mars, they are stunned to encounter a small Midwestern town in which their deceased loved ones are alive once again. How can this be? Are they in heaven? The Earthmen have actually been subjected to a form of Martian hypnosis. They are not seeing the real Mars or the real Martians. It is all a dark mind-game, designed to deceive and to destroy these Earth "invaders." Ray ends the story with a grim Martian celebration: "The brass band . . . marched and slammed back into town, and everyone took the day off."

Next, I have selected Bradbury's end novelette in *Dark Carnival*, "The Next in Line." This story superbly captures the fears and ultimate terror engendered by Ray's 1945 trip through Mexico with his friend Grant Beach (to whom *Dark Carnival* is dedicated). Ray transforms Beach into the protagonist's wife, setting up a series of marital tensions, climaxed by a horrific confrontation with the standing mummies of Guanajuato. Although Bradbury was reluctant to undertake this trip, as a writer it served him well—resulting in stories such as "The Candy Skull," "Interval in Sunlight," and "El Día de Muerte." Never was his brooding poetic style better employed. "The Next in Line" represents Bradbury at the height of his literary powers.

When *Weird Tales* rejected "Homecoming," Ray was delighted to have it accepted by *Mademoiselle,* and that publication built an *entire issue* around it. The best-known of Bradbury's "vampire family" tales, this affecting story deals with the personal alienation of a young boy who does not fit the mold of his outré family, just as Ray himself felt, always, that he was an "outsider." He also wrote several other accounts in this manner, but none was finer than "Homecoming." Prime Bradbury.

The power of "Heavy-Set" resides in Ray's dark portrait of his muscled athletic brother "Skip." For years they shared the same bed, yet were totally opposed personalities. They had nothing in common beyond being related. This story is Ray's attempt to understand his older brother, a burly weightlifter who had no interest whatever in literature. Out of their strained relationship, Bradbury fashioned this dark tale.

In "One Timeless Spring," Bradbury reflects another vital aspect of his basic personality—his desire to escape old age and death, to stay young forever. The boy in this superbly crafted tale fights a lone battle to avoid the curse of adulthood. Adults are the enemy; they want to change him, make him become what they are. Of course, it's a losing fight. In a poetic, moving climax, he finally accepts the fate that awaits him; he had found love:

> I knew it was all over. I was lost. From this moment on, it would be a touching, an eating of foods, a learning of language and algebra and logic, a movement and an emotion, a kissing and a holding, a whirl of feeling that caught and sucked me drowning under. I knew I was lost forever now, and didn't care.

With respect to my sixth selection, I recognize that a wide variety of textbooks have included Ray's cautionary tale "There Will Come Soft Rains" as a part of their curricula. For years, students have marveled at the amazing mechanical house that lives on after its human owners have been burned to atomic ash, an ironic glimpse of a possible destructive future in which man is erased from the complex machine world he has created. The story was a reflection of Ray's fear of atomic holocaust, a theme he explored in greater depth with *The Martian Chronicles* and *Fahrenheit 451*.

"The Lake," first printed in May of 1944, when Ray was twenty-four, is a richly poetic story of loss and remembrance. In this haunting account of a missing child and the man who mourns her, Bradbury finds his style and his true subject matter—his boyhood roots in Illinois. He would celebrate this lost boyhood at length in *Dandelion Wine*; Ray had found his voice, and his past would shape his future.

The *New Yorker* was a tough sell for Bradbury. His usual brand of poetic nostalgia didn't fit their pages. He made just one story sale to the magazine, "I See You Never," in 1947. It dealt with the agony of a fractured family. Short, sensitive, and deeply humanistic, it has rightfully endured as a Bradbury classic, a story with a real emotional punch. I have never forgotten it.

"The Veldt" was first printed in 1950 as "The World the Children Made." In this shocking parable of the future, two hedonistic children literally feed their parents to the lions in a come-alive nursery. Starkly poetic, for me this dark tale retains its power to fascinate and seduce. A stunning concept perfectly executed.

"The Pedestrian" is based on Bradbury's actual late-night walk in Los Angeles with a friend. When stopped and questioned by police as to what he was up to on the night streets, his angry response was: "I was taking a walk!" That walk resulted in a biting futuristic tale in which walking was a forbidden act. A shocking extension of truth into fiction.

So there you have them: Ten shining jewels in Bradbury's crown. My pick of his best, the stories that affected me most emotionally. But the next fifty listed here are all equally fine; I have a warm spot in my heart for each of them. . . . In no particular order, then:

"Zero Hour"
"The Wonderful Ice Cream Suit"
"The Rocket Man"
"All Summer in a Day"
"The Small Assassin"
"Ylla"
"Season of Disbelief"
"The Flying Machine"
"The Exiles"
"Death and the Maiden"
"The Jar"

"Skeleton"

"The Other Foot"

"Dark They Were, and Golden-Eyed"

"The Emissary"

"Jack-in-the-Box"

"The Whole Town's Sleeping"

"The October Game"

"Invisible Boy"

"The Wind"

"Long After Midnight"

"Uncle Einar"

"The Fruit at the Bottom of the Bowl"

"The Miracles of Jamie"

"The Wonderful Poker Chip of H. Matisse"

"The April Witch"

"The Illustrated Man"

"And the Rock Cried Out"

"The Black Ferris"

"The Playground"

"Forever and the Earth"

"Way in the Middle of the Air"

"The Dead Man"

"The Haunting of the New"

"Hail and Farewell"

"The Wilderness"

"The Fog Horn"

"The One Who Waits"

"And So Died Riabouchinska"

"The Big Black and White Game"

"The Meadow"

"And the Moon Be Still as Bright"

"The Naming of Names"

"The Women"
"Punishment without Crime"
"The Wonderful Death of Dudley Stone"
"The Night, Interval in Sunlight"
"The Crowd"
"Powerhouse"
"The Fox and the Forest"

STORIES

The Immortal Ones

[In this satire (my first printed story), I entered Bradbury's world, using his characters, to fashion a fictional tribute to him. It was part of my *Ray Bradbury Review* (1952).—WFN.]

The bone-cold chill of a late autumn night frostily embraces Mellin Town, Illinois, and the studio of one R. Bradbury, word-weaver of fairy spells and magic wonders. A flickering candle glitters like a dead man's eye on a polished desk, its waxen thinness thumbed and fingered to a strangely human effigy. The whirr-whisper of bat wings is in the air and a cauldron of unearthly brew bubbles wickedly at a stone hearth, weirdly shaped mounds and squares of varied hue and odor revolving slowly in its liquid depths. The massive oaken desk casts a somber shadow on the fiendishly carved masks lining the four walls, their demented cries and clamor frozen to a wooden stillness. Behind this oaken colossus sits a man of medium stature whose brown-rimmed spectacles pick up the lights from the fire and spin them in a frenzied whirl-a-gig on shining lenses. The man is writing, and the scratching of the tapered quill he holds sounds not unlike the clawing of long-nailed fingers on a coffin's lid. Heaps of yellowed papers are scattered about the room like oversize decks of playing cards flung from a giant's hand. Small, metallic insects make subtle squeaks and rustlings through their midst, and in one corner an exquisite golden spider endlessly spins its mechanical web to catch a metal fly.

The slender, bone-white hands of the word-magician pause in their mystical inscribing. The keen eyes flash angrily as the extrasensory organs of the ears warn of approaching sound. Footsteps. Slow. Regular. Plodding.

"Not *again* tonight! Damn it no—NO!" One of Bradbury's hands balls itself into a fist and viciously strikes the desk-top, jar-

175

ring the grinning teeth of the small candy-skull paperweights. A knock. Heavy and tired and frustrated . . .

"WELL?" The door swings reluctantly back.

An old man is there, gaunt-faced, with dark, sad eyes.

"Me again, sir. I've tried everything and nothin's any good. I come to ask—"

"Damn it, man, I know well enough why you've come, but you're wasting your time. It's no use."

"I even laid there and pretended—shut my eyes and told myself I was really dead again, but the coffin was cold and my back itched and it was just no good. You created me to be a corpse, Mr. Bradbury. Why can't I be like I used to before you raised me in 'The Dead Man'? Why won't you let me rest again, Mr. Bradbury?"

"I'm sick of telling you that it is not *possible* for you to be dead now. I CAN'T send you back. It's not my fault, man. You'll exist as long as time itself and on after that. My gift is immortality. You've received eternal life and there's nothing to do but make the best of it! Now get out!"—and the door swung shut with pistol-shot finality.

Sadly the old man turned away, his withered arms like wooden sticks dangling loose and helpless at his sides. With trembling steps he made his way down the path.

"And don't come back—you hear me, old man—don't EVER come back!" shouted Bradbury from the window as the ancient disappeared into the woods. Above the black net lacework of the trees he saw 'Uncle Einar' still flapping in slow spirals and impatient circles, his great green wings outstretched. His voice came piping-thin down through the autumn air.

"Please let me land, Mr. Bradbury. Since you made a kite of me with your accursed words I cannot rest—always flying—flying. I'm SOoooooooo tired . . ."

Bradbury strode angrily from the window. "Listen to that old fool! He ought to be glad he's immortal. He'll fly there forever and

there is not a damned thing anyone can do about it. Never satisfied, these characters of mine; I'm sick to death of their weeping
and complaining."

And he thought of Cecy, another member of the "Homecoming," her delicate body relaxed and still on a bed of snowy soft-
ness—her mind a thousand miles away in the eye of a needle, in
the brain of a dragonfly, in the dust motes of a sunlit noon; sometimes even in his own skull, pleading for release, for an end to all
this wandering. But there would be none. None.

"You there, on the shelf—" He faced an ominous "Jar" wherein
two eyes seemed to be staring out through the glassy sides, ever
shifting and moving in the murky fluid of the interior. "No com-
plaints from you, I see. No mouth to complain WITH! Just you
keep on floating 'til Hell freezes over, 'til Gabriel blows his trumpet, 'til the stars and moons and planets all come tumbling down
in a silver shower. Just float, and float . . . Wish to the devil they
were *all* like you."

But there were *some* who had found happiness. He looked to
the heavens. "Catherine the Great is up there," he smiled, "having
a hell of a good time. I put her there in 'The Square Pegs.' And
Napoleon, and Caesar, and Henry the Eighth—all there—all content. Why can't you others be like them?"

The skeleton in the corner did not reply. The tiny golden spider silently spun its endless web and the metal cleaning mice
darted out in tireless effort to carry away the last fragments of
grave-mud left by the dead man's shoes.

"Yes, and my electrical house out there too, across those
wooded hills—baking its own bread and making pies and reading
nursery rhymes to itself. It's happy. No trouble there."

But then he thought of Mars!!

"Oh God, what I did to that lovely planet! Destroyed its jewel-
bright cities, killed its people, filled its air with rocket fire, threw

beer-cans into its lovely canals . . . And *they* are still up there, on that 'Million Year Picnic,' more like a trillion year one now. Still though, the negroes are there, and they deserved the chance to start all over."

He walked across the room to the big closet.

There was his mother, looking as pretty as ever, and his father—strong and tall and still very proud, and the girl he'd known in high school, and the ruddy-cheeked fruit seller that had trusted him when he'd needed an apple or two to keep going in those terrible early days. All there and more, standing neatly in rows waiting to come out and talk and dance and sing to him.

"But you aren't real—none of you . . . My mother died years ago and dad too. You're *all* dead. I brought others back, for all eternity, but they were *mine*, my own original creations. None of *you* were molded out of words on a written page— You were God-fashioned and I *can't* bring you back, not REALLY."

The flesh-perfect marionettes smiled and said nothing. They waited. He slammed the door and took his place at the desk. He wrote. . . .

He wrote of rocket ships, of tombstones, of were-things and bats in the night.

He wrote—while white-hot far-off suns dimmed out and vast civilizations matured and perished.

He wrote—and the stars wheeled in slow majesty over an aging earth.

He wrote—while earth curled up and died beneath him—until Mellin Town was no more, Illinois no more, the earth no more . . .

And still he writes out there among the whirling gulfs and galaxies and black pits of space with his fabulous creations still around him—immortal, imperishable, and continuing on and on and on.

Forever.

—*Ray Bradbury Review* (1952)

Mr. B. Goes to Hollywood

[This story was written in 1952, for a San Francisco fan publication, *Rhodomagnetic Digest*. I was on its editorial board as editor/writer/artist. "Mr. B. Goes to Hollywood" is a satire, in which I send Ray Bradbury to battle the powers-that-be in the very surreal film industry. Does it still hold up as wild humor in our own century? You tell me.–WFN.]

"Mr. Weewig, sir. There's a man outside."

J. B. Weewig, production head of Superscreen Pictures, Inc., dramatically crushed a wet cigar to death in a mammoth kidney-shaped ashtray and fixed an evil eye on his blonde secretary. "That's a wholly ambiguous statement, Miss Muss, which I might interpret in many ways."

"I—I mean a man—to *see* you." Miss Muss had just graduated Hollywood High, was only nineteen, and flustered easily.

"Does he have an appointment?"

"No, sir. And I told him—"

"—that it was impossible to see me without an appointment. Nobody, NOBODY, Miss Muss, sees me without an appointment except my bookie. Is he my bookie?"

"No, sir. He's—"

"By God! Not even Louie B. Mayer can see me without an appointment!" He was waving clenched fists in the air, mentally comparing his performance to that of Charles Laughton in *The Big Clock*.

"He—he says you asked about seeing one of his scripts. He brought one with him."

"Ohmahgawd! Another writer!" Weewig stormed across the office, papers fluttering from the desk in the wind of his passage. "Dime a dozen. Every bum in town's a writer. What in Sam Hill

179

would I be doing reading his script? You know, I PAY people to read." He leveled a Humphrey Bogart gun-barrel finger at the trembling girl. "Has he got a spectacle? We're in the market for spectacles."

Miss Muss was confused and on the verge of tears. "Oh—I'm not sure. . . . He . . . he wears glasses."

"Are you trying to be funny, Miss Muss? You know, I PAY people to be funny."

"Oh, no, sir. I didn't mean—" She was openly sobbing.

"I must insist you pull yourself together! Now what is this fellow's name?"

"R-Ray Bradbury. He—he mentioned something about scenic friction."

Weewig lit up like a Christmas tree. "Science fiction, my dear girl! Science fiction. Up and coming thing these days. And we here in the film capital are proud to say we discovered it *first!* Why, they'll be printing the stuff next. Spectacle. That's what it is. Spectacle. Send this fellow—whatzis—in."

Hands folded behind his back, Mr. Weewig pleasurably scrutinized his secretary's trim legs as she left the room, congratulating himself on the choice of office personnel. He felt very much like James Mason in *The Seventh Veil.*

The door opened. A young man with a crew haircut and bow-tie entered. He smiled at Weewig. "We met at a party. My name is . . ."

"Yes, yes, I know." Weewig gripped the other's hand and pumped it up and down, violently, until he heard bones snap. "Sit down, Ralph. Have a cigar."

"The name is Ray," Bradbury said, massaging his right hand. "I don't smoke, thanks." He sat down.

"So you've brought me a script—eh?"

Bradbury handed the producer a manila envelope.

Weewig re-seated himself at the desk, rolled a freshly-lit cigar across his ample mouth, and glanced over the typed pages. "Mmmmmm. Umph. MMMMMM. Not bad. NOT BAD! No title. What do you call it?"

"I thought *The Outer Ones* might convey the feeling of loneliness, of sadness, which is the dominant theme of . . ."

"Lousy title, Ralph. No zip. No zing. No sales appeal." Weewig paused to belch. "No sex! But forget the title. You know, I PAY people to think up titles."

Bradbury squirmed in the chair. "Maybe I'd better—"

"Whydja bring it ta me?" The producer's speech occasionally lapsed into that of a Brooklynesque gang leader, once enacted by Richard Widmark.

"At this party I attended some weeks ago, you expressed interest in the idea."

Weewig chuckled slyly. "When I'm at a party, I am drunk. And when I am drunk, I am interested in everything. Especially," he winked knowingly, "—women."

"Maybe I'd better take my script and . . ."

"Nonsense, my boy. Sit down. I think you've GOT something here. I might even call it a rough-hewn classic!"

The adjective disturbed Bradbury. "I did seventeen drafts before bringing it in."

"Of course, of course. It's in good shape. By God—" Weewig arose and smashed his fist on the desk to punctuate his decision. "I LIKE the idea. And what I like—I buy. Ralph, how about thirty thousand?" He picked up a fountain pen and began to scratch rapidly in a checkbook.

"Uh—the name is Ray," corrected Bradbury, somewhat shaken.

"There you are, my boy." He handed the check to Bradbury and pressed a wall button. "Our catastrophe man'll be here in a jiffy."

"Your what?" asked Bradbury.

"Joe Niblick. Does all our catastrophes. Great guy, Joe. Damn sensitive, too. When we want an earthquake—a tidal wave—a typhoon, he's our boy!"

The door flew open and a voice, vast and thunder-throated, boomed across the room, setting Bradbury's teeth on edge. "HIYA, J. B.!"

Weewig rushed to embrace the smiling newcomer. For a moment they exchanged obscenities regarding Weewig's secretary. Then—

"Joe, I want you to meet a talented boy—Ray Bogbury."

Before Bradbury could supply the proper name correction, he felt one of his bones crack under Niblick's handshake. After that he didn't care. Niblick, a small greasy man with a tic in his cheek, suddenly quit smiling. "Let's get down to business. You got a catastrophe in this script?"

Bradbury, again seated and massaging his hand, replied uncertainly, "Well, I wouldn't actually call it—"

The sensitive Niblick exploded. "What the hell, J. B. Have you got a catastrophe for me or haven't you?"

Bradbury had the uncomfortable feeling that the man's skull, lobster-red and nearly hairless, would, at any moment, pop its skin like a suddenly squeezed grape.

Niblick was ruffling through the typed pages, his cheek ticing furiously. "A-hhhhhhaaaaa—here's one. Rocket crash!"

"Mr. Niblick, if you read further I think you'll find the—"

"Never mind—never mind. I can see it now." Niblick's eyes glazed and he began to tip back on his heels in an ecstasy of creation. "Times Square on Saturday night. Throngs of people. Neon lights. Music. Sex. And then—WHAM!!!" Niblick smacked the desk top with a ruler. "Five rockets come out of deep space and obliterate half of New York."

Bradbury was out of his chair, hand raised in protest. "It's only one-small rocket, and it lands in the Arizona desert."

Weewig swept past Bradbury and threw both arms around his friend's neck. They wept together. "My God, Joe—IT'S GREAT!" Niblick, clutching part of the script, retired to a corner of the office and slid down the wall to a sitting position on the floor. He began red-pencilling the pages with savage intensity. Weewig pressed another button.

Within seconds, a tall, loose-jointed man with sideburns rushed into the room. He wore a seersucker suit.

"Ralph, I want you to meet Sid Siss. Does all our Illinois dialogue. Sid, this is Ralph Bedbury."

"Hello," said Bradbury, not offering to shake hands.

Siss was facing J. B. Weewig. He had eyes for no one else. "I can't tell you how much this means, J. B. A whole year and no Illinois pictures. Sitting in that office—day after day. Darts and checkers. Checkers and darts! I thought I'd go crazy. But now, NOW, I can get my teeth into something." A strange light glittered in his eyes as he turned to the script.

"Uh, wait a minute." Bradbury was on his feet once more. "The Illinois section is very brief and entirely visual. You just get a subtle glimpse of—"

But the hungry-eyed Siss was already at work on his section of the script and another button had been pressed. The new arrival was gaunt and silent, with deep hollows under bird-bright eyes. His name was Pike.

"Does all our cracker-barrel sequences. That sort of thing. Good to break the mood of a spectacle with a little down-to-earth country store human interest."

Bradbury nodded, numbly trying to recall a cracker-barrel sequence in his story while he watched Pike extract another section from the diminishing script. The tall man grunted twice and walked slowly to the window where he seated himself.

More buttons were pressed.

Bradbury was introduced to a squirrel-faced individual sporting a set of highly burnished plates whose smile was an overrich and dazzling affair, not unlike a display of glittering china under lights. His name was Grist and he had worked with Cecil B. DeMille before signing with Superscreen. Poking a sharp elbow in Bradbury's ribs he repeated, with obvious relish, his favorite pun: "Grist for DeMille. Get it, pal? Grist for DeMille!"

It seemed his specialty was comedy production numbers encompassing hordes of chorus girls and huge revolving stages.

Mr. Chester was summoned next, a singularly ill-mannered fat man whose personal attractiveness was further handicapped by bad breath and a nasal drip. Bradbury couldn't recall his organizational function, but it had something to do with the fact that he had been divorced seven times and was supposed to know all about women. The office was gradually filling. The increasingly argumentative rumble of voices mixed with heavy swirls of cigar smoke made Bradbury slightly ill. Someone mentioned Martin and Lewis and Weewig's scream of delight rebounded from the walls.

Bradbury had begun to edge toward the door when a uniformed waiter, emerging from the press of bodies, belligerently thrust a tray of sandwiches in his face. In order to avoid attracting undue attention, Bradbury apprehensively selected a small triangle of odorous bread smeared with a sickly-hued paste which stuck in his throat like melted chalk when he attempted to swallow. Face flushed and almost gagging, he made his way through the cigar haze to a large kidney-shaped potted plant near the window, wherein he furtively deposited the soggy remnants of the delicacy.

Both hands clutching at his stomach, he finally reached the hallway. It stretched ahead of him cool and inviting.

No one noticed the door close.

Six weeks later, the completed script of *Vampires from Outer Space* lay on J. B. Weewig's desk. The producer was on the phone, discussing the picture with Louis B. Mayer.

"Who wrote it? A fellow named Redbury. Very funny guy, with a great sense a' humor, but, just between you and me, L. B.—a SLOPPY writer. That original script he handed me had no polish whatever, L. B. But the minute I read it I knew we had something. A classic I called it—yessir, L. B.—a rough-hewn classic!"

—*Rhodomagnetic Digest* (January 1953)

The Joy of Living

[When Bradbury went to Ireland in September of 1953 to work on the screenplay for *Moby Dick* for director John Huston, he told me: "When you finish a story that you feel is truly professional, send it to me and I'll give you my critical opinion."

I'd never made a sale at that time, though I'd been writing for several years. Then, late that same year, I finished the final draft of "The Joy of Living" and deemed it professional enough to merit Bradbury's attention. He read it and wrote back to tell me how much he liked the story. He felt it was a true breakthrough for me, that it was my entry into pro ranks, *but* . . . the ending was emotionally flawed.

In my story I had a human male hire a humanoid robot female to take care of his children. He returns from a trip and decides to take over raising the children. At which point he returns her to the robot factory.

Ray pointed out that this ending was "all wrong." He said I was cheating the reader. I had made the robot so emotionally "real" that she must *not* be taken back to the factory. The protagonist must realize he truly loves her and cannot discard her. I rewrote the ending, based on Ray's letter, and it became my first sale (to *If: Worlds of SF* in 1954).

Ray had "saved" my story. And I was, at last, a pro.—WFN.]

"It's just around the next turn," Rice said, peering from the tinted windows as the car skimmed over the warm summer streets of the city.

The vehicle slowed, took the long curve with fluid grace, and whispered to a stop. A silver door panel sighed back and Ted Rice stepped into the heat of morning. His suit-conditioner immediately circulated an inner breath of cool air to balance the rise in temperature.

"I won't need you for the rest of the day," he told the car. "I'll be walking home."

"May I have your location number, sir, in case a member of the family should wish to contact you?"

"No, dammit, you may not!" This was Free-Day. He needn't tell the car anything. "Go home."

"Very well, sir." The machine slid obediently from the curb. Rice watched it glitter briefly, like a lake trout in the moving wash of morning traffic, and disappear.

On Free-Days he told the car what to do. No predetermined destinations. No predetermined activities. Today the bars were open.

He intended getting very, very drunk.

On this morning, the sixth anniversary of his wife's death, Ted Rice had made two highly important decisions. He would quit his job and he would turn Margaret in to Central Exchange. The job he hated, but it had been his life and quitting took courage. It meant beginning anew in an untried field and, at thirty-eight, that wasn't easy. Margaret he did not hate, finding it impossible to cata-logue his exact emotions where she was concerned. But his final decision to turn her in was the only one possible under the cir-cumstances.

His reason for getting drunk, however, had nothing to do with his job or with Margaret. He was not, had never been, a drinking man. Intoxication was an anniversary ritual performed in memory of his late wife, Virginia. He exercised extreme care in his yearly choice of drinking quarters, avoiding pretentiousness because he wanted the surroundings to reflect his own inner loneliness.

Louie's Place was anything but pretentious. Ceaseless towelings had worn the bar top to a circular whiteness. The mirror behind it, in the shape of a giant passenger rocket, hung chipped and black-ening at the edges. Even the mural, depicting Man's First Landing on the Red Planet, was dust-dimmed and faded, the paint crack-ing, peeling gradually away. The shabby stools fronting the bar were all unoccupied.

"Mornin'," greeted the bartender. Rice nodded, took a corner stool, and pressed the straight-whiskey button. The drink glided into his hand and he downed it, grimacing.

"Ain't seen you around before on Free-Days," the barman ob-served, swabbing idly at an already dry glass ring. "Just move inta th' neighborhood?"

"I don't drink often," Rice said, re-pressing the button.

"Wanna tell me about things?"

Rice shifted his attention from his shot glass to the man behind the bar. Beefy, slack-jawed, with a broken nose and a pair of wa-tery, protuberant eyes over which lids folded like canvas sails. The face of mourning. The professional kindred soul, salaried receiver of woes and sad lament. Rice regarded him suspiciously, twirling the shot glass between thumb and forefinger.

"Well, Mac?"

"Turn around," said Rice.

The big man grinned broadly, his solemn face splitting as though a paper-knife had slit the skin across. "Now I *know* you don't drink much. Believe me, I'm the real McCoy. In my racket you have to be."

"Around."

Still grinning, the bartender complied. Law provided that evi-dence of a mechanical could not be concealed and there was no metal switch behind the man's right ear.

"Like I toldja, th' McCoy."

"It's been a year," Rice said, by way of apology. "I wasn't sure they hadn't replaced you fellows too."

"Bars'ud go broke if they did. Who wants to tell their troubles to a bunch a' springs an' cogs?"

Rice glanced at his wrist watch and thought of Margaret, standing in the living room of their modest home, a smile illuminating her delicate features. She had been standing now for fifteen hours, thirty-seven minutes—since he'd switched her off the previous evening in an angry display of temper.

"Six years ago today my wife died in a copter crash," Rice said, meeting the barman's sad eyes. "I've put the memory of that crash away in the back of my mind and once each year I take it out and I remember." He tipped the shot glass at a careful angle, holding it quite still, as though he might capture Virginia's tiny image there within the dark liquid, as a fly is caught in amber. "I remember how she looked when they brought her up to the house, as if her bones had suddenly run wild under the skin, the way her face looked, the face of someone I'd never met."

Rice finished his fourth straight whiskey, feeling it burn down through his body, loosening inner tensions, making it easier to say what he subconsciously *had* to say.

"That can be rough." The big man looked wonderfully, professionally sympathetic, with those mournful red-rimmed eyes, which seemed about to flood into tears. "Didja have any kids?"

"A boy, Jackie. He'll be nine this Game-Day. Lot like his mother. The other children, Timmy and Susan, are mechanicals. Got them after Virgie's death, when I bought Margaret."

"Musta been tough on th' kid, losin' his real mother an' all."

"Jackie doesn't remember much about Virgie. He was only three. Fact is, I've been half a stranger to him myself, on the road most of the year. Margaret's all right, I suppose, but she doesn't think the way you and I do."

"How come you stuck yourself with this Margaret?"

"Authorities. Had to furnish a decent home for the boy or lose him. I couldn't stay settled then, with my wife gone. She was still so much a part of things, of our house, the streets, the places we used to go . . . I went on the road, tried to forget. That kind of life was out of the question for a three-year-old. I had no choice. Either I bought a mechanical or I lost my son. I could find no one to take Jackie. Virgie's parents were dead and my own mother was in no position to raise a child. So I bought Margaret and since we'd originally planned on a brother and sister for Jackie I decided to do it up brown and go for the package deal. After all, I got 'em wholesale."

"Hey!" The barman cocked an eyebrow. "You a mech sales-man?"

"Until tomorrow. I'm quitting. My next job will be right here in L.A. and won't have a damn thing to do with mechanicals!" Producing his wallet, Rice handed the bartender a card. "Read that."

"Theodore A. Rice," the beefy man pronounced carefully, "Authorized representative for World Mechanicals."

"No, no. The slogan at the bottom."

"'A Dollar a Day Keeps Childbirth Away.' So?"

Rice leaned forward, steely-eyed. "So the damned fool who originated that ought to be roasted over a slow fire!"

"Just a slogan, Mac. Everybody knows it."

"Exactly! Do you have any real conception of what that slogan and others like it have done to our national birthrate?" Rice asked, a fresh whisky in his hand. "Childbirth has been converted into a horror, a form of medieval torture in the minds of women today. For thirty bucks a month any woman can have a bouncing baby made to order and delivered fresh-wrapped to her door. For less than it used to cost just to *feed* a human child, she can share the pleasures and joys of motherhood and avoid all the responsibilities.

"'Madam,' I'd say, 'don't risk your figure. Don't tie yourself down and miss all the fun. Get a mechanical! No baby-sitters needed, no dirty diapers or squalling at three in the morning. No measles or mumps or tonsils out. Just a bonny little brat with a switch behind his ear. What'll it be, madam? A fat little bambino with dark eyes and an angel's smile—or a saucy-eyed little Irisher with freckles on her nose?'

"'Or howz about you, fella? Tired of looking for the right girl? Want a ready-made cutie who'll be 100 percent yours? How did the old song go? "I want a paper dolly I can call my own, a dolly other fellows cannot steal . . ." Well, here she is, chum—a full-size babe with the old come-hither look reserved especially for you. Blonde? Brunette? Redhead? You name 'er, we've got 'er. Yours on easy payments!'"

Rice paused, breathing heavily, his glass empty.

The bartender, wise in the ways of his profession, maintained a listening silence.

"Ya know how this electronic illusion got started?" Rice demanded, tongue somewhat uncertain in his mouth, speech beginning to slur. "Well, lemme tellya. People got lonesome. An' when somebody's ole man died 'long comes a mech to replace him. When a woman was sterile she got her baby anyhow. When a Mr. Shy Guy wanted some female company 'long comes a sponge-rubber job right outa th' pinup mags. Jus' a few at first, here an' there, an' expensive as hell. But pretty soon the good ole American commercial know-how takes over and competition gets rough. Prices go down. A lotta people stop havin' babies. In nothin' flat everybody is buyin' mechanicals . . . you . . . 'n' . . . me 'n' everybody . . ."

"Hate ta spoil your fun, Mac, but you're really loadin' one on. I'd ease up on them straight shots."

"An' you know what th' tragedy is?" Rice continued over a filled glass, ignoring the advice. "Th' trashdy is, we're all dyin' an' nobody cares! Pretty soon you 'n' me will be in the same league with the goddam ole water buffalo an' the dodo bird. Th' trasbdy is that everybody is dyin' in a century designed for easy livin'. Say! Lesh drink a toast to th' joy of livin'."

The bartender extended a cautioning hand. "No foolin', Mac, if I was you— Look out! You're gonna . . ."

Rice felt the room tip, rock crazily for no apparent reason. Faintly he heard the bartender's shout of warning, saw his face receding like a toy balloon down the length of an immense corridor which ended abruptly in a high fountaining of colored lights.

Margaret was her usual cheery self when Rice finally switched her on.

"Morning, Ted darling." She bussed him on the cheek. "Sleep well?"

"This is July tenth," he replied sullenly, nursing the remnants of a colossal hangover.

"Goodness! Have I been off *that* long? Honestly, Ted! I'll never get the housework done if you continue to leave me off for days at a time. How are the children?"

"Fine. Still sleeping."

"If this is the tenth, then you've had your . . . your—"

"'Toot' is the word. And I feel lousy."

"What's that cut above your eye? Did someone hit you?"

"My assailant was the floor of the Third Avenue bar. I came off second best."

She was instantly solicitous. "You could have a concussion!"

"I'm fine."

"You're angry again."

"I'm fine and I'm not angry. Now, go wind the dog while I wake the kids."

If only she would react, thought Rice, watching her silent withdrawal. If only *once* she would stomp her feet, throw things, scream at him. But always, always this everlasting indulgence! The spark which ignites a marriage, makes it glow, was missing. In love, he knew, there is violence, and Margaret's love was a calm, manufactured emotion, which left him unsatisfied and edgy, a love unreal, intolerable. When he and Virgie had quarreled, had things out and reconciled, they were actually much closer to each other for having weathered a personal storm. But, with Margaret, the case was different.

Rice thought of the latest incident, two nights ago, when he had been with Skipper encouraging the dog to beg for a plasto-bone. Skipper was outdated, as modern dogs go, but he represented a link with the fading past which Margaret seemed bent on severing. She renewed the familiar subject of his purchasing a modernized, electronic canine to replace the shaggy wind-up model, and he all but hit the ceiling, thundering at her, gesturing, swearing. But she had remained impassive, turning aside his rage with her calm smile. Then, savagely, he had switched her off, as one might extinguish a glaring light. How frozen she had stood! How instantly drained of personality and movement! In that moment, facing her perfect, motionless body, he experienced a recurrent sense of guilt which invariably accompanied such action, as though he had taken a life, had murdered. Damning his own weakness he had left her there, smiling, in the silent room.

"Daddy, Daddy, Daddy," squealed Timmy after he was activated. "Hooray, hooray, it's Picnic-Day! Hooray, hooray, it's Picnic-Day!"

"Hooray, hooray," Rice repeated without enthusiasm, envisioning a hectic afternoon of child-noise and forced amusement.

"Now, quiet down. Your father's not feeling well," Margaret cautioned from the hall as Timmy zoomed and swooshed about the house playing Rocket.

Little Susan's enthusiasm matched that of her mechanical brother. She hopped around the living room, circling Rice, screaming out her delight in a voice that pierced his head like a driven needle.

"For the love of heaven, STOP!" he shouted at the whirling children, "or I'll switch you both off!"

Under his stern threat they quieted.

Margaret returned with Skipper. The dog had run down the previous evening chasing the electronic cat next door. He scampered rustily across the floor, high falsetto bark betraying the damaging effect of morning precipitation.

"Good ole Skip . . . You need some oil, fella," Rice told him, tickling his ears. "Have you fixed in a jiff. Timmy, get the oilcan from the shelf."

Rice was in the act of administering the proper lubricant when Jackie emerged from the hallway, rubbing sleep from his eyes.

"Hi, Mom. Hi, Dad. Morning everybody." He yawned.

"Hi, scout," Rice greeted him, roughing his already thoroughly tousled hair. "Have a good rest?"

"Sure. Hey, this is Picnic-Day isn't it? When are we leaving?"

"Soon as little sleepy-heads like you get out of their pajamas and into some breakfast." He playfully swatted Jackie's bottom. "Now git."

Margaret took the boy's hand. "Come on, dear. I have breakfast on the table." And over her shoulder to Rice: "I do think we should get an early start."

Susan and Timmy bounded into the yard with Skipper, leaving Rice alone with his thoughts.

He said, Hi Mom, first, before Hi Dad. And the look in his eyes when she took his hand! Jackie is too young to see Margaret as I see her; he can't realize that she can never really love him as he loves her. The longer she's here the harder it will be for Jackie when the break comes. I mustn't put off telling Margaret any longer. I'll tell her today. Today.

The bullet-car flowed soundlessly over the highway, blurring the trees, rushing the houses past, but to Rice the speed was illusion, stage trickery. His impatient mind, reaching for the moment when he would be alone with Margaret and able to tell her what he *must* tell her, changed minutes to hours. Head back against the seat, eyes closed, he imagined the car in lazy slow-motion, wheels barely turning, each blade of roadside grass available and separate to the eye if one chose to look.

The ride to the picnic ground seemed endless.

"I'm bushed," he said to Margaret after the car had parked it-self. "Let's skip the games today and just relax in the shade."

"But, Ted, the children . . ."

". . . can play without us. I have something to say to you, some-thing important."

She hesitated, watching the activity on the playing courts. The children, three elves in their picnic-jumpers, fidgeted, desperately anxious to join the games, their eyes darting like imprisoned min-nows in small white pools.

"In order to be enjoyed to the fullest the games require *family* participation."

"Nonsense."

"Young and old, Ted. The games . . ."

"To hell with the games!" he snapped. "Are you going to listen to what I have to say or not?"

"Of course, darling. If you really *want* to talk . . ." She smiled, pressed his hand. "The children can join the Hartleys." She pointed across the wide picnic lawn to a group of rioting players engaged in a vigorous game of Magna-Ball. "Run along you three. And be careful."

"Wheeeeeeee!" pealed little Susan, and hands linked in a daisy-chain, the happily released trio sprang toward the courts.

"If we're going to talk we can at least be comfortable," Margaret said, unpacking a blanket and spreading it over the prickling grass.

Every gesture perfect, thought Rice, watching her hands, *every movement graceful and sure. She's so alive, so amazingly human, possessing such vibrancy and warmth, that sometimes even I find it difficult to think of her as artificially created of wire and circuit and cog. Certainly Jackie has come to love her. She's good and kind and smiles a great deal. These things matter to Jackie. The fact that she isn't human does not matter. Not at all. The situation, therefore, is grave.*

"What are you thinking about, Ted?" Her blue eyes were steady on his.

"About you. About how beautiful you are." He plucked a single dandelion from the grass and held its orange-gold face, like a miniature sun, in the cupped palm of his hand. "This is a weed masquerading as a flower. Beautiful, possessing many virtues, but actually a weed which must be removed before its deep tap root smothers the surrounding grass. Unless it is, there will eventually be room only for the dandelion."

"What has all this . . ."

"You're like the dandelion, Margaret. You're smothering Jackie's love. He has grown to love you far more than he does me. Up to now I've been just a visiting relative who comes home from some distant place to spend Christmas and summer vacations with you. When he was younger he cried whenever I shut you off, as though I had beaten him. Even now he watches me lose my temper, swear, bang the furniture, and I see him looking at me, and I know he's comparing us, weighing us. The scales are in your favor. I'm home to stay now, and as long as you're here he'll always be comparing. I can't, I won't, compete with a mechanical for my son's affection!"

She sucked in her breath, sharply. He could see that his words had struck with the force of hurled stones.

"Have you thought this all out, Ted? Isn't there some *other* way?" She was actually trembling. "You know how much I love you."

"You only *think* you love me, Margaret. What you mistake for love is only conditioning. Receptors can be re-fed, patterned responses erased, new ones substituted. At Central Exchange they'll alter you, Margaret. You'll never know I existed."

"Ted, you can't!"

"There's no other way."

A silence between them.

Despite himself, Rice again experienced a twinge of guilt. Perhaps he had broken the news in too ruthless a fashion, but it was imperative that she understand his position, and he had considered it impossible to pierce her shell of calm. That she would be visibly shaken by his words was totally unexpected. Of course, he reasoned, no mechanical likes the idea of complete re-orientation. On these grounds her behavior seemed less surprising. But still . . .

"Why have you told me all this?" she asked him. "Why didn't you turn me in suddenly, without my knowing in advance? I'd have preferred that." Her hands moved nervously on her skirt, toyed with the locket at her neck, now touched at her hair like two restless birds unable to fly away from her body.

"Because I need your help. Jackie mustn't know the truth . . . Not now. Later, when he's older, better able to evaluate facts for himself, he'll understand. I'll tell him something about your having to go on a long trip for reasons of health. He'll believe me if you'll back me up. Will you?"

"If that's what you want," she replied softly, head down, her fingers turning and turning the dandelion he had discarded. "I'd do anything you want, Ted . . . because I love you."

"Timmy and Susan can stay with Jackie for awhile," he hurried on, "to make your leaving easier for him. In time, he'll adjust."

"Yes . . . he'll adjust."

The drowsy rustle of leaves in summer air. The distant hum of voices from the playing courts.

"Well, then it's settled."

"All settled. You'd better call the children in for lunch."

After lunch, Rice gamboled in the scented grass with the whooping children, imitating, to their vast delight, a bear, a gorilla, a whale, a jet train and a moon rocket. He ran races with them and organized a rodeo, in which he doubled in brass as a fiercely snorting brahma bull and a bucking bronco.

On the way home they sang folk songs and watched the sun go down over the ocean. The day, everyone agreed, had been a huge success.

But, that night, Rice could not sleep.

The headboard whispered, "Three, A.M., sir," when he questioned the hour. He lay on his back, hands laced behind his head, staring into the ghost darkness of the room. In the moon-painted sky a copter whirred past like a giant night insect seeking distant city lights, and Rice thought of Virginia. In past weeks he had been finding it remarkably difficult to remember many of the things about her that he wished to remember; time had hidden her image as a coin is hidden in deep waters.

The drone of the copter faded into Margaret's quiet breathing from the bed beside his, and now *her* face drifted into his mind, superimposed over the dim reflection of Virginia. He saw, in infinite detail, each curling black hair of her down-swept lashes, long and trembling against the rose of her cheek. He saw her quivering lips form words, four startling words of the afternoon: ". . . because I love you."

Impossible, that a mechanical could love as Virginia had loved; that a being of metal and glass, of wires however cunningly woven could fathom and experience such deeply genuine emotion.

Yet, was it conceivable, Rice wondered in the pressing darkness, that somehow an unknown process had taken place in Margaret, that far back in the green cave of her brain, among the delicate spider webbing of silver wires and hidden circuitry, an emotion had come into being above and beyond that of the purely mechanical?

Rice re-lived his initial shock of the afternoon, when, in direct vocal assault, he had unexpectedly found a chink in her armor, when he had all but moved her to tears—ridiculous in itself, for a mechanical, lacking both inclination and tear-ducts, cannot cry! But now, despite his earlier rationalization of her strange behavior, he was puzzled, vaguely disturbed.

At seven, a robin's sweet song awoke him. He felt a breath of air against his closed eyes from the passing flutter of small wings. Burying his head deeper in the snow-soft pillow he tried to ignore the insistent twitterings. However, he knew the damn thing would begin a banshee shrieking if he didn't get out of bed. Irritably he staggered into his slippers, and the robin settled with feathered grace upon his outstretched hand. Rice flipped the body-switch and placed the immobilized Alarm-bird on the night stand.

He dressed before waking Margaret.

"I've had breakfast." He lied to her when she asked. Today he wasn't hungry.

She nibbled toast and drank orange juice in silence. He avoided her eyes, finding inconsequential kitchen duties to occupy his hands while she ate. After half finishing her food she said, her voice very distinct in the morning room, "I guess it's time."

"Early yet," he said, not meeting her eyes. "No hurry at all."

"They open the doors at eight-thirty. We can set the car for a slow drive."

A silence.

"Did you . . . tell the children good-bye?" he asked.

"Last night. We won't need to wake them. They'll be fine until you get back." She put on black gloves, carefully fitting each finger, pulling them tight.

"Margaret, I'm sorry. Honest to God, I'm sorry it has to be this way."

"Don't say anything else, Ted. Just let's go."

"All right," he said. "Let's go."

A brief shower had cleansed the sky, and the morning was fresh and clear. The trees, their leaves still pendant with rain jewels, glittered in the warming sunlight.

Through the open car window Rice inhaled the rich after-scent of rain, and sighed. He wished it had not turned out to be such a damned fine day. The sky outside should have been gray, the trees stark and cold, like mourners along the street as the car, a silver coffin, passed them by.

He tried to think of something to say to Margaret as the car bore them steadily through the crystal morning toward the massive white stone building which housed Central Exchange. He tried to think of words which would not sound wrong the moment they were uttered, as all his words had sounded of late. But he found none and remained silent.

It was she who turned to him in the moving car and spoke first. "Ted, what are you doing?" Her voice was strange.

"Doing?" he echoed, facing her.

"To me, to Jackie, to yourself."

"Margaret, you're not going to question me *now?* We've gone all over this, the reasons for my decision, the factors involved. Surely you must realize—"

"Damn your reasons!" she exploded, eyes blazing at him, gloved hands clenched. "Are they fair? Do they take *my* feelings into consideration? Do they, Ted? Answer me! Do they?"

He couldn't answer her. A door was opening somewhere deep inside him and light was miraculously flooding in to illuminate a room he had never allowed himself to enter. He was blind, and her words were sight.

"I'm a mechanical, isn't that the answer, Ted? A bloodless machine that can be switched off at will, ignored, cursed, shouted at and destroyed, a creature without emotion, without feeling. Well, you're wrong, Ted. So very wrong. Men built me, gave me human impulses, human desires, put into me a part of themselves, a part of their own humanity. I feel hunger and thirst and cold and pain. But more, Ted! I feel a *human* hunger, a *human* thirst, a desire to be respected for myself, as an individual, as I respect others, a desire to be loved as I love others. Can't you see how wrong you've been? I've held all these things within because I was taught enduring humility and consummate patience by those who fashioned me. I was taught to behave rationally and calmly, to accept, to always accept and never question or rebel. But now it's ended and I've lost. . . . You've rejected me, Ted, and I wasn't prepared for this. . . . I can't accept this, but I don't know *how* to fight. . . . I only know I must and I don't know how . . ."

Her lips were trembling, her whole body swaying in the tide of released rage and sorrow.

"Lord, Lord, Margaret . . ." He placed a gentle hand beneath her chin and lifted her bowed head slowly. "You're *crying!*"

But of course there were no tears.

Rice stopped the car and took her, trembling, into his arms, saying her name over and over, quietly, trembling himself, and softly, tenderly, he kissed her.

Then, setting the controls at manual, he turned the car around and with one arm holding her close on the seat beside him he drove carefully home through the warm summer streets, knowing that never again, never ever again in all the years to come, would he switch her off.

–If: *Worlds of* SF (August 1954)

And Miles to Go Before I Sleep

[Written in March of 1957, when I was still under the spell of Bradbury's poetic prose, this story contains all the elements associated with a typical Bradbury tale. When it was printed (in *Infinity SF* in August 1958) the legendary radio giant (director/producer/writer) Norman Corwin told me that his favorite Bradbury story was "And Miles to Go Before I Sleep."

"But Norman," I said. "That's *my* story. I wrote it, not Ray!"

And we both had a laugh over it.

Yet Corwin was right in thinking it was by Ray. The mood was his. The whole aura was his. As were all the elements: the small Midwestern town, the boy who dreamed of Deep Space, the poetic rockets, the robot family—all these were right out of *The Martian Chronicles*.

Without meaning to, I had written a new Bradbury story. Read it and you'll see what I mean.—WFN.]

Alone within the humming ship, deep in its honeycombed chambers, Robert Murdock waited for death. While the rocket moved inexorably toward Earth—an immense silver needle threading the dark fabric of space—he waited calmly through, the final hours, knowing that hope no longer existed.

After twenty years in space, Murdock was going home.

Home. Earth. Thayerville, a small town in Kansas. Clean air, a shaded street and a white two-story house near the end of the block. Home after two decades among the stars.

The rocket knifed through the black of space, its atomics, like a great heartbeat, pulsing far below Robert Murdock as he sat quietly before a round port, seeing and not seeing the endless darkness surrounding him.

Murdock was remembering.

He remembered the worried face of his mother, her whispered prayers for his safety, the way she held him close for a long, long moment before he mounted the ship's ramp those twenty years ago. He remembered his father: a tall, weathered man, and that last crushing handshake before he said goodbye.

It was almost impossible to realize that they were now old and white-haired, that his father was forced to use a cane, that his mother was bowed and wasted by the years.

And what of himself?

He was now forty-one—and space had weathered him as the plains of Kansas had weathered his father. He, too, had fought storms in his job beyond Earth, terrible, alien storms; worse than any he had ever encountered on his own planet. And he, too, had labored on plains under burning suns far stronger than Sol. His face was square and hard-featured, his eyes dark and buried beneath thrusting ledges of bone.

Robert Murdock removed the stereo-shots of his parents from his uniform pocket and studied their faces. Warm, smiling, *waiting* faces: waiting for their son to come home to them. Carefully, he unfolded his mother's last letter. She had always been stubborn about sending tapes, complaining that her voice was unsteady, that she found it so difficult to speak her thoughts into the metallic mouth of a cold, impersonal machine. She insisted on using an old-fashioned pen, forming the words slowly in an almost archaic script. He had received this last letter just before his take-off for Earth, and it read:

> Dearest,
> We are so excited! Your father and I listened to your voice again and again, telling us that you are coming home to us at last, and we both thanked our good Lord that you were safe. Oh, we are so eager to see you, son. As you know, we have not been too well of late. Your father's heart doesn't allow him to get out much any more. Even the news that you are coming back to us has over-excited him. Then, of course, my own health seems none too good as I suffered another fainting spell last

week. But there is no real cause for alarm—and you are not to worry!— since Dr. Thom says I am still quite strong, and that these spells will pass. I am, however, resting as much as possible, so that I will be fine when you arrive. Please, Bob, come back to us safely. We pray God you will come home safe and well. The thought of you fills our hearts each day. Our lives are suddenly rich again. Hurry, Bob. Hurry!

All our love,
Mother

Robert Murdock put the letter aside and clenched his fists. Only brief hours remained to him—and Earth was *days* away. The town of Thayerville was an impossible distance across space; he knew he could never reach it alive.

Once again, as they had so many times in the recent past, the closing lines of the ancient poem by Robert Frost came whispering through his mind:

> *But I have promises to keep,*
> *And miles to go before I sleep . . .*

He'd promised that he would come home, and he would keep that promise. Despite death itself, he would return to Earth.

"*Out of the question!*" the doctors had told him. "*You'll never reach Earth. You'll die out there. You'll die in space.*"

Then they had shown him. They charted his death almost to the final second; they told him when his heart would stop beating, when his breathing would cease. This disease—contracted on an alien world—was incurable. Death, for Robert Murdock, was a certainty.

But he told them he was going home nonetheless, that he was leaving for Earth. And they listened to his plan.

Now, with less than thirty minutes of life remaining, Murdock was walking down one of the ship's long corridors, his boot heels ringing on the metal walkway.

He was ready, at last, to keep his promise.

Pausing before a wall storage-locker, he twisted a small dial. The door slid back. Murdock looked up at the tall man standing motionless in the interior darkness. He reached forward, made a quick adjustment. The tall man spoke.

"Is it time?"

"Yes," replied Robert Murdock, "it is time."

The tall man stepped smoothly down into the corridor; the light flashed in the deep-set eyes, almost hidden under thrusting ledges of bone. The man's face was hard and square-featured. "You see," he smiled, "I *am* perfect."

"And so you are," said Murdock. But then, he reflected, everything *depends* on perfection. There must be no flaw, however small. None.

"My name is Robert Murdock," said the tall figure in the neat spaceman's uniform. "I am forty-one years of age, sound of mind and body. I have been in space for two Earth decades—and now I am going home."

Murdock smiled, a tight smile of triumph which flickered briefly across his tired face.

"How much longer?" the tall figure asked.

"Ten minutes. Perhaps a few seconds beyond that," said Murdock slowly. "They told me it would be painless."

"Then . . ." The tall man paused, drew in a long breath. "I'm sorry."

Murdock smiled again. He knew that a machine, however perfect, could not experience the emotion of sorrow—but it eased him to hear the words.

He'll be fine, thought Murdock. He'll serve in my place and my parents will never suspect that I have not come home to them. A month, as arranged, and the machine would turn itself in to company officials on Earth. Yes, Murdock thought, he will be fine.

"Remember," said Murdock, "when you leave them, they *must* believe you are going back into space."

"Naturally," said the machine. And Murdock listened to his own voice explain: "When the month I am to stay with them has passed, they'll see me board a rocket. They'll see it fire away from Earth, outbound, and they'll know that I cannot return for two more decades. They will accept the fact that their son must return to space—that a healthy spaceman cannot leave the Service until he has reached sixty. Let me assure you, all will go exactly as you have planned."

It *will* work, Murdock told himself; every detail has been taken into consideration. The android possesses every memory that I possess; his voice is my voice, his small habits my own. And when he leaves them, when it appears that he has gone back to the stars, the pre-recorded tapes of mine will continue to reach them from space, exactly as they have in the past. Until their deaths. They will never know I'm gone, thought Robert Murdock.

"Are you ready now?" the tall figure asked softly.

"Yes," said Murdock, nodding. "I'm ready."

And they began to walk slowly down the long corridor.

Murdock remembered how proud his parents had been when he was accepted for Special Service. He had been the only boy in the entire town of Thayerville to be chosen. It had been a great day! The local band playing, the mayor—old Mr. Harkness with those little glasses tilted across his nose—making a speech, telling everyone how proud Thayerville was of its chosen son and his mother crying because she was so happy.

But then, it was only right that he should have gone into space. The other boys, the ones who failed to make the grade, had not *lived* the dream as he had lived it. From the moment he had watched the first moon rocket land, he had known, beyond any possible doubt, that he would become a spaceman. He had stood there, in that cold December, a boy of twelve, watching the rocket fire down from space, watching it thaw and blacken the frozen earth. And he had known, in his heart, that he would one day follow it back to the stars. From that moment on, he had dreamed only of moving up and away from Earth, away to vast and alien horizons, to wondrous worlds beyond imagining.

And many of the others had been unwilling to give up *everything* for space. Even now, after two decades, he could still hear Julie's words: "*Oh, I'm sure you love me, Bob, but not enough. Not nearly enough to give up your dream.*" And she had left him, gone out of his life because she knew there was no room in it for her. There was only space—deep space and the rockets and the burning stars. Nothing else.

He remembered his last night on Earth, twenty years ago, when he had felt the pressing immensity of the vast universe surrounding him as he lay in his bed. He remembered the sleepless hours before dawn—when he could feel the tension building within the small white house, within himself lying there in the heated stillness of the room. He remembered the rain, near morning, drumming the roof and the thunder roaring across the Kansas sky. And then, somehow, the thunder's roar blended into the atomic roar of a rocket, carrying him away from Earth, away to the far stars . . . away . . .

Away.

The tall figure in the neat spaceman's uniform closed the outer airlock and watched the body drift into blackness. The ship and the android were one; a pair of complex and perfect machines doing their job.

For Robert Murdock, the journey was over, the long miles had come to an end.

Now he would steep forever in space.

*   *   *

When the rocket landed, on a bright morning in July, in Thayerville, Kansas, the crowds were there, waving and shouting out Robert Murdock's name. The city officials were all present to the last man, each with a carefully rehearsed speech in his mind; the town band sent brassy music into the blue sky and children waved flags. Then a hush fell over the assembled throng. The atomic engines had stilled and the airlock was sliding back.

Robert Murdock appeared, tall and heroic in a splendid dress uniform which threw back the light of the sun in a thousand glittering patterns. He smiled and waved as the crowd burst into fresh shouting and applause.

And, at the far end of the ramp, two figures waited: an old man, bowed and trembling over a cane, and a seamed and wrinkled woman, her hair blowing white, her eyes shining.

When the tall man finally reached them, pushing his way through pressing lines of well-wishers, they embraced him feverishly. They clung tight to his arms as he walked between them; they looked up at him with tears in their eyes.

Robert Murdock, their beloved son, had come home to them at last.

"Well," said a man at the fringe of the crowd, "there they go."

His companion sighed and shook his head. "I *still* don't think it's right, somehow. It just doesn't seem right to me."

"It's what they wanted, isn't it?" asked the other. "It's what they put in their wills. They vowed their son would never come home to death. In another month he'll be gone anyway. Back for twenty more years. Why spoil what little time he has, why ruin it all for him?" The man paused, indicating the two figures in the near distance. "They're *perfect*, aren't they? He'll never know."

"I guess you're right," agreed the second man. "He'll never know."

And he watched the old man and the old woman and the tall son until they were out of sight.

—*Infinity SF* (August 1958)

To Serve the Ship

[This story ties into Ray's moody, deep-space tales, with no single model. One thing for sure: if I had never read Bradbury I would never have written this story.—WFN.]

He entered the dim chamber, pausing just inside, his back pressed against the door. In the soft semi-darkness the room smelled of iron and aluminum and brass. Ahead of him, dials glowed faintly. Lord, but this is fine, he thought, breathing deeply, hands clenched. He closed his eyes in the warm, familiar dark, thinking, this is where I belong; here I am complete:

Norman Jerome Hollander, Servant of the Ship.

He opened his eyes, pupils adjusting to the dimness. Across the length of the chamber, a rising wall of tiny, multicolored lights winked and gleamed. Needles steadied at correct pressure levels; round dial faces hummed softly, regulating the vast power of the Ship, guiding it through space toward—

Norman Hollander swore, knuckling his forehead with a clenched fist. He didn't want to think about the Ship's destination. It seemed so grossly unfair. But that was how it must seem to all the Servants at such a time. Each thinking the same sad thoughts, each cursing the impersonal machine which had passed its irrevocable judgment.

He moved slowly toward the glowing panel and lowered himself into the cushioning depth of the control chair. Around him he savored the immense breathing presence of the Ship, its muted atomics, deep-buried in their ribbed and layered metal tons, sending out an almost imperceptible vibration which trembled along each nerve and muscle of Norman Hollander's body. In front of him, dials whirred, wheels spun, clicked; wires sang. The Ship was alive, but he was no longer a part of her life. He was now simply a passenger on the way to a destination he hated to reach.

Hollander sighed, removing the slotted metal card from his uniform pocket. He didn't need any light to read the words; they were graven on his brain. He would always remember them:

OUTCOME OF TEST L176X: June 29, 2163
OPERATIONAL STATUS: NEGATIVE

The silver needles had entered his veins. Electronic devices had measured his heartbeat, his hearing, his blood pressure. His reaction time was checked, his entire body combed for the slightest imperfection. And, finally, that imperfection had been found, the verdict rendered. Negative. The one word he'd been dreading, the one word which meant that his job was over, that he was no longer a part of the Ship, could no longer serve her. For eighty-five years, while she hovered in space, suspended above alien planets, mining the rich ores from a thousand strange worlds, Norman Hollander had lovingly guided her efforts. His human hand had moved her delicate metal spider-hands that probed the surfaces of those far-flung worlds for storable riches. She was a Hundred Year Ship, designed and built to remain in space for ten full decades while her great storage compartments were gradually filled. Then, and only then, would she come home. Unless . . .

Unless her Servant fails a test, thought Norman Hollander. Unless she finds her Servant wanting, imperfect. Then she rejects him, takes him back to Earth.

Hollander was 105, barely middle-aged by current Earth standards, but old for space. Ideally, though, he should have been able to remain with the Ship for those last fifteen precious years. But human weakness had cheated him of this. Hollander leaned forward, peering at his own reflection in the circular dial to his right. Not an old face. A strong face, marked with duty, but not old. Science had kept him young, but even the wonders of science could not make him perfect, as the Ship was perfect. And so she was taking him home.

No, not home, he thought bitterly. My home is here, with the Ship; I was born and bred for this and nothing else. Earth is simply a place, faintly remembered, which I'll reach in forty-eight hours—after all these years as strange as any world I've ever visited. No, not home.

"When is he due?" asked Dr. Burack.

His assistant, David Miller, placed the schedule on Burack's desk. "Tomorrow morning," Miller said.

Burack looked at the schedule. Then he met Miller's cool gaze. "I hope we have some luck with this one," he said. "Are your men posted?"

Miller nodded. "He'll be observed from the moment the Ship touches down. Personally, I'm not optimistic. The pattern seems fixed."

Dr. Burack tapped one finger gently against the schedule. "Patterns can be broken. That's the biggest part of our job. I want the usual hourly report on Hollander. We've got a lot to learn yet, but we may be getting closer to a solution. This time, David, we may win."

"I wouldn't count on it sir," said David Miller.

Lying on his side in the bed, Hollander stared out at the stars pricking the dark night sky beyond his window. The stars were telling him that he should be up there with them, that he had no business on this world called Earth. The stars understood him. No one here, on this stifling planet, understood him. No one.

Oh, they'd tried to make him feel at home. He was given this modern house, equipped with every electronic comfort; the latest

Jetcar waited in the garage; a full wardrobe of clothes had been provided—all gifts for his service from a grateful government. They gave him everything except the chance to go back.

His family also tried. They had done all they possibly could to assure him that he was wanted, welcome, that he was now a part of their society once again, that he *belonged*. Yet his parents were strangers to him. He'd been a boy of seventeen when he'd seen them last; now they were smiling, friendly strangers, and he found nothing of himself in them.

From the moment his feet touched Earth he had begun to hate.

He hated the crowds shouting at him; he hated this house, the car, the clothes . . . He even found himself hating his mother and father. They were part of the society that had taken him from space. He felt trapped and betrayed by all these smiling people, the men and women who shook his hand, who told him how heroic he was, how noble he had been, serving alone "out there" for all those years. They gave him medals; they made speeches about him and, through it all, he wanted to damn them, to loose his hatred for what they had done to him.

Hollander often wondered about the Servants who had landed before him. Dozens of them, at the very least. Yet no one seemed to know anything about them; no records existed to prove that any of them had ever come back. Was he, in fact, the only man to have survived the Ships? When he asked questions about other Servants his inquiries were shrugged aside. No, they told him, there were no others. He had questioned his parents, but they said they knew nothing about the Servants. In their denials, however, Hollander had detected a guilt, an uneasiness.

The first month had been hell.

Five days after his homecoming he'd knocked down a man in the street. The man had made an insulting remark about the Ships and those who served them. He could still hear the fellow's mocking voice: *"You have to be insane to stay out there all that time on those damned tubs. You have to be crazy to do a thing like that!"* And Norman Hollander had knocked him to the street. If he hadn't been pulled away he might have throttled the man.

The fool! Hollander could feel the angry heat rising in his body.

During the second week he'd gone to the Psyc Center and allowed the machines to put him through analysis. Adjust, they advised him. Learn to adjust to your society. But Norman Hollander had rejected them, as their Ship had rejected him.

In the third week he had attacked a Lawman. Only his status as a retired Servant had kept him from severe punishment.

I had my reasons, Hollander recalled. When I asked him why there were no other Servants he had smiled like some kind of sly cat—and I wanted to smash that smile, destroy it.

And last week; that had been the worst. He drank for an entire morning, then took out the car. The afternoon ended in near-disaster when a schoolgirl had crossed the traffic strip ahead of him and he hadn't seen her. In avoiding her, he crashed. They took the car away from him. From him, the man whose hands had guided the great Ship!

What next? Hollander asked himself, what will I do next? I can never accept this exile, this living death. If they keep me here I'll end up killing somebody. Anybody. They're all to blame.

Sighing wearily, he closed his eyes, shutting out the bright, beckoning stars. . . .

"He isn't responding," said David Miller. "He's like the others. And we've done everything."

Dr. Burack put aside the folder marked HOLLANDER and stood up. He walked past his assistant to the window. Ninety stories below traffic moved swiftly along the jet strips.

"I've called him in," Burack said, the tone of defeat evident in his voice. "He knows that he can't go back into space. But he also knows that he's a freak here in our world. That's the price a Servant pays. Abnormality is a virtue with the Ships; a normal man would be useless to us. Perhaps, some day, we can reverse the pattern. But not yet. Not now."

"Then you're going to commit him?" asked Miller.

"What else can I do at this point? If I don't commit him he'll break, turn violent. Hollander's a potential killer."

"He's also a public hero."

Burack smiled without warmth. "So were all the others. At least the public is well aware of our problem. That's why they built the Servants' Institution. Here the Hollanders can find peace. They won't find it anywhere else on Earth."

Miller nodded. "Maybe we can save the next one," he said. "We're advancing with each case. Maybe, next time, the Ships won't win."

Dr. Burack said nothing. He continued to stare at the distant ribbons of traffic.

Hollander walked down the long, brilliantly illumined corridor, arms swinging loosely at his sides, his fingertips brushing the regulation stripe on his trousers. It was wonderful to be wearing his uniform again, and the close-fitting jacket gave him a sense of security he hadn't felt since the landing. He enjoyed the echoing slap of his boots against the smooth marble floor. Yes, it was good of them to give him back his uniform.

"Here we are, Norman," said Dr. Burack, indicating a heavy door. "This is where you'll stay from now on. I think you'll find we've thought of everything."

"Thank you," said Hollander. "I'm sure you have."

The two men shook hands.

"Goodbye, Doctor."

"Goodbye, Norman."

Dr. Burack watched Hollander go into the special room. He drew a long breath, then turned away.

He entered the dim chamber, pausing just inside, his back pressed against the door. In the soft, semi-darkness the room smelled of iron and aluminum and brass. Ahead of him, dials glowed faintly. Lord, but this is fine, he thought, breathing deeply, hands clenched. He closed his eyes in the warm, familiar dark, thinking, this is where I belong; here I am complete:

Norman Jerome Hollander, Servant of the Ship.

−*Gamma* (May 1963)

Dead Call

[This one relates to Ray's Martian tale, "Night Call Collect," dealing with a dead man's voice over the phone. I took off in a whole new direction, but the model belongs to Bradbury.—WFN.]

Len had been dead for a month when the phone rang.

Midnight. Cold in the house and me dragged up from sleep to answer the call. Helen gone for the weekend. Me, alone in the house. And the phone ringing.

"Hello."

"Hello, Frank."

"Who is this?"

"You know me. It's Len . . . ole Len Stiles."

Cold. Deep and intense. The receiver dead-cold matter in my hand.

"Len Stiles died four weeks ago."

"Four weeks, three days, two hours and twenty-seven minutes ago—to be exact."

"I want to know who you are?"

A chuckle. The same dry chuckle I'd heard so many times.

"C'mon, ole buddy—after twenty years. Hell, you *know* me."

"This is a damned poor joke!"

"No joke, Frank. You're there, alive. And I'm here, dead. And you know something, ole buddy . . . I'm really glad I did it."

"Did . . . what?"

"Killed myself. Because . . . death is just what I hoped it would be. Beautiful . . . gray . . . quiet . . . no pressures."

"Len Stiles' death was an accident . . . a concrete freeway barrier . . . His car—"

"I *aimed* my car for that barrier," the phone-voice told me. "Pedal to the floor. Doing over ninety when I hit . . . No accident, Frank." The voice cold . . . cold. "I *wanted* to be dead. And no regrets."

I tried to laugh, make light of this—matching his chuckle with my own. "Dead men don't use telephones."

"I'm not really using the phone, not in a physical sense. It's just that I chose to contact you this way. You might say it's a matter of 'psychic electricity.' As a detached spirit I'm able to align my cosmic vibrations to match the vibrations of this power line. Simple, really."

"Sure. A snap. Nothing to it."

"Naturally, you're skeptical. I expected you to be. But . . . listen carefully to me, Frank."

And I listened—with the phone gripped in my hand in that cold night house—as the voice told me things that *only* Len could know . . . intimate details of shared experiences extending back through two decades. And when he'd finished I was certain of one thing:

He *was* Len Stiles.

"But, how . . . I still don't . . ."

"Think of this phone as a 'medium'—a line of force through which I can bridge the gap between us." The dry chuckle again. "Hell, you gotta admit it beats holding hands around a table in the dark—yet the principle is the same."

I'd been standing by my desk, transfixed by the voice. Now I moved behind the desk, sat down, trying to absorb this dark miracle. My muscles were wire-taut, my fingers cramped about the black receiver. I dragged in a slow breath, the night dampness of the room pressing at me.

"All right . . . I don't . . . believe in ghosts, don't . . . pretend to understand any of this, but . . . I'll accept it. I *must* accept it."

"I'm glad, Frank—because it's important that we talk." A long moment of hesitation. Then the voice, lower now, softer. "I know how lousy things have been, ole buddy."

"What do you mean?"

"I just know how things are going for you. And . . . I want to help. As your friend, I want you to know that I understand."

"Well . . . I'm really not . . ."

"You've been feeling bad, haven't you? Kind of 'down,' right?"

"Yeah . . . a little, I guess."

"And I don't blame you. You've got reasons. Lots of reasons. For one . . . there's your money problem."

"I'm expecting a raise. Shendorf promised me one—within the next few weeks."

"You won't get it, Frank. I *know*. He's lying to you. Right now, at this moment, he's looking for a man to replace you at the company. Shendorf's planning to fire you."

"He never liked me . . . We never got along from the day I walked into that office."

"And your wife . . . all the arguments you've been having with her lately . . . It's a pattern, Frank. Your marriage is all over. Helen's going to ask you for a divorce. She's in love with another man."

"*Who*, dammit? What's his name?"

"You don't know him. Wouldn't change things if you did. There's nothing you can do about it now. Helen just . . . doesn't love you any more. These things happen to people."

"We've been . . . drifting apart for the last year—but I didn't know why. I had no idea that she . . ."

"And then there's Janice. She's back on it, Frank. Only it's worse now. A lot worse."

I knew what he meant—and the coldness raked along my body. Jan was nineteen, my oldest daughter—and she'd been into drugs for the past three years. But she'd promised to quit.

"What do you know about Janice? Tell me!"

"She's into the heavy stuff, Frank. She's hooked bad. It's too late for her."

"What the hell are you saying?"

"I'm saying she's lost to you . . . She's rejected you, and there's no reaching her. She *hates* you . . . blames you for everything."

"I won't *accept* that kind of blame! I did my best for her."

"It wasn't enough, Frank. We both know that. You'll never see her again."

The blackness was welling within me, a choking wave through my body.

"Listen to me, old buddy. Things are going to get worse, not better. I know. I went through my own kind of hell when I was alive."

"I'll . . . start over . . . leave the city—go East, work with my brother in New York."

"Your brother doesn't *want* you in his life. You'd be an intruder . . . an alien. He never writes you, does he?"

"No, but that doesn't mean—"

"Not even a card last Christmas. No letters or calls. He doesn't want you with him, Frank, believe me."

And then he began to tell me other things . . . He began to talk about middle age and how it was too late now to make any kind of new beginning . . . He spoke of disease . . . loneliness . . . of rejection and despair. And the blackness was complete.

"There's only one real solution to things, Frank—just *one*. That gun you keep in your desk upstairs. Use it, Frank. Use the gun."

"I couldn't do that."

"But why not? What other choice have you got? The solution is there. Go upstairs and use the gun. I'll be waiting for you afterwards. You won't be alone. It'll be like the old days . . . we'll be together . . . Death is beautiful, Frank. I *know*. Life is ugly, but death is beautiful . . . Use the gun, Frank . . . the gun . . . use the gun . . . the gun . . . the gun . . ."

I've been dead for a month now, and Len was right. It's fine here. No pressures. No worries. Gray and quiet and beautiful.

I know how lousy things have been for you. And they're *not* going to improve.

Isn't that your phone ringing?

Better answer it.

It's important that we talk.

–*Frights,* ed. Kirby McCauley (1976)

Fair Trade

[The "dialect" stories in *Dark Carnival* (in particular "The Dead Man"), plus Ray's horror work in EC Comics, inspired this dark tale.—WFN.]

He tole me to speak all this down into the machine, the Sheriff did, what all I know an' seen about Lon Pritchard an' his brother Lafe an' what they done, one to the other. I already tole it all to the Sheriff but he says for sure that none'a what I tole him happened the way I said it did but to talk it all into the machine anyhow. He figgers to have it all done up on paper from this talkin' machine so's folks kin read it an' laugh at me I reckon. If you don't believe it why should I talk it all down I wanted to know but he says it's for legal when they stan' me afore Judge Henry for Lon Pritchard's killin' which I sure never done. I witnessed it done, with the blood an' all, but I never done it personal.

Well, anyways, here goes . . .

First, my name is Jace Ridling. I guess that's Jason but none as ever called me the name formal. I was born right here in this part'a Virginia where I been all my life but I'm not rightly sure about my years due to my bein' alone an' all with no kinfolk alive to testify my age. I don't recall I ever had no blood kinfolk—'cept my Ma and my Pappy an' I never knew 'em proper. Not enough to hang a recollection on 'em. They both took off when I was a tad an' left me at the county home an' I run away an' jus growed as best I could, livin' off the woods an' what you find there. Guess I've et everthin' that grows there in my time—grub worms an' wiggly bugs under dead logs an' squinch owls an' frogs an' crickets an' skittery squirrils an' what all else I can't rightly recall. Don't matter none to this story, 'cept that's why I saw what I did. Livin' out in deep woods like I do I see what goes on when town folk are abed of a night. Lotsa funny things go on in deep woods if yer a mind to look for 'em.

Like I tole Sheriff Meade this here story begun a week back, at the tail end'a that real mean rain spell we had. Hard black rain, the worst anybody kin recollect, worst ever in this county, slicin' inta that yella clay out there on Cemetery Ridge, makin' the ground all soft an' slidey. It was the rain, jes comin' down an' comin' down what done it—what caused the box they had Lafe Pritchard nailed inside to bust open at the bottom'a Calder's Hill. Rain loosed it—an' that wet clay run like yella blood down the hill, carryin' the box hard onto the rocks. Knocked the top clean off, lettin' the rain in onto Lafe an soakin' his nice black fifty-dollar store-bought suit, the one they buried him in.

Now comes the part Sheriff Meade says is looney talk—but as the Lord A'mighty is my witness it happened jes like I tole him it did. 'Bout Lafe Pritchard I mean, 'bout how the rain—God's Tears some call it—come peltin' down into that cold split-open wood box an' woke ole Lafe till he rose up to sit straight as a soldier there in his fine black suit . . .

I was no more'n ten feet away—huggin' the side'a the hill the way I was to shelter me some agin' the storm—with my shiny rain slicker curled 'round me like a tent there in the blowin' dark—watchin' that dead man blinker his dead eye an' move his dead mouth like he was testin' 'em to see if they still worked proper.

I was down wind'a him—an' even past the smell'a the rain I caught his scent, strong as sin on Sunday. I could nose him plain, all sour an' gone to rot, the kinda smell a crushed rat gives off inside a barn after the wagon wheel has run him over an' him bein' there on the barn floor a while.

For sure, I was scart. Never seen me no livin' dead men afore, but I'd heard tell of 'em a'plenty an' knew it could happen, that the dead could raise up if they had a mind to do so. An' a *reason*. They's a reason behind everythin' men do, livin' an' dead. An' Lafe, he sure *had* hisself a reason. The rain was the thing that woke him from his uneasy rest, gave him the chance to do what he had to do. It jes happened I was there to see it.

I tole myself Jace, you calm on down now, boy, 'cuz Lafe was yer friend an' it don't figger he means to harm ya none. Jes speak up to him kindly.

Lafe, I say . . . standin' close to him an' lookin' down at him sittin' there in that cold wet box with his rain-slicked hair all plastered along the dead white of his face. His one eye rolls up to look me over. There's jes a hole where the other was. Worms got it likely. His face is half gone. Parts of him have fell off, parts'a his nose is missin' an' his upper lip is been most et away till the teeth shine out at me like he's smilin' even when he's not.

He's a plain fright, Lafe Pritchard is—but I say to him, Lafe, oh sweet Jesus, Lafe, you're the first livin' dead I ever come across. What brung ya back?

He don't answer right off. First, he stands up slow, looks around with that one eye at the dark on Calder's Hill an' up at the other graves on Cemetery Ridge an' at the wind-shook trees an' he stretches like a long-asleep cat, his arms up above his head, stretchin' those dead muscles an' I stand there a'side him wonderin' if there's still any blood in him. For sure not. But *somethin'* keeps him there, tall in the dark. Somethin' fires his dead flesh an' moves those long arms a'his.

Lon. He says that name to me, soft an' raspy, deep as a well. It's Lon I want to see. Where's Lon?

To home, most likely, on a night like this I say back to him.

Lon. I must see my brother Lon, he says. Can't sleep proper till I do. That voice a'his was somethin' to remember. Like no voice I ever heard afore or since or ever will agin' I'd guarantee.

Can the dead walk? Can they move through hollers an' gullies an' through deep woods? Oh yes they can!

Lafe did, that night, walkin' his dead legs along steady as you please past drippin' oak and evergreen, through tangle-weeds an' waist-high grass, his shoes suckin' at yella clay or lost in leaf loam an' me with him an' the black rain peltin' down like buckshot on us both an' neither of us sayin' nary a word as it final gave way to a smoky-burnt sun which come up slow over the trees.

Sure enough, the storm was over. Over an' spent. Jes like it had stayed long enough to wake ole Lafe an' havin' done that job took off for other woods. A bird, kingfisher most likely, sang high an' sweet for us, an' frogs moved morning-soft in the marsh.

We're almost into town I say to Lafe.

He nods an' I step back a mite from the scent of him. The sun makes him smell worse as it heats him up. Already our wet clothes is steamin' like smoke.

I ask him do you aim to walk right down the main street? Somehow it don't seem proper to me.

I aim to, he tells me in that raspy voice that sounds like it comes from inside a holla log.

What'll folks say, seein' as how you look an' all? Seein' as how they know you belong dead an' buried on Cemetery Ridge?

They'll be none up to say, he tells me. They'll most be abed.

You intendin' to go straight through town to Lon's?

Straight through. That's my proper intent.

Now he stops at the edge of the wood, lookin' toward the town with that one spit-shiny eye, with his teeth gapin' an' his dead white skin all flaked half away to raw bone.

I coulda cut an' run, right then. I didn't hafta go in an' see what I saw, witness what I witnessed, an' sure as God's grace I'd be safe off this minute in the deep woods if I'd done jes that' 'stead'a bein' here inside this jailhouse talkin' at this machine an' not bein' believed by nobody. But I never run.

I went in with Lafe.

The town was dawn-silent 'cept for a big splotchy dog that came snuffin' an' barkin' outa Red's Cafe toward us, till he got a whiff'a Lafe an' down-tailed it quick back inside. Lafe paid him no mind.

We walked the length'a that street to Lon's house at the far side where the road turns back to deep wood. Lon he's lived there alone since Lafe died. Nice, with climbin' vines along one side an' big sunny windas.

I had no fear in me then, jes a burnin' curiosity to see what Lafe would do when he found Lon, an' what Lon would do when he laid sight'a him seein' his own dead brother standin' there fresh from the grave.

Jace boy, I tole myself, keep yer eyes wide open 'cuz it ain't never 'afore happened that a dead man walks bold as brass beside you toward a brother he hated more than Satan himself 'afore he died.

Because see, it was *hate* that brung Lafe here, hate fer Lon that druv him up from that coffin to walk the woods here to face the brother that deviled his woman an' ruint his life an' drove him to fire that bullet into his own heart.

Hate was the blood that filled Lafe Pritchard's body that mornin'—hate was the coal that fed the furnace of him.

What you gonna do when you find Lon to home I asked?

You'll see, Lafe says to me an' knocks on that door as calm as you please, a dead man knockin' to be let in an' Lon comin' up from sleep in his gray long-johns to open the door an' seein' his horror of a brother standin' there—an' screamin' like a stuck pig as Lafe reaches out to take him by the throat.

It all happened fast.

Lon claws at those bone-white fingers an' staggers back inside, eyes bugged, an Lafe, all swole up an' stinkin' from the sun havin' been at him, drags Lon down the hall by the neck, me follerin' to the kitchen. Not a word betwixt 'em. Just the horror of it, the stench of it, in that dark mornin' room with the shades down an' the light still outside.

Now comes the part that got me sick, so I don't rightly want to dwell on it.

Sheriff Meade says he's certain convinced that what I'm really doin' here is confessin' up to killin' Lon Pritchard an' that this is my way'a tryin' to slip past the law's penalty by blamin' a dead man for what I done.

He's wrong. Lafe done in Lon, right there in front'a me that mornin' in that kitchen an' it was Lafe that cut the hole in him with the carvin' knife. I didn't do it. I jes watched it gettin' done, gaggin' the while, sick with the raw sight of it all, yet with my gaze plain fixed to it.

After it was done Lafe steps back an' says to me, we're even now, me an' Lon. I got what I come fer. I can sleep proper now. It's a fair trade. He owed me an' I collected.

So that's all there is to it. If you don't believe me you go out an' see fer yourself. Out to Cemetery Ridge where he's sleepin' now inside that box agin with the lid nailed shut an' a fresh hole dug an' him at the bottom where he asked me to put him.

I done it fer a friend. I buried him proper so's he could finally rest easy.

I don't judge him fer what he done. Lon Pritchard was bad clean through, we all knew that. Stealin' other folks wommin, an' cheatin' at his store business an' getting' sod-drunk on God's Sunday. Deserved what he got, if truth be tole. It's the Lord's own justice what Lafe done to him.

An' the trade's been made. You'll find it in there, in the box with him. He's a'holdin' it fast in those bony fingers, claspin' it to his bosom like a lost pup. I didn't take it. Not me. Nosir. It's down there with him—the thing that was missin' when Sheriff Meade found the deceased.

Lon Pritchard's heart.

—Whispers (March 1982)

The Dandelion Chronicles

[This is a parody, my attempt to capture the essence of Bradbury's style, dialogue, and characters. All wildly exaggerated, demonstrating (I would hope) a bemused affection for Ray's work. In no way was this parody meant to demean or diminish Bradbury's talent. It was written out of a desire to laugh *with* Bradbury, not *at* him.

Many parodies are cruel.

This is not one of them.—WFN.]

"Look!"

"Hey!"

"Ah!"

The Waukegan crowd sighed, gasped, choked, cried out, the look of the great dream-colored climbing strawberry rocket in their round Illinois eyes, the thunder sound in their ears, mouths, on their pink tongues, all warm-ice and cool-fire and October carnival explosions, fading, fading . . .

Gone.

"Mom!" A bramble-headed boy shouted, yelled, pointed. "Are they going to Mars, eh? Is that where? All the way to Mars, Mom?"

"Yes," said the mother. "That is where they are going, Timmy. To Mars. All the way to Mars."

"Ah!" breathed the vast crowd, softly, watching and watching the calliope rocket fire away and away into the immense black velocities and depthless depths of Space.

Their ship was named *The Golden Dandelion*, and it was a good ship with a good crew, and it flew straight and true and did not slow down, ever. On board were Irish priests and simple Mexican peons and robust lightning-rod salesmen and rag-tag Dublin beggars and robots who cunningly resembled Irish priests and simple Mexican peons and robust lightning-rod salesmen and rag-tag Dublin beggars. And, of course, there was the crew: men named Littel and Bigg and Small and Able and Fine and Wright.

"Well . . ." said Captain Icarus Montgolfier Good. "So." He smiled. "Do you know what the old sun looks like from up here?" he asked, gazing and gazing through the strawberry porthole into Space, gentle hands folded behind his back. "It is like an immense dip of soft good lime sherbet, an immense dip of soft good lime sherbet indeed," said Captain Good, smiling and smiling through the strawberry port.

"Oh, you're *right*, sir!" agreed anthropologist Small. "It is like the kind of sherbet Mom and Uncle Ned used to have heaped and waiting on our plates when we'd come home for lunch, all hot and tired and full of school, smelling of fresh-cut summer grass and cool vanilla."

"And yet, sir—" marveled Bigg, "—it is *hot!* It is as hot as ten thousand furnaces going all at once and never stopping. It is as hot as ten thousand wiener-fires on ten thousand picnic beaches."

"It is indeed," said the captain. He checked the gauge: Fahrenheit 451. "Ah," he said.

And they all stood silently, looking at the hot, hot sun.

"Jeepers, you know, Captain . . ." sighed crewman Littel. "I've been thinking a lot about deep space lately, of how you have to be crazy to voyage out here ten zillion light-years from Earth—"

"Good grief!" exclaimed Captain Good, an exasperated tone in his voice. "We aren't *nearly* that far out! I suggest you consult your star charts before you indulge in wild metaphor."

"Anyway," stubbornly continued crewman Littel, "a person still has to be nuts to fly out here, facing all the terrors and dangers of space. Believe me, Captain, it's a graveyard for lunatics."

"You're a big man, Littel," said the captain. "You can stand up to it. We all must. We're a *team* out here in the void."

"Yet we die alone," said Littel.

"Yes, and it doesn't matter *where* we die," shrewdly observed the captain, staring down at his tennis shoes. "On Mars, or on some remote God-forsaken asteroid, or on good old Mother Earth . . . death is always a lonely business."

The Golden Dandelion feather-drifted toward Mars, blown by frosty polar winds and immense tidal moon winds and winds the color of old wine, which smelled of Time and Eternity, winds which blew and blew and never stopped blowing.

"Sound the solar foghorn," commanded Captain Good. "We are rapidly approaching the Red Planet. Prepare—" said the captain, nervously cracking his knuckles, "—for dis-embarkation."

"May the saints preserve us every one!" sighed Father O'Faith, the rusty old Irish robot priest.

The Golden Dandelion descended, feathered, dove-drifted, hawk-settled, eased down from Space, balancing on a pillar of fire, baking the red dust of Mars with its angry furnace mouth.

The airlock hissed like a carnival snake, and they stepped out onto the waiting desert.

"Got a dime on ya, pal?" asked a greasy little rat-like man. He wore only a loincloth and his body was covered with illustrations that shimmered and writhed with a life of their own. Otherwise, he looked just like anyone else.

"Gollywhillerkers!" exclaimed crewman Bigg. "A humanoid!"

"Look," said the greasy desert rat, "you got no dime, you get no mirage. But—put a dime in my grubby palm, jump, hop, skip, run to the top of that rise, gaze out to your heart's content and sure as my name's Will Strange—you'll see Kubla Khan or New York or Port O'Spain. For a dime!"

"I'm all out of change," confessed Captain Good. "But I have a solar credit card. Or do you accept personal checks?"

But before Strange could reply, crewman Wright quickly fired seven deadly pellets from a bee-shaped hand weapon. Will Strange dropped to the red sand, twitched, gasped, choked, sighed, and said "Damn."

"There'll be *no* swearin'!" said Father O'Faith.

Then Will Strange died; all his illustrations went dark.

"Sorry I had to waste him, Captain," said crewman Wright sheepishly. "But that was probably no humanoid at all. That was, in my opinion, probably a hideous, ugly, revolting, spider-like, slithery, green, unnatural-looking, disgusting alien who hypnotized us all, clouded our minds, warped and distorted our thinking—all in an effort to entrap us, throw us off our guard, and destroy us to a man."

"Well, you're wrong, Mr. Wright," snapped Captain Good. "And frankly, I'm annoyed at you. Killing these aliens is *not* the answer. There *must* be another way to deal with them—and I intend to find it!"

Wright scuffed his toe in the sand. "Fooey!" he said.

"We don't have room for hotheads on board this ship," mused Good. "Remember, men, *we're* the aliens now!"

The captain looked down at his feet and smiled. "It is good that I have on tennis shoes," he said. "Because they make my feet feel fine and good and there is a smell about them like going home after baseball."

All the men looked at the captain's fine black tennis shoes.

"Well, glory be!" breathed crewman Littel. "You know where I'd like to be right now, sir? I'd like to be out on the tippy-top of a tall, windy hill flying that old paper kite Dad made for me when I was ten and needed my backside switched."

"Me, I'd like to be running and running," cried Fine, "under the summer vanilla-night trees with the Illinois moon like a teardrop crystal in the sky."

The others joined in now, their voices blending, rising, surging, falling. And fire balloons were spoken of, and ripe lemon-yellow bananas, and Baby Ruth nut bars, and tall frosted cones fresh and dripping from the Ding-a-Ling wagon that came belling by each evening when it was warm-cool and the stars were winking on like so many yellow porch lights all up and down the long summer street. Like so many yellow porch lights, indeed.

And through it all Captain Good stood smiling down at his soft black tennis shoes, remembering and remembering.

Juan La Noche stepped like a dark shadow from the clockwork interior of the ship to stand beside the captain. He removed his broad, sweat-stained straw sombrero. "Maria, my common-law wife, is big with child," he said. "She will soon honor me with a fine son or a miserable daughter, as the case may be."

"It is good to be a father," said the captain. "Each tiny tot forms yet another link in the universal cosmic chain. We must all grasp the rope of life and not allow it to slip through our fingers. Yet we dare not hold too tightly, lest it burn our hands. The way to do it is to kind of hold it loosely, and then you won't—"

La Noche slunk away, confused and bored, his eyes like dead coins in his penny-brown skull.

"A city! A city!" cried Billy Able, pointing to the horizon. "Hurrah! Hurrah!"

The captain put a long spy-glass to his eyes and peered at the distant strawberry hills rising like the back of a great white whale.

"It *could* be that greasy alien desert rat's mirage," he said.

"No! No! A city! A city!" cried Able. "Oh, hell, sir, we've *done* it!"

"Faith, an' willya stop the damn swearin'!" shouted the Irish robot-priest.

"Look alive, men," snapped the captain. "We'll soon see what's to be seen. Double-time! Hip-hup! Hop! Skip! Jump!"

The crew hop-skip-jumped into the city.

"Lordy!" breathed Fine. "It's—it's—"

"Greenboil, Illinois, on a Sunday afternoon in 1928," said Captain Icarus Good. "But it *can't* be!"

It was.

There, before them, was a maple-and-oak-shaded street, urine-colored dogs, legs defiantly raised near sun-red fire hydrants. Here, bellowing Stutz Bearcats full of dish-faced, flask-swigging college youths in long, foul-smelling raccoon coats. There, giant billboards advertising Carter's Little Liver Pills, and old, rotting rococo houses with senile grandmothers dozing on porch swings, spittle a-looping from their half-opened mouths—filthy kids in filthy knickers playing Mibs and emptying rancid garbage cans onto spotless front lawns.

"I don't like the look of this," mused Captain Good. He frowned darkly.

"Maybe," suggested crewman Small, "we've gone through some kind of time warp, ending up back in 1928 when things were clean and fine except for racial prejudice, and the stock market was booming."

Three odorous Irish beggars shuffled forward, all rags and open sores. "Let *us* go out an' make the test," they begged. "If nothin' terrible happens to O'Donnovan and Mike Fogarty and meself, Jamie O'Hennessey, poor blind dirty ignorant hoop-and-holler Dublin beggars that we are, then it'll be safe enough fer the rest a ya!"

"What these dirty ignorant Irish beggars are mewling makes good sense to me," said Fine. "Let's send them into the city."

"Fair enough, Fine," nodded Good. "Out they go!"

Yet, before they could slink an inch, crewman Wright rushed forward and began spraying the filthy kids and the urinating dogs and the drooling grandmothers and the flask-swigging college

youths with deadly pellets from his bee-shaped hand weapon.
Moaning, groaning, sighing, choking, clutching at their chests,
they fell dead every one.

Silence.

"I was *afraid* of something like this," mused Captain Good.
"Wright is, it seems, trigger happy. This sort of thing certainly
won't win us many friends here on Mars."

Wright swung around, his bee-shaped hand weapon still smok-
ing. "Don't you *see*, Captain? It was a trick. All a cunning, evil, not-
so-good trick. They ran away with our minds. This street wasn't
here, isn't here, not really, not truly really. It was all—"

"Mr. Wright, you may consider yourself under ship's arrest,"
snapped Captain Good. "Confine yourself to quarters. Double-
time. Hip-hup! Hop! Jump!"

Wright hop-jumped back to the rocket, muttered "Fudge!" and
slammed shut the airlock.

Good stepped forward, into the church-quiet corpse-littered
blood-spattered maple-and-oak-shaded street. "Gosh!" he said.
"What a mess!"

"Hey!" shouted Billy Able, waving excitedly from a distant
corner. "Look! Hey! Over here!"

"Hip-hup, men," said Captain Good.

As they rounded the corner they all stopped, awed at what lay
before them. . . .

An Irish cobbled thoroughfare, rattling carts drawn by phlegm-
eyed sway-backed horses, old men in grime-stiffened caps and thick
unwashed mufflers, clay pipes afire between toothless gums,
thatched huts and tall stone churches, and drunken Irish songs
drifting like gentle smoke from the pubs.

"Dublin!" breathed Father O'Faith. "'Tis none other!"

Captain Good frowned darkly. "It doesn't make sense," he said.
"It just doesn't add up."

Crewman Small ran to the swing door of Dooley's Pub. "Ale!" he shouted. "Stout! Black Irish whiskey!" He dipped his head inside the batwing door. "Shall we sample it, Captain? Oh, *shall* we, sir?"

"Poison!" a familiar voice announced behind them. It was crewman Wright again. He rushed past crewman Small and sprayed the pub's interior with a burst of deadly pellets from his bee-shaped hand weapon. "So," he said. "And *so!*"

The Irish songs had ceased. Inside, there was only . . .

Silence. The silence of an oh-so-deep Illinois ravine under a frosted Halloween pumpkin moon the color of orange sherbet when even the crickets have called it quits. *That* kind of silence.

"By golly, Wright," snapped Captain Good. "Didn't I just put you under ship's arrest and confine you to quarters?"

"But, sir, *someone* must protect you. I, therefore, chose to disregard your order."

"Then consider yourself under *double* ship's arrest," said Good. "Now, back to the *Dandelion*. Off you go! Hip-hup! Jump!"

Father O'Faith stepped up to Good. "They's one poor soul left alive in there," he said. "A fine broth of an old lady with a harp all silver like an angel's wing."

"Then drag her out," snapped Good. "We'll question her. Oh, and tell her she has nothing to fear from us. We come in peace."

"Aye!"

Father O'Faith fetched the old woman. She came side-blinking out into the soot-colored day, dragging a tall silver harp behind her.

She belched loudly. Again. And then again. And yet again.

"I am Captain Icarus Montgolfier Good, and this is my loyal crew and we have come all the way from Earth to you in a really neat spaceship—the first of many who will eventually descend upon your planet like so many silver locusts, like so many silver locusts indeed." He hesitated, out of breath. "Just who *are* you?"

"Me name's Molly Malone, yer honor," she said.

"Occupation?"

"Sure an' I play me harp fer a bit of drinkin' likker an' a pinch from a laughin' boy."

She dove-drifted a withered stick hand over the silver harp strings.

"Rain!" sighed crewman Bigg. "Sounds for all the world like a fall of clear and gentle rain."

"It sounds," said Tom Fine, "like ten thousand crystal drops on ten thousand sleeping roofs. It sounds like all the rain that ever was or ever will be!" And he burst into tears.

"Yes," said the captain, eyes closed. "And yes."

The old woman smiled toothlessly and danced her spider fingers through "Limerick Is My Town," "The Lovely Isle of Innisfree," and "Doin' It in Dublin."

"Hey, and do you know 'Laughin' on the Liffey'?" asked crewman Small.

"I do indeed!" The harp notes quivered on the cool air.

"Ah!" said Captain Good. And *he* burst into tears.

"Ah!" said Able and Fine and Wright.

"Ah!" said Littel and Small.

They *all* burst into tears.

Then the cheerful old lady pitched forward flat on her face to the street.

"Dead, an' gone to her sweet reward—mortally wounded by one a' them pellets from that pesky bee-shaped hand weapon," said Father O'Faith. "Sure, an' she was dyin' a little with every harp note, bless her withered old stick body."

"Darn!" said Captain Good. "I really *like* good music."

"Hey!" shouted Billy Able from the end of the murky Dublin street. "Come! Look! See!"

"Hip-hup, lads."

They ran. They stopped. They looked, mouths agape.

"Good God!" said Good.

"Maria!" cried Juan La Noche to his sweating wife. "See! Savor what your eyes tell you! Feast your sight like summer wine. We are Home!"

"Aa-eeee!" cried Maria, wobbling ponderously forward, her shawl close about her. A great quivering black hair grew ferociously from her left nostril. She was large with child and her hair was a color found long after midnight when the streets are black with things darker than old Mr. Death himself, but not as dark as the great pits of Space where there is no up or down or sideways, only the great pits. She burst into tears. "Juan speaks truth," she cried. "This is indeed our home. It is Guadalajara! Ae-eeeeee!"

Before them: sod shacks, crude roads of baked black adobe, a wedding-cake white graveyard, walls of handlaid stones. And—next to the graveyard, the catacombs.

Juan rushed forward, yanking back the great wooden door sunk in rich earth.

He fell back, gasping. "Down there," he said softly, "the dead stand like so many frozen soldiers, wired to the walls, horror-mouthed and stark-socketed. Their screams are silent, but one can *hear* them; their skull sockets are eyeless, yet they see Death. Bone fingers claw fetid air. Bone legs arch and writhe like so many breadsticks in an oven. Ayeeeee! The dead ones—the standing mummies of Guadalajara! It is good to be home!"

"I don't like the smell of things, Captain," said Tom Fine.

"Aye," breathed Maria, holding her nose. "The dead do not smell so sweet. Good grief, Juan, shut the door!"

The big door whammed down like a drum. Bang!

"There's something about all this I don't understand," said the captain. "This isn't . . ." He groped for the word ". . . *normal.*"

At that precise moment, a withered old night watchman approached them.

"I'm a withered old night watchman," he said, "an' you fellas have got to get the hell off the lot and quit killin' the extras."

"Lot . . . extras . . ." breathed Captain Good. "Great Scott! I think I'm *beginning* to understand!"

The men all held their breath, waiting for their captain to figure things out.

Suddenly, the captain's eyes lit up. He hopped. He danced. He shouted. "Oh, men, don't you *see?* Don't you, each and every one, see the plain and simple truth?"

They all shook their heads, still holding their breath, each and every one.

The captain shouted out the words, the important words, the words that made everything plain and simple: "Mars . . . is *Hollywood!*"

"Waal," spat the old night watchman, "not exactly. This here is Television City. Me, I call it the Meadow of the World, but that's because I'm an old poetic night watchman. But Hollywood *proper* is a few miles off. Tell ya what—ya just take Fairfax up to Sunset, then ya turn right and go past La Brea an' then ya—"

"Good grief," exploded the captain. "Our enormously expensive and incredibly complicated space direction finder must have gone on the fritz. Men, in plain and simple words, we've landed back on Earth."

The men all began breathing again, knowing that their captain had finally figured things out.

"There's only one minor item which still continues to puzzle me," said Captain Good.

"Whazat?"

"Who in blazes was that greasy old desert rat we originally killed near the ship—the illustrated fellow with the mirage?"

"That was a plot complication," said the old night watchman, "an' *nobody* can explain plot complications. Ain't no way out of 'em."

The captain nodded, frowning darkly.

"Well, what do we do now, eh, Captain?" asked Billy Able.

Captain Good rocked slowly to and fro in his black tennis shoes, cracking his white, white knuckles.

Silence.

"Gee, I'm not sure what to do next," confessed the captain, biting his lower lip like a sullen child. "Yet . . . I've always wanted to act. To be a great star. To see my name in lights. To wear a gold Elvis coat and have packs of panting, swarming, full-bosomed young teenaged girls clawing at my body . . ."

The captain looked at his crew.

"What say you all—shall we *act?*"

"Aye! Aye!" shouted the crew. "So shall we all!"

The old night watchman yawned. "The casting office is 'bout half a block west of here," he told them. "Just say that Ed Poe sent you over. What with all the extras that crazy fella of yours killed with that bee-shaped hand weapon, they'll be needin' some replacements."

"Hurrah! Hurrah for Mr. Poe!" shouted Father O'Faith.

And Juan La Noche and Maria and the three dirty ignorant Irish beggars and Billy Able and Tom Fine and crewmen Bigg and Littel and Small, all of them shouted, "Hurrah! Hurrah!"

And they turned their backs on the great golden rocket and ran and rushed and arrowed in a tide, a drift, a freshet, a bright-running river—straight for the casting office.

And, watching them go, the withered old night watchman shook his withered old head.

"Damn bunch of fools!" he said, and spat into the silent dust.

—Included in *The Undead* (1984);
rev. ed. in *The Bradbury Chronicles* (1991)

TRIBUTES TO RAY BRADBURY

Goodbye, Old Pal

That's what I always called him—my old pal. I met him in Venice, California, when he was twenty-nine—and now, at 91, he's gone. By his own admission, he lived a great life, did all the things he wanted to do, wrote his wonderful books and stories, was beloved around the world, won a host of awards, traveled through Europe, laughed and loved with his friends and family, and influenced millions of other writers. What more can life provide?

When I last saw him, in late March of this year, half-blind, half-deaf, slow-voiced, unable to leave his bed, he was still grimly fighting death. But he knew the end was near.

Of course, when we're all gone, his legendary works will remain in print. Golden apples and illustrated men and Martian chronicles and dandelion wine: They are part of us now, part of our culture. They will last.

Yes, Ray Douglas Bradbury died this week, but his literary children will never die.

What a man he was!

Goodbye, old pal.

God bless.

—WILLIAM F. NOLAN
June 6, 2012

Kneeling at the Dandelion Shrine

It is hard to appreciate the living.

Not hard in the sense that we don't admire their qualities, or like their company. . . . Hard in the sense of comprehending their true value to us as individuals. We know them, we love them, we enjoy their witty banter, but until they are absent—whether due to illness, or a long excursion, or, finally, death—we cannot realistically measure their impact in and on our lives. We cannot come to terms with their *imagined* absence: Hard as we may try, we cannot fully grasp what it means to hear their voice in our mind, to remember a certain look or a turn of phrase, and realize that it will always be only the echo of an experience . . . a fond, even cherished memory, subject to the constant erosion of daily life, the relentless forward progression of the clock. Then, one day, a year has gone by . . . and another . . . then ten . . . And we realize all the times we have not been able to pick up the telephone and talk with our friend, our lover, our relative. We grieve anew at the letters we never got to write, and the replies that never cluttered the mailbox . . . or the dinners that were not lingered over, the laughter that went unshared—even the tears that were not shed.

Such is the feeling I have about Ray Bradbury: I met him in the course of filming several documentaries (he was also in our anthology, *The Bleeding Edge*); during the nearly ten years that my wife Sunni and I knew Ray, he was always courteous, never less than fascinating. He had a lightning-fast mind and a huge presence. He was more of an experience! He was gracious with his time, his enthusiasm, his friendship. We considered Ray our friend, and he did likewise in return. We were at his fabled residence many times, several times without Bill Nolan, and many times with him (we met Bill as we were making our documentaries, also, and struck up another lifelong friendship, but Ray came first and was, in fact, the first interview I ever conducted). I am pleased to count Ray, Bill, Richard Matheson, Dan & Diane O'Bannon (Dan: talk about someone sorely missed!), George Clayton Johnson, Frank M. Robinson, S. T. Joshi, Rocky Wood, and Marc Scott Zicree as my personal and professional mentors; as people who took a genuine interest in my ideas, my writing, my work. They all shared advice, read my stories, dispensed criticism, and doled out encouragement: they were inspirations, yes, but also tough, fair, and kind. They each became dear friends to us: Sunni and I love them all (and so many others, such as Forrest J Ackerman, Ray Harryhausen, Greg & Astrid Bear, even Harlan Ellison!).

Most people never got to meet Ray, so I will try to encapsulate his essence for the curious: He was an individual *bursting* with love, with life, with passion. He had an *insatiable* appetite for knowledge, and a sometimes bawdy sense of humor; laughter was important to him, as it should be to us all. He was sparking with ideas, with opinions, brimming with confidence and authority. At times he could be harsh; other times he was an open wound, vulnerable, sensitive. He was rowdy, impish, charming, and intense: his leonine charisma never failed him.

I admit I have been sad during the past day or so, and have wept off and on in remembrance of various gatherings that we shared with Ray, but have tried to maintain a perspective about the passage of someone that was so dear not only to me, but to the world: Ray lived a fantastic life, and a long one. He was a man at peace, and he was not in pain.

What more can one aspire to, but to live your dreams, and dream your life as you hope it should be.

Ray is gone, and long may he live.

—Jason V Brock
June 6, 2012

Ray Bradbury's Good Companions

"A ten-year-old boy still lives inside Ray Bradbury, impatiently scuf-
fling, running, teasing, provoking, and challenging the man he has
become. Similarly, Ray's own literary children, including some of
the first stories he ever wrote, still cry out to him and demand to
be recognized. Now, a half century later, they are not through with
him yet, and he is not through with them, either. Memory and
myth are like that, shape-changing with the gusts and eddies of history's crosswinds."

I wrote those words in 1997, as I prepared an interview article
on Ray Bradbury's newest book publication, *From the Dust Returned*. At the time, Ray and I were driving through the Plaza in
Kansas City, Missouri, on our way to the University of Kansas. We
had just visited the Thomas Hart Benton murals at the Nelson-
Atkins Museum. He had expressly wanted to see them. Now, fifteen years later, and just a few days after his death at age ninety-
one, I remember moments like that and still find myself applying
the present tense. Ray always lived in the present tense. In the
more than forty years of our friendship, which saw his visits to my
home in Kansas City, my many visits to his home in Los Angeles,
our sharing the podium together at several science fiction conventions, touring his work on Spaceship Earth at Disney's WED facil-
ity in Burbank, many interviews, a continuing correspondence—he
was never less than *present*, always in the moment. Until the next,
and the next.

Even today, I still believe in that present, that *presence* . . .

But what is there to say about him that hasn't been remembered, expounded, celebrated, analyzed, critiqued, and talked to
death all this time? I can merely offer up some thoughts of my own

about some of the things I learned that are perhaps not so well known about him.

But, to begin with . . . In a half century of writing fantasy, science fiction, and satire, Ray Bradbury has taken us on safari to hunt Tyrannosaurus Rex, crouch among the mummies in the catacombs beneath Mexico City, chase demons in a Midwestern carnival midway, resurrect ghosts in the Hollywood backlots, sprint through Dublin's streets, and colonize Mars. We met firemen who burn books, vampires who work in mortuaries, robots who resemble grandmothers, and spacemen who trail the Son of God from planet to planet. Ray Bradbury is his own macrocosm and microcosm—by turns touching the sun and probing at his own bones. His more than sixty books—including *Dark Carnival, The Martian Chronicles, Fahrenheit 451, The Illustrated Man, Dandelion Wine, Something Wicked This Way Comes,* and *From the Dust Returned* (along with dozens of plays and screenplays, hundreds of poems, and many consultancies as city planner and Disney Epcot designer) are known to millions all over the world.

So where do I come in? Ray Bradbury had many Good Companions in his lifetime, kindred spirits, beckoning muses. I am not referring to his contemporaries, friends, and relatives, like his beloved Aunt Neva back in Waukegan, Illinois, or cartoonist Charles Addams, or illustrator Joseph Mugnaini, about all of whom I have written elsewhere. And I don't cite the great catalogue of literary influences which he celebrated so frequently and enthusiastically, from the John Carter adventures and Lon Chaney's movie grotesques during his youth, to the *Weird Tales* coterie of Robert E. Howard and H. P. Lovecraft during his apprentice days, and to Walt Disney and Lewis Mumford in his later years of public celebrity. No, I speak here of three other men—a filmmaker, a writer, a composer—whom he certainly never met, but who are no less noted in the Bradbury pantheon of heroes. We sometimes know

ourselves by knowing our heroes. In citing them, I believe I am
further defining Bradbury himself.

To begin with there is the great swashbuckler, Douglas Fairbanks, Sr. . . . He was Ray's Eternal Youth, his Peter Pan. "Douglas" was Ray's middle name. "My middle name is Douglas, named
for Douglas Fairbanks, Sr.," Ray explained in a letter to me dated
22 August 1970 (the day of his fiftieth birthday), "who was at the
height of his fame when I was born in 1920." Seven years later he
signed all three names to my just-published Fairbanks biography.
Indeed, the name "Douglas" appears as the name of many of
Bradbury's characters. Certainly, that name was his own code for
the fleet, buoyant spirit that fueled *The Thief of Bagdad* and *Robin
Hood* and the agile prose that drove his own stories.

And there was Gilbert Keith Chesterton. . . . Gilbert was Ray's
Everyman, his Job grappling with an elusive God. An immense
and curious apostle of logic and lunacy who haunted British letters
until his death in 1937, Chesterton turned the world upside down
and space inside out with his paradoxes. I had no inkling of Ray's
enthusiasm for him until one day I spotted on his bookshelves a
number of Chesterton volumes. The moment was like a stroke
lightning: Of course! How could these men *not* be bound at the
hip! Many happy conversations followed, exchanges back and forth
about the poetry of both (he particularly loved Chesterton's *Ballad
of the White Horse*: "Do you remember when we met / Under a
dragon moon?"), the Father Brown detective stories, and questions
about those famous paradoxes—just *who* or *what* was the character
of "Sunday" in *The Man Who Was Thursday?*

Third, was the French composer Hector Berlioz. . . . Another
bolt from the blue. Mighty Hector was Ray's Barbarian at the
Gate, breathing fire and brimstone. Ray's chance reference one
day to the great Romantic firebrand pricked my attention. In every
expostulation and exclamation point, Ray matched Berlioz's vol-

canic outbursts, the cannon fire, and explosive rhetoric of *The Symphonie Fantastique* and *Harold in Italy*. He knew Berlioz's forays into science fiction, too, in particular, that strange story of a mechanized city of the future. . . .

You see, Fairbanks's flying trajectories were those of Ray's flights to Mars, the sun, and beyond. They sang together their paeans to an almost pagan youth, and nurtured the spirit of the boyman who would never grow old, at least on screen and on the page. Chesterton's sturdy optimism was the smile with which Will Halloway defeated Mr. Dark and Leo Auffmann built his "Happiness Machine." But when the smile turned upside down, we had Chesterton's gargoyles and Bradbury's October People. Significantly, they growled and the grinned, almost interchangeably. Moreover, Chesterton's search for God on earth was like Ray's search for Christ on the planet Mars. They shared the divine paradox of divinity and spirituality immanent in the dust of men. Indeed, I like to think because of Chesterton's topsy-turvy insights and spiritual quests, he knew Bradbury better than Ray knew himself. If you insist, quite rightly, that they never met, read Chesterton's 1911 novel *Manalive* and you will see the best portrait anyone ever did—or ever will—execute of Bradbury. As for Berlioz's bursts of energy, well, just try to avoid one of Ray's big bear hugs. Like the blare of Berlioz's brash trombones, those hugs come at you from everywhere at once. Monsieur Berlioz and Mr. Bradbury shouted, loved, and hated at the tops of their voices. Together, they plunged into the Hell of *The Damnation of Faust* and rode the infernal merry-go-round of *Something Wicked This Way Comes*. Indeed, they were the children of Faust, outsiders, interlopers, damned and exalted. I have no doubt that Ray's early story "The Homecoming" is his own *Damnation of Faust*, evoking a yearning for a dark sublime that would never be satisfied.

Writers, filmmakers, composers all, they were not in the business of shrinking from life or from themselves. I have sometimes wondered how it was that a man like Ray, with little formal education, managed to acquire his experience and love with seemingly remote influences like these, so apart from the more familiar fantasy worlds of *Weird Tales* and the hard realities of space travel. Maybe it's because Douglas and Gilbert and Hector were, like Ray, autodidacts, who deployed their equal-opportunity enthusiasms in the never-ending search for youth, God, and the Devil.

And so, in conclusion, when I bid farewell to the earthly remains of my friend, I want to say, simply, goodbye, Ray-Douglas-Gilbert-Hector Bradbury.

—JOHN C. TIBBETTS

A Master of Symbol and Metaphor

It is a source of keen regret that I never met Ray Bradbury. I had several opportunities to do so, and it would have required a simple plane ride from my home in Seattle to his residence in Los Angeles to meet this living legend of weird fiction, fantasy fiction, and science fiction. Although I was not acquainted with him, I knew several individuals who were, ranging from William F. Nolan and Jason V Brock to Jonathan R. Eller, the author of an exceptional literary biography (*Becoming Ray Bradbury*) and, with William F. Touponce, the director of the Ray Bradbury Center at Indiana University–Purdue University at Indianapolis (IUPUI).

It was through my association with Eller and Touponce that I myself have become involved in the study of Bradbury's life and work. I was not even aware of the Ray Bradbury Center until I received an invitation some years ago to give a lecture there; my topic happened to be on Poe and Lovecraft as pioneering writers of weird fiction, each of whom effected a revolution in the genre; but once I learned that IUPUI was the focus of serious Bradbury studies, my own casual reading of the author of *The October Country* took a much more serious turn. I first became aware that a bibliography, undertaken by longtime Bradbury friend and collector Donn Albright and his colleague James Welch, had languished unpublished for years, although Albright was diligently adding to it as new items by and about Ray appeared in print. (There was an additional serendipitousness to the whole situation when I learned that Donn had a family home in Muncie, Indiana, not two blocks from the home where I myself spent my formative years, and that Donn had gone to the same high school as I had attended. Donn had frequently seen my mother—who still lives in that Muncie house—puttering in her garden, and may well have caught a sight of me on my frequent visits there.) I at once resolved that I could lend a hand in Bradbury studies by putting that bibliography into proper format, and Prof. Eller and I hope to publish this seminal work in due course of time.

The incredibly rich treasures of the Ray Bradbury Center tempted me to contemplate other projects—volumes of his uncollected and unpublished stories, essays, and reviews (how many know that he wrote a review of the *Star Wars* film in the *Los Angeles Times*?), and more significantly, a volume of Bradbury's selected letters. His correspondence with such significant figures as August Derleth (who ushered into print his first book, *Dark Carnival*, under the Arkham House imprint), Robert Bloch, Forrest J Ackerman, his agent Don Congdon, and countless others in the realms of literature and film would shed immense light on his own life and mind as well as that of the figures whose lives he touched so indelibly.

It is by no means too early for an assessment of Bradbury's achievement as a writer. His early work has already achieved classic status by virtue of its intrinsic merits and its immense influence. My own focus has been on Bradbury's weird fiction, and in this field he has proven himself a master, even if he largely abandoned the genre after the first two decades of his career. Chronologically speaking, Bradbury should probably be regarded as the pioneer in the midcentury shift of supernatural horror from the flamboyant cosmicism of Lovecraft and his colleagues to the mundane social realism that in some ways continues to dominate the field today. Bradbury's letter to the editor in the November 1939 issue of *Weird Tales* briefly praises Lovecraft's "Cool Air," and he retained a lifelong devotion to the exotic prose-poetry of Clark Ashton Smith's fantastic tales; but his own work, while being richly prose-poetic in its own way and deftly fusing fantasy, supernatural horror, psychological horror, and a delicate character portrayal not often found in weird fiction, is as different from Lovecraft's Cthulhu Mythos or Smith's tales of Zothique and Hyberborea as any literature could well be.

What distinguishes Bradbury's work from that of many of his predecessors, contemporaries, and successors—aside from the sheer inventiveness of his imagination and his immense gifts of language and story construction—is his uncanny ability to construct weird scenarios that serve as powerful symbols or metaphors for central human concerns. Perhaps the most obvious—but nonetheless effective—instance of this trait is the somewhat later story "The Dwarf" (*Fantastic*, January–February 1954), which uses Bradbury's patented carnival setting. Here the dwarf of the title is obviously a stand-in for Bradbury himself, as he writes pulp detective stories (Bradbury wrote extensively for the detective pulps as well as for the weird and science fiction pulps). Ralph, the operator of the hall of mirrors at the carnival, switches mirrors so that the dwarf looks, not bigger, but even smaller than his actual dimensions: a more transparent symbol could scarcely be sought for Bradbury's own insecurity as he was transitioning from a pulpsmith to the greater stature he sought as a mainstream writer.

Bradbury's ability to use weird motifs as metaphors for profound human concerns allowed him to shift easily from the pulp market to slicks like *Collier's* and *Saturday Evening Post*, while his hugely popular works of science fiction helped to raise that genre in critical esteem and to elevate his own work to the level of an American classic. It is a bit sad to note that the best of his work had largely been written, with rare exceptions (like *Something Wicked*), by the late 1950s. Bradbury, more than most authors, has written far too much and has also in some senses believed his own press and become a self-consciously literary author. Little that he has written since the 1960s is of any account, but his early work has made an imperishable impression on the fields of science fiction, fantasy, and supernatural horror, and his undoubted talents will establish him as a writer close to the stature of a Lovecraft or a Poe.

—S. T. JOSHI

Afterword: The Return of Ray B.

In the end, Ray's death came gently enough in his sleep. During his last decade life proved increasingly difficult, yet Ray, in my presence at least, never lost his enthusiasm, never indulged in self-pity. This is life. Life is hard. He had learned this while growing up, as Bill Nolan tells us in his fine short biography.

Yet while life is hard, it's also brilliantly attractive, devilishly beautiful. The interplay between pain and death and beauty—and between life and imagination, where all things seem possible—fascinated Ray from a very early age.

I am certain that a thousand years from now, if there are still human beings—and there will be, whatever shape they take—Ray's stories will continue to echo and entrance. How do I know this? Because they address a core condition, a core passion: how dearly we love life, how much we fear and distrust death.

His are not stories for sophisticates in the grayest sense of that word. They are stories for the wondering child in us all. Because of Ray, in large part, and in sympathy with Ray and all his colleagues, because of all the brilliantly diverse and quixotic writers of fantasy and science fiction, I am still that child.

And that brings me to William Nolan, as much an evergreen child as I am, and bless him for that. When Bill and I and our friends get together, we crack bad jokes, fall into lines of patter, look right and left for the sheep-crooks that could yank us offstage at any moment.

And we don't care. We love it.

Bill knew Ray for six decades. I knew Ray for forty-five years. Any connection to our sparkling lack of savoir-faire? You bet. We're part of a tradition. And so, it turns out, is Ray; we are all children of the same culture. We flock together because we recognize something in each other that is difficult to find among the serious, the cool, the cognoscenti: a recognition that Death is best served up with a pun, a bad joke, a silly song, and best delayed with a cracking good tale in which, just possibly, Death plays a central part.

Imagine Dorian Gray living forever not because his portrait ages, while he does not, but because that picture in his attic is Death itself, trapped! Only to be let loose when we are at our most despairing, our most feeble, our most exhausted. When only Death can appreciate our beauty and restore our youth. Make no mistake: to die is to reclaim, at least in the memories of those we leave behind, that youth we once had, the energy and beauty we once enjoyed.

The aging, sickly Ray Bradbury we met with, in those last few months and years, was still our Ray, still vital, but trapped in a failing body. He is no longer trapped. In my mind, Ray is now as I first saw him in 1967, a mature and accomplished forth-six-year-old man . . . fifteen years younger than I am now. He is once again as he appears in his dust jacket photo for *Fahrenheit 451*, thirty-something and buzzcut and staring up at the future with a delighted but skeptical crinkle in his eye . . . that decade's favorite pose for science fiction writers.

He is the boy hawking newspaper outside of Paramount Studios, accosting movie stars, gathering autographs in a small book, scribbling down Gracie Allen's license plate number—stalking fame and celluloid dreams and impossible beauty and wit. It was here just beyond the studio gate—on Gower, as I recall him saying—that W. C. Fields delivered Ray a true blessing. Ever skeptical of youngsters, the brilliant comedian signed Ray's small book and returned it to him, exclaiming, "Here you go, you little son of a bitch!"

Ray told that story often, with delight, and in a damned fine Fields voice. Astrid and I saw and held that autograph book a couple of years ago, on one of our visits to Ray's house, and marveled at Fields's signature, at Leo Carrillo's self-caricatured cowboy (wait, Leo Carrillo . . . Like the state beach? Like the Cisco Kid? Time travel happens!) . . . at Gracie's license plate number. Who wouldn't dream of dating Gracie Allen?

Ray is now as he was at the Studio Playhouse watching his plays being performed—at his happiest, I think—

Or sharing a cafeteria dinner with a crowd of young and rowdy enthusiasts after the first tiny San Diego Comic-Con in 1970.

Or traveling with me in an old Saab in 1983 to Digital Productions to see what the future of film might be like in the computer age, looking at pre-viz of *Little Nemo* and scouting for work.

Or in the late 1960s, venturing with a small tribe of teenagers and my grandmother into Cascade Studios to meet the animators of Alky Alka-Seltzer and the Pillsbury Doughboy and a dancing bottle of Ripple wine—and preview a clip in the studio theater from Jim Danforth's *When Dinosaurs Ruled the Earth* . . . And then driving off for a burger and shake (of course) at Frascati Restaurant in Beverly Hills.

Or sitting on a panel at a 1993 St. Louis science fiction convention with his good friend Ray Harryhausen—and another good friend, Julie Schwartz, chiming in—as I try to wheedle stories of their early days, asking why Ray H. didn't recognize Ray B.'s story while filming *The Beast from 20,000 Fathoms* . . . to which Ray H. responded, with a skilled Oliver Hardy delivery, "I have NOTH-ING to say . . . !"

Or at a celebration of the sixth-fifth anniversary of *King Kong*, when Ray H. and Ray B. join a posse in a van to travel to a steakhouse for dinner. Both simultaneously invoke, with spontaneous precision and eternal wonder, the glorious name of "Gustav von

Seyffertitz!" A ritual obviously performed many times in their youth. (Look him up; Seyffertitz had quite a distinguished and lengthy career.)

Or Ray and I sitting in the beef-haunted semi-dark of a Hamburger Hamlet in the 1990s, complaining about how tough it was to get a movie made. Ray lamented the extraordinary difficulties and even heartbreak of working with John Huston, and later, of facing a friend's directorial Waterloo on *Something Wicked This Way Comes*. And marveling that that film actually turned out pretty good, in large part because of Ray's script.

Or Ray writing a fan letter to John W. Campbell, editor of *Unknown*, published in March 1940: "[Harry Walton's 'Swamp Train'] brought back memories of a not-so-distant childhood, some scant eight years or so ago, of when I lived in a small country town and often found such scenery and such atmosphere as was described so well in Walton's yarn [. . .] the sort of thing that makes you draw a bit nearer the fire or jerk suddenly around to look at the darkness just outside your window or perhaps stiffen at the sound of dry leaves clacking on the panes [. . .] It makes you wonder what it is all about, this life of ours, and if we are really as cocksure about our science as we think we are. It is a splendid antidote for 'scientific poisoning' that one might get from some of the super-science *Astounding* stories. The two mags balance each other. If you pick up Unknown first and get that ice cubish feeling about your spine the best remedy is a quick dash of atoms and doctors with black spade beards and disintegrators at ye olde ship *Astounding*. And when you get tired of feeding molecules to the Martian fuddy-duddies and your brain is so full of mechanics and theories that it squeaks, it is a simple task to open up Unknown and get air-conditioned via the old Salem witchery way."

So wrote nineteen-year-old Ray, "editor of *Futuria Fantasia*," in Los Angeles, California. This young man, ripe with his own future, is back with us now, filled to overflowing with love and energy and startling wisdom.

These and many other Rays have been returned to us, select, hazy, out of sequence, as is good and proper, for this is not history, this is not biography, this is dream and memory. These are the stories we tell when one of us completes his journey and himself becomes a story.

Ray is here.

Ray is back as he was then, and then, and then. And ever will be.

—GREG BEAR

Select Bibliography

I. Ray Bradbury

A. Novels

Fahrenheit 451. New York: Ballantine, 1953.

Dandelion Wine. Garden City, NY: Doubleday, 1957.

Something Wicked This Way Comes. New York: Simon & Schuster, 1962.

Death Is a Lonely Business. New York: Knopf, 1985.

A Graveyard for Lunatics. New York: Knopf, 1990.

Green Shadows, White Whale. New York: Knopf, 1992.

Let's All Kill Constance. New York: Morrow, 2003.

Farewell Summer. New York: Morrow, 2006.

Somewhere a Band Is Playing [novella]. Colorado Springs, CO: Gauntlet, 2009.

B. Short Story Collections

Dark Carnival. Sauk City, WI: Arkham House, 1947. Expanded ed. Springfield, PA: Gauntlet, 2001.

The Martian Chronicles. Garden City, NY: Doubleday, 1950.

The Illustrated Man. Garden City, NY: Doubleday, 1951.

The Golden Apples of the Sun. Garden City, NY: Doubleday, 1953.

The October Country. New York: Ballantine, 1955.

A Medicine for Melancholy. Garden City, NY: Doubleday, 1959.

R Is for Rocket. Garden City, NY: Doubleday, 1962.

The Machineries of Joy. New York: Simon & Schuster, 1964.

The Vintage Bradbury. New York: Vintage, 1965.

S Is for Space. Garden City, NY: Doubleday, 1966.

I Sing the Body Electric. New York: Knopf, 1969.

Long After Midnight. New York: Knopf, 1976.

The Stories of Ray Bradbury. New York: Knopf, 1980.

Dinosaur Tales. New York: Bantam, 1983.

A Memory of Murder. New York: Dell, 1984.

The Toynbee Convector. New York: Knopf, 1988.

Classic Stories. New York: Bantam, 1990. 2 vols.

Quicker Than the Eye. New York: Avon, 1996.

Driving Blind. New York: Avon, 1997.

From the Dust Returned. New York: Morrow, 2001.

One More for the Road. New York: Morrow, 2001.

Bradbury Stories. New York: Morrow, 2003.

The Cat's Pajamas. New York: Morrow, 2004.

Forever and the Earth: Yesterday and Tomorrow Tales. Hornsea, UK: PS Publishing, 2005.

Match to Flame: The Fictional Paths to Fahrenheit 451. Colorado Springs, CO: Gauntlet, 2006.

Now and Forever. New York: Morrow, 2007.

Masks. Colorado Springs, CO: Gauntlet, 2008.

Summer Morning, Summer Night. Hornsea, UK: PS Publishing, 2008.

We'll Always Have Paris. New York: Morrow, 2009.

Marionettes, Inc. Burton, MI: Subterranean Press, 2009.

The Bullet Trick. Colorado Springs, CO: Gauntlet, 2009.

C. Plays

The Anthem Sprinters and Other Antics. New York; Dial Press, 1963.

The Pedestrian. New York: Samuel French, 1966.

The Day It Rained Forever. New York: Samuel French, 1966.

The Wonderful Ice Cream Suit and Other Plays. New York: Bantam, 1973.

Pillar of Fire and Other Plays. New York: Bantam, 1975.

Forever and the Earth. Athens, OH: Croissant, 1984.

Ray Bardbury on Stage. New York: Donald I. Fine, 1991.

Moby Dick [screenplay]. Burton, MI: Subterranean Press, 2008.

D. Poetry

When Elephants Last in the Dooryard Bloomed. New York: Knopf, 1973.

Where Robot Mice and Robot Men Run Round in Robot Towns. New York: Knopf, 1977.

The Haunted Computer and the Android Pope. New York: Knopf, 1981.

The Complete Poems of Ray Bradbury. New York: Del Rey, 1982.

Witness and Celebrate. Northridge, CA: Lord John Press, 2000.

A Chapbook for Burnt-Out Priests, Rabbis, and Ministers. Baltimore: Cemetery Dance, 2001.

I Live by the Invisible. Cliffs of Moher, Ireland: Salmon Poetry, 2002.

They Have Not Seen the Stars. Lancaster, PA: Stealth Press, 2002.

E. Nonfiction

Zen and the Art of Writing. Santa Barbara, CA: Capra Press, 1973.

Zen in the Art of Writing. Santa Barbara, CA: Capra Press, 1989.

Yestermorrow. Santa Barbara, CA: Capra Press, 1991.

Conversations with Ray Bradbury [collected interviews]. Ed. Steven L. Aggelis. Jackson: University of Mississippi Press, 2004.

Bradbury Speaks. New York: Morrow, 2005.

Listen to the Echoes: The Ray Bradbury Interviews. Ed. Sam Weller. Brooklyn: Melville House; Chicago: Stopsmiling Books, 2010.

F. Books for Children

Switch On the Night. New York: Pantheon, 1955.

The Halloween Tree. New York: Knopf, 1972.

Dogs That Think Every Day Is Christmas. Salt Lake City, UT: Gibbs-Smith, 1997.

Ahmed and the Oblivion Machine. New York: Avon, 1998.

G. Edited Works

Timeless Stories for Today and Tomorrow. New York: Bantam, 1952.

The Circus of Dr. Lao and Other Improbable Stories. New York: Bantam, 1956.

II. William F. Nolan

A. Novels

Logan's Run (with George Clayton Johnson). New York: Dial Press, 1967.

Death Is for Losers. Los Angeles: Sherbourne Press, 1968.

The White Cad Cross-Up. Los Angeles: Sherbourne Press, 1969.

Space for Hire. New York: Lancer, 1971.

Logan's World. New York: Bantam, 1977.

Logan's Search. New York: Bantam, 1980.

Look Out for Space. New York: International Polygonics, 1985.

Logan: A Trilogy. Baltimore: Maclay, 1986.

Rio Renegades (as by "Terence Duncan"). New York: Zebra, 1989.

Helltracks. New York: Avon, 1991. Rev. ed. Baltimore: Cemetery Dance, 2000.

The Black Mask Murders. New York: St. Martin's Press, 1994.

The Marble Orchard. New York: St. Martin's Press, 1996.

Sharks Never Sleep. New York: St. Martin's Press, 1998.

The Winchester Horror [novella]. Baltimore: Cemetery Dance, 1999.

The Logan Chronicles [novels and novelette]. North Webster, IN: Delirium, 2003.

Demon! [novella]. North Webster, IN: Delirium, 2006.

B. Short Story Collections

Impact 20. New York: Paperback Library, 1963. Rev. ed. Colorado Springs, CO: Gauntlet, 2002.

Alien Horizons. New York: Pocket, 1974.

Wonderworlds. London: Gollancz, 1977.

Things Beyond Midnight. Santa Cruz, CA: Scream/Press, 1984.

3 for Space. Brooklyn, NY: Gryphon, 1992.

Night Shapes. Baltimore: Cemetery Dance, 1995.

The Brothers Challis. Brooklyn, NY: Gryphon, 1996.

Down the Long Night. Unity, ME: Five Star, 2000.

William F. Nolan's Dark Universe. Lancaster, PA: Stealth Press, 2001.

Have You Seen the Wind? [also includes poetry]. Boalsburg, PA: Bear Manor Media, 2003.

With Marlowe in L.A. [story and poem]. West Hills, CA: Sidecar, 2003.

Nightworlds. New York: Leisure, 2004.

Far Out. North Webster, IN: Delirium, 2004.

Ships in the Night. New York: Capra Press, 2005.

Wild Galaxy. Urbana, IL: Golden Gryphon Press, 2005.

Nightshadows. Bonney Lake, WA: Darkwood Press, 2007.

Seven for Space. Escondido, CA: Park Hill, 2008.

Dark Dimensions. Bonney Lake, WA: Darkwood Press, 2010.

Space Tales [e-book]. Escondido, CA: Park Hill, 2010.

Kincaid: A Paranormal Casebook. Somerset, PA: Rocket Ride, 2011.

C. Nonfiction

Ray Bradbury Review. [San Diego: William F. Nolan, 1952.] Los Angeles: Graham Press, 1988.

Adventure on Wheels (with John Fitch). New York: Putnam, 1959.

Barney Oldfield: The Life and Times of America's Legendary Speed King. New York: Putnam, 1961. Rev. ed. Carpinteria, CA: Brown Fox, 1998.

Phil Hill: Yankee Champion. New York: Putnam, 1962. Rev. ed. Carpinteria, CA: Brown Fox, 1997.

Men of Thunder. New York: Putnam, 1964.

John Huston: King Rebel. New York: Sherbourne Press, 1965.

Sinners and Supermen. North Hollywood, CA: All Star, 1965. San Bernardino, CA: Borgo Press, 1997 (as *Legends and Lovers*).

Dashiell Hammett: A Casebook. Santa Barbara, CA: McNally & Loftin, 1969.

Steve McQueen: Star on Wheels. New York: Putnam, 1972.

Carnival of Speed. New York: Putnam, 1973.

Hemingway: Last Days of the Lion. New York: Capra Press, 1974.

The Ray Bradbury Companion. Detroit: Gale Research Co., 1975.

Hammett: A Life at the Edge. New York: Congdon & Weed, 1983.

McQueen. New York: Congdon & Weed, 1984.

The Black Mask Boys. New York: Morrow, 1985.

Max Brand: Western Giant. Bowling Green, OH: Bowling Green State University Popular Press, 1986.

The Work of Charles Beaumont. San Bernardino, CA: Borgo Press, 1986.

The Work of William F. Nolan (with Boden Clarke; as by "James Hopkins"). San Bernardino, CA: Borgo Press, 1988 (rev. ed. 1997).

How to Write Horror Fiction. Cincinnati: Writer's Digest, 1990.

Let's Get Creative! Writing Fiction That Sells! Sanger, CA: Quill Driver, 2006.

William F. Nolan: A Miscellany. Ed. Jason V Brock. Vancouver, WA: Cycatrix Press/Dark Discoveries, 2011.

D. Miscellaneous

Dark Encounters [verse]. Madison, WI: Dream House, 1986.

Death Drive [screenplay]. Port St. Lucie, FL: Hellbound, 2005.

Ill Met by Moonlight [prose, poetry, and artwork]. Port St. Lucie, FL: Hellbound, 2006.

E. Edited Anthologies

Omnibus of Speed (with Charles Beaumont). New York: Putnam, 1958.

The Fiend in You (with Charles Beaumont [uncredited]). New York: Ballantine, 1962.

When Engines Roar (with Charles Beaumont). New York: Bantam, 1964.

The Pseudo-People. Los Angeles: Sherbourne Press, 1965.

Man Against Tomorrow. New York: Avon, 1965.

3 to the Highest Power. New York: Avon, 1968.

A Wilderness of Stars. Los Angeles: Sherbourne Press, 1969.

A Sea of Space. New York: Bantam, 1970.

The Future Is Now. Los Angeles: Sherbourne Press, 1970.

The Human Equation. Los Angeles: Sherbourne Press, 1971.

The Edge of Forever by Chad Oliver. Los Angeles: Sherbourne Press, 1971.

Science Fiction Origins (with Martin H. Greenberg). Greenwich, CT: Fawcett, 1980.

Max Brand's Best Western Stories. New York: Dodd, Mead, 1981, 1985, 1987. 3 vols.

Urban Horrors (with Martin H. Greenberg). Arlington Heights, IL: Dark Harvest, 1990.

The Bradbury Chronicles (with Martin H. Greenberg). New York: Penguin/Roc, 1991.

Tales of the Wild West by Max Brand. Hampton Falls, NH: Sagebrush, 1997.

More Tales of the Wild West by Max Brand. Hampton Falls, NH: Sagebrush, 1999.

California Sorcery (with William Schafer). Baltimore: Cemetery Dance, 1999.

Off Beat by Richard Matheson. Burton, MI: Subterranean Press, 2002.

Masquerade: Ten Crime Stories by Max Brand. Norfolk, VA: Crippen & Landru, 2007.

The Bleeding Edge (with Jason V Brock). Vancouver, WA: Cycatrix Press, 2009.

The Devil's Coattails (with Jason V Brock). Vancouver, WA: Cycatrix Press, 2011.

www.ingramcontent.com/pod-product-compliance
Lightning Source LLC
Chambersburg PA
CBHW070450030726
47503CB00004B/977